Leonore thought Nicholas had taught her all there was to know of the pleasures of love. Until now.

"You have only read gothic novels, Leonore," he told her. "Shall I show you how vampires really use their teeth?"

Sharp fear and trembling shook her. But Leonore breathed deeply and stilled herself. "You will not, Nicholas. I already know."

His fingers came to caress her cheek and feathered down her neck. His hand gently curved around her throat.

"If you are a vampire, Nicholas," she whispered, "do it."

A deep groan came from him. He pushed her away and she stumbled onto her knees.

"Go away, go away, Leonore, before I hurt you," he said.

"You are not a vampire," she declared.

Nicholas gave a short, mirthless laugh. "Oh, yes, I am."

The Vampire Viscount

by

Karen Harbaugh

A SIGNET BOOK

SIGNET
Published by the Penguin Group
Penguin Books USA Inc., 375 Hudson Street,
New York, New York 10014, U.S.A.
Penguin Books Ltd, 27 Wrights Lane,
London W8 5TZ, England
Penguin Books Australia Ltd, Ringwood,
Victoria, Australia
Penguin Books Canada Ltd, 10 Alcorn Avenue,
Toronto, Ontario, Canada M4V 3B2
Penguin Books (N.Z.) Ltd, 182-190 Wairau Road,
Auckland 10, New Zealand

Penguin Books Ltd, Registered Offices:
Harmondsworth, Middlesex, England

First published by Signet, an imprint of Dutton Signet,
a division of Penguin Books USA Inc.

First Printing, October, 1995
10 9 8 7 6 5 4 3 2 1

I would like to dedicate this book to my good friend, Deborah Wittman, for introducing me to vampires when I thought I wouldn't like them; to Leonore Schuetz for letting me borrow her lovely name; to my local critique group and the GEnie ROMex critique group for their encouragement and nit-picks; and to my agent, Ruth Cohen, who found a home for this odd little book.

Most of all, I would like to dedicate this book to the memory of my father, John Eriksen, who taught me how to read, who introduced me to myths and legends, who gave me a love of books and history, and who knew his daughter would be an author someday.

Author's Note

I hope vampire fans will forgive me for departing from the fairly recent tradition in vampire lore of having the vampires incapable of seeing themselves in mirrors. This idea came mostly from Bram Stoker (who wrote *Dracula* at a much later time than the Regency era), and I thought it better thematically to do something different with mirrors in my story. I am supported in this by Lord Byron, who did not even mention mirrors with regard to his vampires, and Byron's contemporary and personal physician, Dr. John Polidori, whose vampire, Lord Ruthven, was too impeccably dressed not to have looked in a mirror from time to time. However, vampires have been known not to like looking in them, whatever they may or may not see. That piece of folklore, at least, I have included.

There are many conflicting traditions and "rules" in vampire history, and an author must choose with care which ones she will use. I hope I have sufficiently done so.

Chapter 1

The Viscount St. Vire closed his book with a snap and shoved it away from him. He was tired of being reclusive. He would go out tonight instead of staying in his study, reading ancient texts. He eyed his solicitor's report upon his desk and shrugged. At least his research in that direction was finished, and he need select only one—fortunate—candidate. But not tonight.

Rubbing his eyes, he sighed. He would definitely go out. Perhaps mingling with others once again would dispel the memories of the dreams. They were getting worse. The last time he woke, the images continued to move before his eyes even though he knew he was no longer sleeping.

He went to his chamber, donned an impeccably designed waistcoat, tied his neckcloth with precision, and selected a finely tailored coat. He pondered over a selection of walking sticks, then rejected them all. The last time he'd gone to a gaming hell, he had lost one.

He stepped out of his house and walked through the barely moonlit night to a house that he remembered from many years ago; happily, the gaming hell was still there. He knocked at the door, and a burly guard opened it slightly.

"I need the secret word from yer, sir," he growled.

St. Vire only smiled at him and shrugged. The guard hesitated for a long moment, then opened the door wide. He shook his head as if to clear it, then resumed his post as St. Vire walked past him.

The air was heavy with the smell of sour wine, smoking candles, and the heat of crowded humanity. Even he could smell it. The decor had changed since last he had entered this room, for the better, thankfully. Heavy gold curtains draped the windows, and the rugs were relatively new and soft. Clearly, the owner of this gaming hell did very well for himself—or herself. A gaudily dressed woman turned in his direction. She smiled and glided toward him.

"I see we have a new guest, hmm?"

"Nicholas, Viscount St. Vire. I heard there was some interesting play here and thought I'd see what it was about," St. Vire replied. He grinned at the woman, and a dazed look came into her eyes. "I take it you are the proprietress of this establishment?"

"Why yes, my lord. . . ." She moved closer to him and ran her fingers across his chest. "And what is your preference?"

Clearly, she was hoping his preference would not be at the gaming table, and he considered it. No. He had to take care upon whom he slaked his lust, and it would be awkward if it were the gaming hell's proprietress. A tide of ennui washed over him, and he glanced at the gaming tables. He needed something to stimulate his mind tonight.

"Faro or whist," he said. "Or vingt-et-un." He let his gaze wander with relish over the woman's voluptuous figure, however, so that she would know he appreciated her efforts. She gave a little pout, but led him to a table where three men sat, proposing a game of vingt-et-un.

"May I introduce you to the Viscount St. Vire, gentlemen?" the proprietress said.

He bowed, regarded each of the men in a friendly manner, and nodded as each introduced himself: Lord Eldon, Lord Bremer, and Mr. Edward Farleigh. Of the three, Mr. Farleigh seemed out of place; he was a burly older man, whose eyes would have seemed intelligent had they not been so bloodshot. His clothes were stained, and shiny spots appeared at the elbows from wear. Lord Bremer was a well-dressed man with a bored expression; Lord Eldon, also impeccably dressed, could not be over thirty years of age and had a look of good humor about his eyes and mouth.

St. Vire noticed, when he glanced at Mr. Farleigh, how that

man's expression shifted from a vague discontent to speculative greed as he gazed over his wineglass at the newcomer. St. Vire smiled a little to himself as Lord Eldon dealt the cards. It seemed Mr. Farleigh deemed the new player a pigeon to be plucked.

The viscount played, won, lost, and won again. He knew how the game was played, more than mere stakes and the turn of a card. One lured one's opponent with an innocent manner and baited the trap with a lamb's guise. He knew he looked very young, and he almost smiled as Mr. Farleigh's greed caused him to stake more against him than was wise. Lord Eldon put down a modest wager, and Lord Bremer grimaced and made out some vowels.

Half an hour passed in silent contemplation of the cards. The play came around to St. Vire, and he laid down his cards, looking up at his opponents. Wry humor twisted Lord Eldon's lips as he spread his cards on the table. "Your luck is in, St. Vire! Damned glad I didn't get taken in by your innocent looks and stake more than I should have." The viscount grinned at him.

Lord Bremer grimaced and slapped down his cards. "If you'll give me your direction, I'll settle this tomorrow, St. Vire."

"Of course; I shall be here tomorrow night if it's more convenient for you than calling upon me," St. Vire replied.

"Good of you." Lord Bremer's voice was grudging; he regarded St. Vire with an ironic eye, which the viscount returned with one of bland innocence. A laugh broke from Bremer, and he shook his head ruefully.

St. Vire looked at Mr. Farleigh expectantly. A slight sheen of sweat gleamed upon the older man's brow, and his expression was one of anger. He had wagered a substantial amount. He looked up and caught St. Vire's gaze, and his smile seemed forced. "You're a good player, my lord." He placed his cards upon the table.

Farleigh had lost, but his smile remained. "Another game, my lord?" He looked at the other gentlemen as well.

Lord Eldon yawned and shook his head. "I'm out!" F

looked slightly embarrassed. "Promised m'sister I'd attend my niece's wedding in the morning, and it's getting on a bit."

Lord Bremer barked out a laugh. "It is not even nine o'clock! Your sister still pulling you about by your leading strings, boy?"

Lord Eldon raised his brows. "*I'm* not the one living under the cat's foot, my lord."

A guilty expression passed over Lord Bremer's face. "I'll have you know my Hester is a damned fine woman, Eldon." He looked even more uneasy. "I suppose I should look in at her musicale." Lord Eldon only grinned.

Farleigh looked at St. Vire. "Well, my lord?"

The viscount looked at the large number of vowels before him, more than half of which were Farleigh's. He raised his eyes from the pile of paper and caught a brief look of frustration in the older man's eyes. St. Vire put on an uncertain expression. "I . . . don't know, Mr. Farleigh. It seems my luck has been in tonight, but I have no idea how long it will last. It rarely does with me, you see."

Farleigh visibly relaxed, and this time his smile seemed more genuine. "Perhaps a different game will make it last longer," he said.

At a brief touch on his sleeve, St. Vire looked up to see concern in Lord Eldon's face. The young man bent toward him. "Don't bother, St. Vire," he said in a whisper. "It will not be a challenge at all with Farleigh. Worst luck I've ever seen in a man, give you my word!"

"All the more reason to play, don't you think?" St. Vire replied softly. He glanced at Farleigh, but the man was occupied with pouring himself another drink.

Eldon shook his head. "I hear the man's a drunkard and a brute; my brother lives next to him—told me so. Takes his losses out on his wife and daughter. You can hear him rage right across the square. I only wager with him when I've got money to lose."

St. Vire suppressed a smile at Eldon's inadvertent admission to charity. "Perhaps I have some money to lose as well," he said, and a relieved look crossed Lord Eldon's face. The young man straightened himself, smiled, and took his leave.

Lord Bremer gazed after Lord Eldon with some indecision. He grimaced. "Devil take it! I suppose I really should look in at Hester's musicale. She would have my head on a platter if I did not." He, too, rose, bowed, and left.

Farleigh's gaze settled on St. Vire. "Well, my lord? Are you going to leave as well?"

The viscount hesitated, looking at the older man. Farleigh was one of the men his solicitors had mentioned in their report, and Farleigh had a daughter. The words he had read in his study earlier rose before his mind's eye, and a sudden electric exhilaration rushed through him. He had decided to take no action tonight, but perhaps this was a sign that he should. He smiled. "Faro, Mr. Farleigh?"

Relief crossed Farleigh's face. "Of course." He turned around in his chair, searching the room for the proprietress. "Rosie! Bring me brandy!" he roared.

"That's Mrs. Grant to you, Mr. Farleigh!" the woman retorted. "And I'll not be bringing you another bottle until you've paid for the last!" She held out her hand and glared at him.

Farleigh thrust his hand in his pocket and shoved some coins at her. "There, devil take it!"

With a complacent smirk at St. Vire, Mrs. Grant signaled a servant to bring the brandy. When it arrived, Farleigh poured himself a glass and gestured with it toward St. Vire, who only smiled politely and shook his head.

This time St. Vire did not need to pretend unskilled innocence for Mr. Farleigh to wager more and more money. The brandy did that for him. The man's luck was phenomenally bad, and his skill only mediocre. Even when the viscount deliberately discarded some excellent cards, Farleigh still lost.

St. Vire won once more, and boredom crept in. Really, it was finished. He'd won enough in vowels from Farleigh to bargain for the soul of a saint, and this man was no saint. And this in the space of less than one hour. He stood up and smiled.

"Well, it was a pleasure playing against you, Mr. Farleigh. Shall I expect to meet you tomorrow?"

Mr. Farleigh raised a gaze full of confused rage to St. Vire's face. "I am not done yet! Another game!"

"Hush! You disturb the other players," the viscount said softly. The man looked furtively around at the other gamesters, some of whom did indeed stare with distaste toward them.

He grasped St. Vire's sleeve. "Another game," he said hoarsely.

"Please, Farleigh. You are wrinkling my coat."

"Damn you, St. Vire! I want another game!" Farleigh stood up abruptly, and the other guests glared at him.

"No."

Farleigh's fist shot out, but St. Vire caught his wrist almost effortlessly and held it away from his face. The man breathed heavily and struggled. St. Vire did not let go, but smiled, watching the fear grow in Farleigh's eyes.

Mrs. Grant ran to them, alarm clear on her face. The viscount gave her an apologetic glance.

"I am terribly sorry, Mrs. Grant, but it seems Farleigh and I are at some disagreement." He pushed the man backward into a chair. Farleigh rubbed his wrist, staring at St. Vire, who returned the look contemplatively. "Perhaps we should go somewhere more private to discuss this."

"To be sure, my lord, I've got a private parlor if that's what you'll be wanting," Mrs. Grant said, eyeing him uneasily. As she looked at him, her face softened. She leaned toward him and lowered her voice. "He's a bad man, that Farleigh is. I'll send Grundle to you if you need 'im. He used to fight with Gentleman Jackson himself before he ruined his knee."

Farleigh's face flushed red. "Why, you blowsy—"

St. Vire cut him off with a sharp glance, and Farleigh looked down at his feet. The viscount turned to Mrs. Grant and brought her hand to his lips, smiling at her. "You are most kind, Mrs. Grant, but I will not need your servant. Merely a room in which Farleigh and I can be private."

A blush appeared upon her cheeks, and she simpered. "Well, and so you shall have it!" She turned, then looked back at him and beckoned.

St. Vire repressed a smile, then stared hard at Farleigh. "You will come with me if you please."

The man rose and dragged his feet as he followed.

Mrs. Grant opened the door to the parlor and was disposed to linger, but St. Vire put some coins in her hand and gently pushed her away. "Later," he whispered in her ear, which put a gratified look upon her face. He smiled. He had promised her absolutely nothing; it was amusing what meaning people could put into a single word and tone. He closed the door behind her.

St. Vire turned to Farleigh, staring at him meditatively for a while before gesturing to a chair. "Sit, please."

Farleigh complied, eyeing him warily. "I'll pay you, my lord, if that's what you're wanting to talk to me about."

St. Vire's lip curled slightly. "Pay? I doubt it. I have it on good word that you are very much in debt. I wonder that you are not in prison for it already." He sat and leaned his chin upon his hand, gazing at Farleigh's rumpled, worn clothes, his ill-tied and stained neckcloth. The man's eyes were filled with both resentment and fear. A vulgar man, thought St. Vire. Remarkable how an old family such as the Farleighs had come down in the world. He winced inwardly. Did he really want to ally himself with this man? The devil only knew what his daughter would be like. He shrugged to himself. Well, he would find out first.

"What do you want?" Farleigh said. He wet his lips and looked about the parlor as if trying to find an avenue of escape.

"I want to be sure you will pay me what you owe in some way. Either in money or goods. And be honest with me, for I have no hesitation exerting the right amount of . . . pressure to gain my ends."

"I can pay . . . perhaps a sennight from now." The man's eyes shifted and looked away.

"I am not stupid, Farleigh. The moment a few coins drop in your hands you spend it on drink—or game it away."

He looked about to argue, but did not. His eyes held a bleak, desperate look. "I . . . I do not have anything, my lord."

"Nothing?"

"I . . ." He stopped, then a hopeful expression came over his face. "Wait! I have a daughter. . . ."

St. Vire rose and turned away until he controlled the expression of disgust and triumph he was sure was on his face. God, the man needed no prompting at all to offer his daughter for sale. He wondered if perhaps he had made a mistake. One had certain standards, after all, and if the Farleighs had fallen so low as to breed a man like this, it could very well be that he would have to bear more than good taste could stand. He mentally reviewed the rest of the families on his solicitor's list. Really, the Farleighs would cause the least amount of trouble. The rest, however poor they'd become, still had respectable reputations. Farleigh's daughter could probably expect no help from her father if she did not like his agreement with St. Vire. And she would be only a means to an end, after all.

"A daughter." He turned back and looked hard at Farleigh. "Is she a virgin?"

Farleigh smiled sourly. "She's an ape leader, a skinny thing—naught to tempt a man, there—and waspish, too. No reason to suppose she's not a virgin. There's better game in town than a shrew, I'm sure."

"I am looking for a wife, Farleigh. You do not make her seem a very attractive prize."

"A wife!" Farleigh's brows rose in surprise, then greed shone in his eyes. He looked at St. Vire and shifted uncomfortably on his seat. "Well, she ain't a prize. But you wanted the word with no bark on it, so there it is," he said resentfully.

St. Vire considered it. If she was as her father said, she'd be glad to marry at all. He sighed impatiently at himself. He need not be so particular. It would only be for a year, after all, and then he could be rid of her. He'd see her first before he'd make an offer, however. He pulled a calling card from his pocket and flicked it at Farleigh, who managed to catch it.

"Bring her to me tonight, at this address. I want to see what I am buying."

Farleigh's eyes filled with relief. "Straightaway, my lord."

St. Vire rose from his chair. He leaned toward the sitting man and stared at him intently. "And if I find you are lying to me, I shall make sure you suffer for it." He smiled cheerfully at him. "I can, you know."

A shudder went through Farleigh's bulky frame. "Yes, no, of course, my lord."

"Go, now."

Farleigh stood hastily and almost ran from the room.

St. Vire frowned. The whole thing was in very bad taste, but there was no help for it. It was necessary for the spell to work. He sighed. What a pity it was that magic had no sense of good *ton*.

Chapter 2

Tick. Tick. Tick. Tick.

Once more Leonore Farleigh's eyes rose from the book on her lap to the parlor clock. Except for this action, she showed nothing of what she was feeling, for she kept her face emotionless, her posture straight, and her hands steady upon the pages. She gazed dispassionately at her mother, who was embroidering a purse by the light of a branch of candles, and said nothing. It was not necessary. The clock made enough conversation for both of them. She turned her eyes to her book.

A loud voice sounded in the hallway outside the parlor. Mrs. Farleigh gasped. Leonore looked up slowly, her gaze cool as she stared at the parlor door. Carefully, she smoothed the pages down, then closed the book. She clasped it, white knuckled, on her lap. Mrs. Farleigh dropped her needlework and twisted the rings on her fingers.

"Leonore! Martha!" came the voice again, and a large, heavy thump made the door tremble. Leonore caught her mother's frightened glance and looked once more at the clock. It was a little past nine o'clock; early for her father to return from the gaming hells he frequented.

"I think you should open the door for him, Leonore."

Leonore cast an angry glance at her mother. "No. I want to know how inebriated Father is by how long it takes him to open the door."

"Leonore, please—"

But the door opened, and Leonore smiled to herself cynically. Her father must have won something at the gaming table to be less intoxicated than usual. Indeed, his red face was full of smiles as he gazed upon both his wife and daughter.

"Congratulate me, Martha!" He wove his way forward and draped himself upon the sofa on which his wife sat. He gave his wife a smacking kiss on the cheek, and she visibly tried not to wince. "I have got our Leonore here a fine husband."

A cold chill seized Leonore's heart, and she could feel herself grow pale. She could smell the brandy on her father from where she sat. *He is inebriated,* she told herself. *He does not know what he is saying.*

"Did you hear me, Leonore?" Mr. Farleigh turned his wavering gaze toward his daughter. "A husband!"

"Yes, Father."

"Well, are you not going to thank me?"

Leonore caught another frightened, warning glance from her mother, but it was for nothing.

"I am convinced you must be mistaken, Father."

He rose up like an angry bear and cuffed her ear. "I am not mistaken. It is Lord St. Vire, I tell you!"

Leonore put her hand to her stinging ear and stared at him, expressionless. "I am afraid I have not heard of him." Her voice trembled only a little, and she was glad of her control. Perhaps if they were lucky her father would tire soon and leave. A great weariness came over her as she looked at him. She yearned to leave home, and marriage might be an avenue of escape. Being a governess gave her some relief, but it did nothing for her mother or her sister. On the other hand, marriage could be worse; there was no guarantee of relief from her father's rages—or indeed those of a husband—and still it did nothing for her family.

Her father seized her shoulders, pulled her from her chair, and shook her. "Stupid girl! He has an estate near Avebury. It was rich in my father's time, and I am certain it is still so. You will marry him, for I have promised you to him."

"Edward, no!" cried Mrs. Farleigh. "I have heard nothing good about the St. Vires, for all they are reclusive."

He turned reddened eyes to her and raised his fist. "Silence, woman! I know what is best for my family!" His wife shrank away from him. He turned to his daughter again.

"How much money did you lose this time?" Leonore bit her tongue, but it was too late to take back the words she had blurted. Her father shook her again, then pushed her away. Slowly, she sat down on the chair again.

"It matters not—he has agreed to marry you, and he will pay all our debts as well. Do you see?"

"Yes, Father." There was both relief and greed in her father's eyes, and Leonore knew it was not some drunken dream of his, but the truth.

Her stomach turned, and she pressed her lips together to keep down the rising nausea. She had been sold to this St. Vire, no doubt an old, lecherous man, one who had probably worn out his prior wife, trying to get sons on her. Why else would he want to wed a young woman like herself, whom he had never seen?

"Good girl," Mr. Farleigh said, and he released her. "We will go to him now."

"Edward, it is very late! Why, it is not decent to have a girl go to a man's house at this time of night! Indeed, not at any time at all!" his wife cried.

This time it was his wife whom he seized by the arm and shook until she sobbed. "Decent! Not decent! She is my daughter, and she is going with me, woman!"

"Father, stop!"

He turned, staggering.

"I will go with you. I cannot promise I will marry him, but I will at least see him for myself." *Perhaps if he thinks I am willing, Father will not cause trouble. Then I will take my savings from my wages and take Mother and Susan with me to Aunt May's house to visit—to gain a little quiet for once. No one can object to that, not even Father.* She wished she had taken a governess's post away from London, so that she need not feel obliged to come home on her days off. She sighed mentally. She had, after all, chosen to stay close to home; it was useless to regret it now.

"You will keep your mouth shut and say nothing, do you hear?"

"Yes, Father."

Mr. Farleigh was all smiles again. "Good."

Leonore had not even time to nod at her mother reassuringly before her father seized her arm and pulled her out the parlor door.

The hackney took Leonore and her father to a fashionable part of town—Pall Mall, she believed, looking at the new gas lamps. The lamps lighting the street were brighter than the moon and shone upon the gleaming brass fixtures on the door of the house. About that, at least, thought Leonore, her father had not lied. St. Vire must indeed be wealthy to live on this street. She wet her dry lips as her father nearly dragged her up the steps to the door, his fingers digging into her arm. She closed her eyes briefly, more from shame than from the pain. No matter how many times she had been humiliated by her father and his actions, each new humiliation was as nauseating as the last.

The door opened slowly at Mr. Farleigh's pounding, and the butler acknowledged them with a slight bow. He led them through the silent house, and Leonore could not help staring all around her, for the walls were covered with brocade, the draperies heavy and rich. Fine paintings lined the hallway, suggesting finer ones within the rooms. The clean smell of beeswax and polish came to her, and as she went up the stairs, she felt the smooth and sturdy banister beneath her hand. Lord St. Vire must be very wealthy indeed.

Lightly knocking at the door in front of them, the butler announced their presence.

"Come in." The door muffled the voice, and Leonore could not tell from it if the owner was young or old. Shame and anger overcame her in that instant, heating her face, and she felt she could not look at her host without showing it. She stared down at her hands clasped tightly in front of her instead and stepped into the room.

"Welcome, Mr. Farleigh, Miss Farleigh. Please sit down."

The voice in front of her was soft and deep and did not quaver with age. Perhaps he was middle-aged, instead of old, thought Leonore . . . not that it made her situation any better. She pressed her lips together firmly, choosing a chair well away from her father. It was best to face things as they were instead of guessing and pretending, she knew, however much less it hurt to pretend and imagine. But still she did not want to look at him; just for a moment she wanted to pretend she was not here. Leonore swallowed and castigated herself. She would control her emotions once again, and show a face as serene as she could make it.

"Miss Farleigh," the voice said, soothingly. "Do look up. I would very much like to see your face." Somehow she could not take offense at his words, for his voice pulled at her, the sound of it curling up around her ears so that she felt impelled to do just as he asked. For one moment she fought it, then took a deep breath and looked up.

He was beautiful.

Her breath left her in a rush. He was tall, much taller than herself, and she was considered well over average height. He could not be much older than her own five-and-twenty years, Leonore thought. His hair was dark and glinted red in the candle-light—it would show dark auburn or chestnut in the sun, she was sure. Two dark, arched eyebrows were set in a face per-fectly oval and smooth of lines. Beneath those brows were eyes, large and of an impossible green—grass green, almost— fringed with thick lashes. His lips, smiling gently, were aus-terely formed and yet oddly sensual. She would have thought him too beautiful to be a man, except that the lines of his face escaped the feminine with a firm, cleft chin, a strong jaw, and a classically straight nose.

But he was pale, pale as a marble saint in a medieval church, and there were shadows beneath his eyes. The cause of that must be dissipation, Leonore thought, or illness. Her mother had said that there had been little good said of the St. Vires; perhaps that was why he wished to marry her, sight un-seen. Perhaps his reputation put him beyond the pale for mar-riage with any well-born young lady, although his wealth and looks must have attracted many. Here was a puzzle, she thought.

St. Vire gazed at her up and down, his eyes lingering upon her figure, but with the coolness of an experienced horse trader. A blush warmed her cheeks, though Leonore kept her face impassive. How dare he! she fumed inwardly, then thought, how dare my father! For she was being sold as surely as a well-bred horse would be at Tattersall's. She began to resent him, almost as much as she did her father.

Something of her thoughts must have reflected in her face, for St. Vire smiled at her gently, saying, "I understand how awkward this must seem, Miss Farleigh. But you see, I need a wife quickly and could not wait to do it in the usual manner." He glanced at Leonore's father and returned his gaze to her. "I believe you came here willingly?"

"I came to see what you were like. So yes, I suppose you might say I came willingly. I made no promises to my father, and neither do I make any to you."

Her father rose from his chair in a stumbling rush. "I told you to keep your mouth shut, you little—!"

"Silence!" The room filled with an almost palpable threat as St. Vire leaned across his large desk toward Mr. Farleigh. The older man shrank down upon his chair again.

"Thank you," St. Vire said. His tone was cordial, and Leonore realized with surprise that his voice had never risen above a conversational level. He returned his gaze to her.

"Now then. Your father told you I wished to marry you?" He smiled at her, almost sympathetically, she thought.

"Yes. But unlike you, I did not want to make a decision that would affect the rest of my life without seeing what I would be living with."

St. Vire's smile turned into a wide grin. "Fair enough." He stood up and spread his arms wide. "You may look all you wish."

Leonore felt a blush rising in her cheeks again, but she looked him over as purposefully and as assessingly as he had her.

"Are you satisfied?"

She gave him a level look. "Not yet."

A low grumble came from her father. St. Vire gave him a sharp look, and Mr. Farleigh subsided. The younger man seemed to come to a decision and pulled the bell rope. "I think, perhaps, it is best if Miss Farleigh and I talk alone."

"Leave her alone with *you*!" Mr. Farleigh exclaimed. "You said you'd marry her right and tight, and I'll not have you tell me this night she's damaged goods!"

Silence reigned for one tick of the clock on the mantelpiece.

"I think it is best if Miss Farleigh and I talk alone," St. Vire repeated. The door opened, and the butler looked respectfully at his master. St. Vire nodded his head toward Mr. Farleigh. "Our guest wishes to wait in the parlor. Do provide him with some refreshment if you please, Samuels."

"Very good, sir."

Leonore's face grew more heated with mixed shame and wonder as she watched her father follow the butler out the door. If she did not know her father better, she would have said he had been cowed into submitting to St. Vire's wishes. She had never seen her father submit to anyone. How had St. Vire done it? She dared glance at him and found him looking at her again, seated and resting his chin on his hands.

"Interruptions are distressing, are they not?" he said.

A reluctant smile lifted the corners of Leonore's lips.

"Ah, that is better. You have a most charming smile."

"Are you relieved?"

St. Vire raised his eyebrows in question.

"That I am not an antidote," she explained.

This time he laughed—a pleasant, husky sound. "Truthfully, I did not think about it, although I must say to be wed to a lovely woman cannot be unpleasant."

Leonore's smile faded, and she looked away, remembering the times that sort of comment did her harm.

"You do not like to be complimented upon your looks?"

She raised her eyes and found him looking at her intently. "Attractiveness is not a useful attribute in a governess."

"Ah. Your father neglected to mention this."

"My family is poor," she said bluntly. "As the eldest, I

thought it better I earn my way in the world than be a burden upon my family's slight resources."

"And a respectable way to escape, I imagine." He pushed himself from the desk and leaned back in his chair, his expression contemplative.

Leonore looked at him in wary surprise. The man was perceptive; she needed to keep herself from displaying much of her feelings, lest it make her vulnerable in some way.

"Your father told me you are five-and-twenty. How is it that you are not married?"

"Quite easily: I am poor, have no dowry, and no entrée to the higher circles of society, despite my lineage. I am very much a creature betwixt and between."

"And yet you are clearly a lady of good breeding and intelligence."

She smiled wryly. "The first is of little worth when compared with the lack of other attributes, and the second is a liability, I assure you."

"But not, I assure *you*, to me."

Leonore blinked. To him? Of course. He wished to marry her. It was odd how she had been lured into talking with him as if she were actually considering it, responding almost automatically to his soft, sympathetic voice. Her intention had been to say little or nothing. Quickly, she went back through their conversation in her mind and realized she had revealed a great deal about herself, but he had said little of himself. How had he done it? She seldom spoke of her feelings, her thoughts to anyone. It had been his voice, perhaps, for it was deep and musical, lulling her into a comfort she seldom felt around people, dissipating the resentment she'd felt earlier.

"Why?" she asked. "Why do you want to marry me?"

There was silence as he watched his finger trace an aimless design upon the surface of the desk. Then he looked up at her.

"I need a wife. Soon. For . . . the usual reasons."

She watched him, his pale perfect face and the faint shadows under his eyes. A tired expression crossed his features, then a certain sad frustration replaced it. Clearly, he was not telling her everything. But she could guess, and pity for him rose within her. He was not well, it seemed. Perhaps that was why he wished to wed so quickly, to beget an heir before his illness overcame him. She shook her head, however. Regardless, he had no right to require that she marry him in return for her father's gaming debts.

"No. I am sorry, but no. I do not know you, and though I understand your troubles must be grievous, I am not the one. I am sure you will find another young woman more than happy to become your wife."

The frustration in his eyes grew, and he said, "May I ask why?"

"Simply this: I will not be sold."

He hesitated, then said bluntly: "My dear lady, do not all marriage arrangements concern a certain trade of favors? However much a pair may proclaim affection for each other, one gives and the other takes, and vice versa. A woman may bear her husband children in exchange for a comfortable living. In return, the husband protects her from all harm. Sometimes property is involved. I am offering that same comfort to you and will extend the same to your family. I only ask that you be my wife and live with me for a year. In that respect, it is no different from what any other man might ask in a proposal of marriage."

Leonore shook her head again. "I have no guarantee that you will deliver what you promise."

"Come here, please, Miss Farleigh."

She would have preferred staying in her chair, but she rose, nevertheless, and came to him. Lord St. Vire rose as well; he was tall, indeed. The top of her head came to his chin, and she had to tip back her head to look at him. Leonore felt suddenly small in front of him, and she did not like the sensation. She looked away from him.

A light caress circled her sore ear and then her chin, gently lifting her face so that she looked at him again. A fleeting expression of anger crossed his face, and Leonore took a quick step back.

"Your father hit you." It was not a question.

Shame suppressed all her words and she turned away from him.

"I promise, he will never do so again. And I swear I will never lift my hand to you, for as long as we are married."

Leonore looked at St. Vire, into his impossibly green eyes and thought she saw honesty there. Should she trust it? She thought of not having to constantly school her features so that an unguarded expression would not spark her father's wrath. Glancing about the room, she noted the beautiful tapestries that hung on the walls and rubbed her feet upon the soft richness of the carpet. Here she would have some comfort and would be surrounded by beauty instead of ugliness. Perhaps, also, she could ask that Susan stay with her, for she knew her shy and sensitive sister had almost become a recluse in her own room in an attempt to escape their father's drunken rages. St. Vire offered generous settlements; certainly a steady flow of money would keep her father's rages under control most of the time, and thereby offer some peace to her mother and sister. Could going to St. Vire be any worse than returning home? No, it could not. A tendril of hope pushed through her resistance, and she let out a breath she did not realize she'd been holding.

"Do you promise, then? Truly?" Leonore gazed at him intently.

"Yes, I do. I swear it." He looked straight and solemnly at her, then hesitated, glancing away briefly. "I hope to be a good husband to you. However, in all honesty, I must warn you that my habits are not those of other men."

Her brows rose in question, but her body tensed. The prospect of marrying St. Vire was so terribly tempting in many ways, and though she believed she could bear anything that resembled her father's intoxicated outbursts, she was not sure if she could bear anything worse.

"I cannot squire you in any daytime activities, although I can accompany you to all the society functions at night. I have a . . . condition that prohibits me from going out in the sunlight. I am very sensitive to it and will become quite ill."

Leonore wet her lips nervously. "Is . . . is it catching?"

Wry humor suddenly sprang into St. Vire's eyes. "No, I assure you, you will not catch it from me."

She smiled at him then and felt an odd regret. She had wondered what his hair would look like in the sun, and now she would never know. Regret turned to pity, and she extended her hand comfortingly to him.

"Very well, then. I shall marry you." The words came from her abruptly, rattling the brief silence between them. She surprised herself. She had not thought about it at all, but had spoken on impulse. It was a thing she rarely did; she was far more used to measuring her words carefully with people she did not know. Governesses did not keep their posts, else. But then, what did she have to lose? She would be away from her father and his drunkenness and be able to offer at least some support for her mother and sister. Marriage to St. Vire could be considered a form of employment, to be sure.

There was silence again, while St. Vire watched her. "Do you say that willingly? Your father has not forced you to agree? And I have not put undue pressure upon you, I hope?"

Leonore made sure to think carefully now. She thought of the advantages and looked at St. Vire's pale, earnest face. Perhaps he was, indeed, quite ill, and the one year he had spoken of was the amount of time he had left to him. Her pity for him grew stronger, overcoming the resentment she had felt earlier. Regardless of the way he took advantage of her father's debt to him, he still offered her more choices than she had ever had before. Though she was not so naive as to think he would tell her all, she felt that what he did tell her would be the truth. It was a thing she could sense about people, a skill she had built from sheer observation and from necessity. An urge to become free pressed from inside her, and the direction it pointed was away from her father's house and from his influence. She would have a measure of freedom here, with Nicholas St. Vire, more so than she would at home, or as a governess. She closed her eyes briefly, then said: "Yes. I say it willingly. I agree to marry you."

This time it was St. Vire who sighed, and his shoulders visibly relaxed. "Thank you," he said. "You have helped me im-mensely." He took her hand in his, lifting it to his lips. "I shall do my best to make sure you will live in comfort."

"And I shall do all I can to be a good wife," Leonore replied, letting out a breath as he released her hand. His touch was cool and soft, yet there seemed to be a controlled strength in his grasp. She almost shook her head, puzzled. Was he ill, or not? She gazed at his pale skin and decided on the side of illness.

He smiled brilliantly at her, almost dazzling her. "I am sure you will," he said.

Chapter 3

She was lovely.

St. Vire had not expected it, for surely someone like Farleigh could not have sired anything except brutishness and vulgarity in his offspring. But Miss Leonore Farleigh was tall and slender, unlike her burly father. Indeed, he would have almost thought her one of the *sidhe*, rather than human, with her gray eyes set in an elfin face and her delicate hands.

He contemplated the idea, as he put on his waistcoat. Perhaps it was her eyes that made him think strongly of the fairy folk, for though her expression had been neutral almost throughout their interview, her eyes had a wary, wild look in them. She belonged, not amongst the cobblestones and bricks of London, but in the wildwood, dancing beneath the moon.

St. Vire shook his head and smiled at his fancy. He was too old to be enthralled by a pretty face. Yet, he had always loved and admired women, the way they looked, the way they talked and laughed and moved. It had been, in the end, his downfall. All that was past, however, and the remedy for his . . . condition was in the present, and he hoped in his future with Miss Farleigh.

Taking a neckcloth from his valet, he wrapped it around his collar, keeping his eyes firmly on his hands reflected in the mirror. Glancing to the side, he noticed his young valet watching his actions carefully and almost smiled again. Edmonds was well on his way to becoming an excellent valet, for he was diligent, memorizing all he could about the tying of neckcloths, the polishing of boots, and the general care of clothes. He would definitely deserve a praise-filled reference when the time came to discharge him. It was too bad, but he could not afford to keep his personal servants for too long a time.

The *ton*, thankfully, was less observant. He never went to social functions, preferring his own company, but now he was to be married, and it was necessary that he enter society once again. He should recompense Miss Farleigh in some way for becoming his wife, after all. Thinking of his betrothed brought her image to mind again, her soft white-blond hair and slender form—especially that slender, womanly form. He chuckled at himself. He was truly incorrigible.

St. Vire turned away from the mirror with a last tug on his neckcloth. Lady Jersey, he had heard, would be at Lady Bremer's card party tonight, to which he had been invited. He had won a bit of money from Lord Bremer. He smiled cynically. Lord Bremer had been all too eager to issue him an invitation in return for debt, as the man was known to live in fear of Lady Bremer's stringent eye and sharp tongue. Once there, St. Vire would cultivate Lady Jersey's acquaintance. He had known her father long ago, and was sure he could claim the acquaintance once again—obliquely, of course.

He dismissed Edmonds, then changed his mind and stopped the young man with a raised finger. "Oh, by the way, I understand you did not request a clothing allowance when you were retained."

"No, my lord," replied the valet. "The wages were generous enough, I thought."

St. Vire smiled. "You are an honest man, Edmonds. But I give all my servants a clothing allowance. I will write my solicitor later, but meanwhile, do take that yellow waistcoat from the wardrobe—I have taken a sudden dislike to it."

"Not . . . not for me?" stammered the man.

"Yes, for you." His smile grew wider. "The color offends me."

Edmonds grinned in return. "Thank you, my lord! I'll take care not to wear it in your presence."

"Good. Is the carriage ready?"

"Yes, of course, my lord."

"Excellent." He turned and left the room.

St. Vire descended the stairs to the waiting carriage. Gaining entrance once again into the heart of the *ton* should be easy. He had the initial entrée through Lady Bremer's card party, and he could employ the special talents he had gained so long ago if he had to. He would only need to be persuasive. There should be no trouble obtaining vouchers for Almack's from Lady Jersey, after all.

The lights from the Bremers' town house shone almost as bright as day. But as the lights had nothing to do with the day, and everything to do with staving off the night, St. Vire did not mind it. A brief hush came over the room when he made his entrance, startling him, but he supposed it was because he was a stranger, and odd-looking. Lord Bremer greeted him as if he were an old friend and introduced him to his wife, a stern, aristocratic matron. St. Vire smiled his best smile for her, and she turned pink, fluttering her fan like a young girl. She, in turn, brought him to Lady Jersey.

Sally Jersey. She had aged well. St. Vire could see the little girl he had once known in this mature and pretty lady. He bowed most gravely to her.

"Do I know you?" she said after Lady Bremer introduced them. Lady Jersey had a puzzled, interested look on her face as if she were trying to recall him. "You seem familiar to me."

He smiled. "Yes, of course. I knew you when you were a little girl. I see you have not changed at all."

Lady Jersey looked as if she did not know whether to be affronted or amused. "Nonsense! You cannot be more than five and twenty, if that!"

St. Vire put on a concerned expression. "Have I offended you? You did say I seemed familiar, and it seemed to please you. So, I decided to be even more familiar, to see if it would please you further." He let his gaze linger avidly over each of her features as he bowed over her hand.

She burst out laughing, lightly tapping his hand with her fan. "I see you are a rogue! Now I am certain I have seen you before! Tell me!"

He smiled. "I think you may have seen my . . . father. He

was acquainted with yours. Perhaps you might have seen him once or twice. I am said to resemble him greatly."

Lady Jersey's face cleared. "Of course! I do remember your father! A most charming man, even to the child that I was. I never did hear of him since, though. Is he well?"

St. Vire shook his head. "I am afraid he passed away years ago, when I was young. I hardly knew him."

"Ah! I am sorry. But you!" She gazed at him assessingly, and a determined light grew in her eye. "Why is it I have not seen you in London?"

He took her hand, put it on his arm, and led her to the supper table. Another, older man—apparently Lady Jersey's supper companion—gave him an angry glance and started forward, but St. Vire only smiled sweetly at him. The man stopped, and though he continued to glare, he did nothing. Lady Jersey did not seem to notice, for all her attention was on St. Vire.

"Alas," he said. "I did not know such beautiful ladies abounded in London, else I would have hurried here, hotfooted." He was pouring the butter boat over her, and he was certain she knew it. He gave her a mischievous look, and she tapped his arm smartly with her fan again.

"Double rogue! I do not know why I am even speaking with you, for you seem incapable of answering me straightly. Indeed, where is Colonel Stoneworth? *He* was to be my supper companion!"

"Was he? He is a poor soldier, then! One glance from my fiery, jealous eye, and he was thoroughly routed, I assure you." He brought her, unresisting, to a table.

Lady Jersey burst into laughter again and tried to stifle it beneath her hand. "Oh, dear! You really must come out more often, St. Vire!"

"I would, Lady Jersey, but I have been so secluded on my estates, that I know no one, other than poor Lord Bremer and his most charming wife."

She gazed at him, her lips pursed in consideration. "I *could* give you a voucher for Almack's, but I suspect *that* is why you cultivated my acquaintance."

"No!" He put a hand over his heart. "You wound me, saying such a thing! Have I asked for one, after all?"

Lady Jersey pressed her hand against her lips again to stifle her laughter and failed. "How vexatious you are! I am *certain* now you only wish entrée to Almack's." She gnawed her lower lip and considered him. He put a ludicrously expectant, hopeful look on his face, and she laughed again. "I vow, you look like a naughty boy with that expression! Oh, very well! But you must promise to be amusing, and *no* naughtiness."

St. Vire gave an exaggerated sigh of relief and gazed soulfully into her eyes. "I can but try, my lady."

The patroness of Almack's tried to look stern but failed. "You are *incorrigible*!"

"Yes, my lady," St. Vire said obediently and grinned.

It would be two months until they married. Leonore fingered the delicate lace of the dress she had laid upon her bed. She did not know whether the time before her wedding was too long or too short. She dreaded the marriage, as anyone would dread the unknown, but she dreaded more staying much longer with her family, wondering when the next violent outburst would happen. At least her father was all smiles now and his temper well in check; St. Vire had advanced him some money from the settlements.

Leonore stroked the fine silk gown she had bought. The cloth was pink and shimmered in the late afternoon sunlight, one of the few bright spots in her drab and faded bedroom. She was not to be shabbily attired, it seemed. St. Vire had sent her a note, recommending a particular dressmaker, Madame Etoile in New Bond Street. When she had gone there with her mother, the dressmaker had looked upon her drab clothes with some disdain. But then her mother had timidly announced their names, and the woman had become eager to do business with them. Apparently, St. Vire had sent a note to Madame, saying all purchases Leonore and her mother made would be charged to his account.

There were more dresses coming in the next week, but Leonore wanted the pink silk one soon, even though she knew she would have no occasion to wear it. The dress was lovely, lovelier than anything else she had ever owned, and she was content to look at it, letting its smooth folds slide through her hands. She felt daring at the indulgence and would put the dress away again, only to pull it out not a few hours later.

A knock on the door startled her from her thoughts.

"Who is it?"

"It is I, Leo," came her sister's voice.

"You know you can come in, Susie. You need not wait." Leonore rose from the bed and opened the door, smiling affectionately at her sister. The girl was seven years younger than Leonore, her parents' last attempt at siring a boy after years of stillbirths. Perhaps it was fortunate that her father generally ignored Susan's existence after his initial disappointed rage.

Susan smiled eagerly at Leonore. "I came to see your new dress. Mama said you had brought one home, and I did so want to see it." She hesitated. "It is permitted, isn't it? For me to see it, I mean."

Leonore laughed. "Of course, silly! I was just looking at it myself." She picked up the dress from her bed and held it up against her. "See?"

"Ohhh. . . ." Susan's eyes were round with awe. "May . . . may I touch it?"

"Here." Leonore held out the dress to her. "Indeed, you may even try it on."

The girl stared at Leonore, then broke out in laughter. "Oh, you are such a tease, Leo! You know it would never fit me! You are so tall and pretty, and I am just a little squab of a thing."

Leonore looked at her sister's golden blond hair and large, beautiful blue eyes. True, Susan was six inches shorter than herself, and very slight of frame, but she was very pretty.

"Nonsense, Susie! You are just turned seventeen, and I did not reach my height until I was nineteen. You shall undoubtedly be as tall as I, and beautiful, besides."

Susan shook her head, blushing, and Leonore smiled. She turned to a chair at the side of her bed and picked up a package from it. "And this, my dear sister, is for you." She held it toward Susan.

The girl did not touch it, but looked uncertainly at Leonore. "Is it allowed? For me to have it, that is?"

"Yes. Yes, it is." Leonore leaned toward her. "*I* bought it, do you see? St. Vire wishes me to buy whatever dresses I like, and for you, too." Her sister still hesitated. "Open it, Susie!"

Susan looked once more at Leonore, then took the package. She unwrapped it and let out a long, awe-filled sigh. "Ohhh. Is this really for me?" Pulling out the blue round-gown, she gazed at it with wide eyes.

"Have I not said it?" Leonore said. "Do try it on! I want to see if it fits you properly."

Hastily, the girl pulled off her clothes and put on the blue gown while Leonore lit a branch of candles, the better to see in the growing dimness. She tied the ribbon at the back of the dress, then pushed her sister in front of a mirror. "Now look!" she said.

Susan stared at herself in the mirror. "This is mine," she whispered. "This is truly mine." Tears welled up in her eyes, and she turned to Leonore. "Oh, Leo, thank you! I don't know . . . I've never had Ohh!" The girl cast herself into her sister's arms and hugged her fiercely. "You are the *best* of sisters! You should be *sainted*!"

Leonore burst out laughing. "Hardly that, silly! Now, don't cry, please! You will stain your very pretty dress, and I shall then regret giving it to you."

Wiping away her tears with her fingers, Susan smiled mistily at her sister. "Well, *I* think you should be sainted. I am sure you cannot love St. Vire in such a short time, so I know you are sacrificing yourself for our family."

Leonore glanced away. "Oh, it is hardly a sacrifice! St. Vire is a gentleman and seems kind besides. And I shall be living in luxury, to be sure! Why, if you could only see his house! It is full of the richest draperies, and the furniture is of the finest. Not only that, but—"

"But you don't *love* him."

"What has that to say to anything?" She glanced impatiently at Susan. "People marry for many other reasons than love."

"You will be unhappy; I know you, Leo. We have talked of this, I remember, long ago."

"Oh, well, long ago!" Leonore replied. "It has been a long time since we have read fairy tales together and, after all, that is all they were—fairly tales. You cannot base your life on made-up stories."

"But you told me there was a seed of truth in all those stories!" Leonore could hear a note of bewilderment in Susan's voice.

"Well, there might be, but *only* a seed. And, as I said, that was long ago. I am older now and must face facts: We cannot all have the luxury of marrying where there is love." She gazed at Susan and saw the lost look in the girl's eyes. "Oh, Susie! It will be different for you! Why, you will receive a dowry and will be able to choose whom you will wed! And you are so pretty, I am sure you will have many suitors from which to choose."

"It isn't right, Leo, it isn't right!" cried the girl passionately. "I cannot be happy that you are marrying an old, ugly man! Not for *my* sake!"

"Oh, my dear Susie!" Leonore took her sister in her arms, hugging her tightly, glad Susan couldn't see the tears in her own eyes. "You are mistaken! Did no one tell you? St. Vire is young and handsome. Exceedingly handsome! Why, I am sure everyone will think me an absolute hag when I stand next to him."

"Oh!" Susan moved away from her, blushing. "I have been very stupid, I think."

Leonore sighed. "No, my dear, you have only been good-hearted and loyal, and the best of sisters." Susan was so reclusive that apparently not even their mother had bothered to give her any of the particulars of Leonore's betrothal. Their father barely spoke to Susan at all. She felt a pang of guilt. Neither had she, for she had avoided thinking of her impending wedding, and so was not wont to talk of it.

"I am certain he will come to love you, Leo. He must know

how beautiful you are and will come to see how good you are, too, and then will love you forever, I am sure of it!"

Leonore smiled slightly. "Perhaps." Just a little longer, she would allow Susan her dreams. Certainly, the girl would have a better chance at it than herself and would marry a man who would adore her as her little sister deserved. Such a thing was not for Leonore, herself. Was she not making an arranged marriage? And she did not, truly, know St. Vire. In real life, beasts often lurked under the face of a prince, rather than the other way around. No spell would change that, and neither was she a princess to kiss away an enchantment.

"And, if he is indeed as kind as he has been so far," Susan continued, "and since he is so handsome, *you* will come to love him, too."

"Perhaps," replied Leonore, forcing herself to smile wider still.

A knock on the door startled the young ladies, and they both looked at the door, then glanced at each other. "Come in," Leonore said. A maid entered.

"Excuse me, miss, but there's Lord St. Vire wishing to speak with you."

Leonore rose, her hands clasped tightly together. It was past the hour for callers, just beyond twilight. What could St. Vire want of her? "Yes, Annie, of course. Do let him know I shall be down directly in the drawing room." The maid bobbed a curtsy and left.

"Do . . . you wish for me to be with you, Leo?" Susan asked anxiously. "Mama is not well today; she has the headache."

Through the years Mama's headaches had increased in frequency and duration. Leonore bit her lip and wished she did not feel so nervous; there was something about St. Vire that intimidated her, and this angered her. She had had enough of intimidation throughout her life and had sworn she'd never be under it again. No doubt it was his undeniable handsomeness, or his exquisite elegance; she felt a drab mouse beside him, and he disconcerted her with his words and his manner, and the lingering way he looked at her.

She tried to smile at her sister reassuringly. "Only if you

wish to see what St. Vire looks like. I am betrothed to him, after all."

Susan bit her lip, considering the idea. She glanced at Leonore, then nodded. "I think I shall, just for a little, for perhaps he would like to be private with you, and I would not like to intrude."

Leonore almost sighed with relief. It was proper for her to be alone with her betrothed, but she did not feel comfortable about it yet. She smiled. "And I am sure you would very much like to see if he is as young and handsome as I have said he is," she said, teasing.

A blush suffused Susan's cheeks, but a dimple appeared as well. "Well, I only wished to see who our benefactor is . . . and all the better if he is young and handsome."

"Minx!"

Susan only grinned.

It had been two weeks since Leonore had seen St. Vire for the first time, and that late at night. She sometimes thought perhaps she had exaggerated his handsomeness and his youth, that wishful thinking had tainted her memory of him. But she only had to look at her sister's awe-filled gaze upon their entrance into the drawing room to confirm her own perception.

For St. Vire was more handsome than she had remembered, perhaps because she was not so tired now as she had been two weeks ago. He was impeccably attired, apparently for some evening event, instead of in the more casual fashion she had seen him that night. His well-fitted jacket showed off his broad shoulders, and a silver-chased waistcoat peeked beneath it. A single ruby pin glowed in the midst of the immaculate folds of his neckcloth. In all, he looked magnificent, even more so in contrast to the faded wallpaper and the worn furniture around him.

He greeted her and bowed over her hand with exquisite grace, and then over Susan's, which made the girl giggle.

"Miss Susan Farleigh, I presume?" he said smiling.

The girl nodded shyly. "I am pleased to meet you, my lord." She looked at Leonore and then back to St. Vire. "Shall I leave, now, sir?"

"Susan!" Leonore exclaimed at her sister's abruptness. She was hoping Susan might stay a little longer, at least until Leonore felt more comfortable in St. Vire's presence.

St. Vire chuckled. "Only if you wish to leave, Miss Susan."

Susan cast a mischievous glance at her sister. "Oh, I think I shall. I have some mending to do."

"Susan—!" Leonore hissed as the girl passed her on the way out the door. But Susan ignored her and shut the door firmly.

Her face was hot, and Leonore was sure she was blushing furiously. She could not look at St. Vire, could not say one word because of her embarrassment and her frustration at being put at such a disadvantage. Silence was a wall between them, and she tried to breach it with a small laugh.

"You must excuse her, my lord. She is young and full of romantic notions."

"And you, of course, are an ancient, too full of years to have such ideas."

This time she could not help smiling, and this gave her courage to glance briefly at him. He was also smiling at her, and his gaze was kindly. "Of course not," she said.

"Ah! I have hope that you, too, have romantic notions."

Blushing, she shook her head. "You mistake me. I meant I am not an ancient. But I have enough years to know our match is not at all romantic."

"One never knows how anything will turn out. You should have enough years in you to know that." He took a step closer to her. She looked up at him then. Their eyes met and held. "You are lovely, Miss Farleigh—Leonore. I could easily have romantic notions about you." He took another step closer.

She was but a handbreadth away from him. His eyes shifted from her own and focused on her lips.

"Nonsense," Leonore said, surprised her voice came out in a whisper. "Nonsense," she said more clearly. "We have met only once, and that two weeks ago." She hated herself for her weakness, for showing even slightly that he discomposed her.

He grinned. "I see you have been counting the weeks, Leonore."

She took a step backward and breathed deeply. "Not I! I have been too busy for that. And . . . I have not given you permission to use my Christian name."

"How remiss of you. I, however, will do my part: My name is Nicholas. You may use it whenever you wish." He took another step toward her, but when she stepped back, she found herself against a wall. She dropped her gaze from his.

His hand came up to rest on the wall next to her head. The other touched the same ear he had touched when they first met. A finger traced a tingling line from ear to jaw, making her face flame hot again.

"In fact, I would very much like to hear you say it. You have a lovely voice, you know. I have always like my name, and I think I shall like it even better if you were to say it."

"Nicholas."

"Ah. I was right. I do like it better when you say it."

An unwilling chuckle bubbled up from within her and made her look at him again. It was a mistake. St. Vire had bent his head toward her so that his face was very near hers. A considering look crossed his countenance.

Her breath came and went quickly, making a sound like a little moan. A spurt of anger at herself for her loss of control came after it.

He moved away from her. "You are frightened of me."

"No, I—"

"You need not be, you know. I have said I will never raise my hand to harm you. I keep my word."

"It . . . it is just that I do not know you, my lord." Leonore glanced at him and saw he was not angry. Her heart slowed its hammering beat, and she let out a slow breath.

He smiled and took her hand, kissing it. "Then my errand to you is most opportune. In the interests of getting to know one another better, perhaps I can persuade you to come to the opera with me?"

"The opera?" She felt a little dazed at this change of subject. "When?"

"Tonight. Now. And, if you feel uncomfortable about being

alone with me, you may ask your mother and sister to come with us."

"Tonight?" Her mind was in a flurry of confusion. "The dresses I have ordered have not come yet—or wait! There is one I brought home, and Susan can wear her new one. But my mother—oh, she is ill with the headache. I do not know—"

"Then you and your sister can come with me," he said patiently.

Susan would be ecstatic at a chance to go to the opera. Leonore gazed up at St. Vire and smiled gratefully at him. "You are very kind, my lo—Nicholas. I shall tell my sister, and be ready quickly."

" 'My Nicholas.' I like the sound of that." He took her hand again and kissed it. His lips were soft against her skin.

Again the thoughts scattered in her mind. "I didn't mean . . . That is to say . . ." She looked at him, saw laughter in his eyes, and pulled her hand away, saying, "You are teasing me!"

"I?" His expression was wounded. "You accuse me unjustly, my dear."

This time she could not help laughing. "You *are* teasing, and for that I shall take my time dressing and make you late for the first act." She went toward the door.

"Oh, horror!" he cried and put his hand theatrically to his forehead.

Leonore did not reply, but laughed again before she shut the parlor door behind her.

St. Vire stared contemplatively at the closed door for a moment. He sighed. His betrothed was a truly delectable woman, but she was as elusive and as easily startled as a wild deer. The wooing of her would take some time, and he had only two months before the wedding. And it was necessary that she give herself willingly on their wedding night.

He grinned suddenly and widely. At the very least, he would enjoy the pursuit.

Chapter 4

Leonore captured one's gaze, thought St. Vire, and made it linger. He was conscious of the speculative looks at their box in the theatre, and knew she and her sister were attracting much attention. There was something gratifying about it, after his lengthy seclusion from society.

He watched Leonore, who leaned forward in her chair, her whole focus on the stage. It was more amusing watching her than the opera itself. Her face, ordinarily quite controlled, now clearly showed the emotions the opera evoked in her. Gone were the guarded look and the wary watchfulness, and he thought her more lovely for it.

As for himself, he had seen Mozart's *Don Giovanni* many times before. Since Lord Byron had published his poem *Don Juan*, all things even remotely related to the story were revived for public consumption. Perhaps he was becoming jaded from overexposure to the character, but St. Vire thought Don Giovanni—Don Juan, for that matter—singularly stupid. No man who truly appreciated women would treat them as that character did.

His lip curled as he watched Don Giovanni struggle upon the stage to escape from the seduced Donna Anna and end up killing her father in the process. What a fool the man was, with no finesse whatsoever. A woman was to be wooed gently, seduced into understanding that nothing mattered but the moment; and a wise man chose experienced women who expected nothing else. Don Giovanni had no discrimination whatsoever. St. Vire shrugged. He recalled the music was sublime, and if he did not reflect on the story, he could concentrate on the sounds coming from the stage and perhaps recapture the experience he'd once had.

St. Vire let his gaze wander appreciatively over his betrothed, considering her. He *had* wooed her gently this evening, giving Leonore most of his attention when he was not playing host to both her and her sister. And yet, though this usually would have thawed the iciest of dowagers, it only brought the wary look into her eyes again. Should he not press his attentions upon her as much? But then, he had only two months until their wedding day. It was not much time, to be sure.

The second act ended, and he watched Leonore sigh and lean back in her chair. She turned to look at him, her expression still unguarded.

"Are you enjoying the opera, Leonore? Miss Susan?"

"Oh, Lord St. Vire!" Susan exclaimed, her eyes glowing with wonder. "It is the most wonderful treat! And such a story! I cannot wait to see what happens next."

A light laugh came from Leonore, and she leaned toward St. Vire. "I agree and would add to that the wonder of such beautiful music." She put out her hand in an impulsive gesture and touched his sleeve. "Thank you. It was very kind of you to bring us here."

An odd warmth rose within St. Vire, surprising him. "Nonsense," he said. "I wished for company. Who else more appropriate than my betrothed?" He almost wished he had not spoken, for his voice sounded cool and abrupt. He had been surprised out of his customary urbanity, and he frowned briefly.

Leonore gazed at him, her wary expression returned, and then it disappeared again with a wide smile. "You need not have asked Susan to accompany us, however. I still think it very kind of you to do so."

St. Vire gazed at her, arrested. Here, now, was Leonore's expression open again, and for what? Not flattery, but a simple act of what she termed kindness. He had thought he'd seduce her with his words and his manners, as he had done with other women. But one simple invitation for herself and her sister had sufficed to have her look upon him more favorably.

He smiled and raised her hand to his lips. "No, again it was merely self-interest. I merely wished the whole *ton* to be envious of me that I have two lovely ladies in my box."

Leonore withdrew her hand from his, but this time her gaze was uncertain rather than wary. A blush rose in her cheeks, and she shook her head. "You are too kind."

St. Vire leaned back in his chair. "I am not, really. In truth, I am a selfish fellow, concerned only with my own wishes. However, if you are determined to think me otherwise, please do so. Indeed, I will give you another reason to heap praise upon my head: I have ordered refreshments be brought here, so you needn't venture forth and be mobbed by the enormous number of gentlemen who have been training their quizzing glasses for the last half hour upon you both."

"*Have* they?" Susan inquired, her eyes round. She leaned forward and looked out of their box, then shrank back. "Oh, no!"

Leonore put her hand on Susan's arm. "It is only that we are strangers, I am sure. Once we are better known, they will not stare so." Her sister relaxed and continued looking about the opera hall with more interest. Leonore seemed to hesitate, then leaned toward St. Vire and lowered her voice. "My lord, my sister is normally reclusive and only agreed to come because music is so dear to her heart." She pressed her lips together and looked at him uncertainly. "I do not want her to . . . she needs to . . ."

St. Vire took her hand and squeezed it gently. "She is not used to society, eh?. And the attentions of strangers tend to frighten her a little and make her more reclusive?"

She sighed and smiled at him gratefully. "Yes, that is it. Susan is not at all used to having attention paid to her, and she would not know how to respond to it."

"Very well then. I will be careful in what I say, so we may ease her into society with as little trouble as possible." He noticed Leonore had not pulled her hand from his grasp and, indeed, pressed his hand in return. "Am I wrong in thinking this might be true of you, also?" he asked.

A flustered expression briefly flickered over her face, and she withdrew her hand. The refreshments came, and as she sipped a bit of wine, she seemed to gain some measure of composure. She looked at him, a bit of defiance in her gaze. "Oh, I shall manage quite well, I am sure."

He merely nodded and suppressed a smile. He really could not resist teasing her. "I am certain of it. But there are so many rules and restrictions, it would be easy even for me to falter."

"Oh, really?" Leonore's eyebrows rose. "I would not have thought it." Her voice was ironic.

"Truly. I received one set-down after another from Lady Jersey the other night, and there was nothing for it but I must persist in blundering toward my goal."

"And that was . . . ?"

He opened his eyes wide in innocence. "Why, procuring vouchers for Almack's of course."

There was silence.

"Almack's?" Leonore croaked.

"Yes. Do you not wish to go?"

"For me? I . . . I will go to Almack's?" She stared at him, hope and disbelief crossing her features. She shook her head and smiled ruefully. "No, of course not. You are teasing me. If you are such a blunderer, and if Lady Jersey gave you set-downs, then you cannot have received any vouchers."

St. Vire shook his head as well. "Alas, it's true. She called me a rogue and double rogue and slapped my hand with her fan time after time."

"No doubt you deserved it . . . and I suspect, my lord, that you are a hopeless flirt."

"Never hopeless, Leonore," he said. He took her hand and smiled into her eyes.

It was an intimate smile, and Leonore could feel her face grow warm. But she could not look away, for his gaze held hers as firmly as his grasp on her hand. The lights dimmed, St. Vire turned to glance at the stage, and Leonore was able to look away. She tried to move her hand from his, but he held it firm.

"Don't pull away, Leonore," he whispered as the music started. "No one will see. I would like to hold your hand. It . . . pleases me to do so."

She gazed at him again, at his face that showed nothing but kind friendliness. Surely it was not such a terrible thing to allow him to hold her hand for a while. He was her betrothed, after all, and he had been kind to her and Susan. What he asked for was little compared to what he had given. She relaxed, nodding slightly.

"Thank you," he said and gently pressed her hand.

Leonore gave him a hesitant smile, then leaned back in her chair, letting the opera's music flow over her. But this time, she could not immerse herself in the story of Don Giovanni. She was too conscious of St. Vire's hand upon hers. He pulled her hand toward him, lacing his long fingers through hers, and settling it upon his knee. She could feel the firm muscles of his leg upon the back of her hand, glad the theatre was dim enough to hide her blushes.

She did not know how such a simple, innocent thing could seem so intimate to her. He released his fingers slightly from hers, and though she could not see it in the shadows of the theatre box, she could feel his thumb rubbing gently the palm of her hand. It was at once distracting, soothing, and oddly comforting.

His thumb stopped for a moment, and then she felt her glove slipping off. His hand came down upon hers again, flesh upon flesh, for he was gloveless also. His skin was dry and cool, growing warm as his thumb again caressed the hollow of her hand; but this time a fine tingling shimmered across her palm, radiating through her fingers and up her arm.

She trained her gazed upon the stage, but it was as if she saw nothing. All her attention was upon his bare hand entwined with hers, alternately still and caressing, the sensation of knitted silk breeches over muscle pressing upon the back of her hand.

"Don't," she said at last and was annoyed at the breathlessness in her voice.

St. Vire turned to look at her, his brows raised in question.

"What you are doing," she explained, beginning to feel foolish. He took his hand from hers and she felt strangely bereft.

"You do not like me to hold your hand?"

Leonore glanced at Susan, but the girl was oblivious, totally absorbed by the music and the singers on the stage.

"Your sister has noticed nothing," he said, smiling.

"It is just . . . you were not just *holding* my hand," she said, feeling even more foolish for protesting what now seemed a trivial thing.

His smile turned apologetic. "I am sorry. You seemed to find it soothing, perhaps comforting in a way. It was at least to me."

A strange sensation, a soft tenderness, unfurled within Leonore, and she drew in her breath, half afraid of the feeling. It *had* been comforting, and therefore seductive, for there had been little tenderness in her life, except for Susan's sisterly affection. He had said it was comforting to him, too. Suddenly, she remembered why he wanted to marry her, and sadness came over her. He probably had not long to live and took comfort in what signs of affection he could find. She smiled at him and took his hand again. "You need not be sorry. It was foolishness on my part. I am not used to signs of . . . affection."

St. Vire cocked his head a little to the side in a considering manner. "Could you become used to it, in time?"

Leonore could feel her face grow warm, but nodded. "I think I could learn. It is not . . . unpleasant."

He smiled widely at her. "I am glad," he said, and brought her hand to his lips.

It was almost dawn by the time St. Vire readied himself for sleep. It had been a good evening. Apparently Leonore had decided to allow him a first step toward intimacy, and it seemed likely he could, indeed, persuade her to come willingly to him on their marriage night. He thought of it, the coming marriage, with a mix of anticipation and dread. He would know then, that night, if he could be cured eventually of his condition. And even if he found he could, there was still no telling whether it would all end in regaining full use of his senses or if he would die at the end of a year. How ironic it would be if all his efforts resulted in achieving all he held dear in life, only to be snatched away.

St. Vire took off his robe and caught sight of the cheval mirror, hidden under the curtain he had specially made for it. Turning, he stretched out his hand toward it, hesitated, then jerked the curtain aside.

Pale, pale as death. The familiar urge to smash the mirror rose in him, but he thrust the feeling down. He forced himself to look upon his reflection: feet, legs, sex, stomach, arms, and chest—all normally formed, all that was necessary to a living, breathing man. Yet the sight of his body mocked him, for other than the fact that he breathed and was standing, there was no other sign of life upon him, no fleshly color to his skin.

And then his face. St. Vire made himself stare into his reflected eyes, and his hand rose up involuntarily, as if to strike the reflection. He lowered his clenched hand and made it relax. It was an alien face, the only alive thing in it his eyes—an old man's eyes set in a face obscenely young.

Why did no one see it? Was it that everyone else was stupid, blind, or was it himself? *He* could see his pale, translucent skin, his teeth just as white, the canines sharp and longer than in humankind. Sometimes he thought he had gone mad, for no one had ever commented on his looks, and indeed some seemed to gaze upon him with favor.

Yet every time he hunted, and every time he came upon his prey, he would be shocked into sanity again, for certainly he'd glimpsed the horror in the eyes of his victims—the horror that should be there in anyone else who looked upon him. But it was not.

Perhaps he was mad. St. Vire shuddered and thrust the thought away. God, no. Not yet, not before he could feel, hear, smell, and taste of life again. Even an hour of it would be enough for him, after sixty years of being one step removed from life. Sixty years of touching but scarcely feeling, of eating but not tasting. Music, with its sublime sweetness and agony, could not pierce through the confusion of noise his ears heard; the glory he had heard so long ago was only a memory. Not even sexual desire could stand against the wash of thirst that overcame him, the thirst for blood.

"A vampire," he whispered. "I am a vampire."

There, he had said it. Anger and despair muddied his emotions, but he pushed the feelings aside. There was no use bemoaning his fate. He smiled slightly. Besides, it was of more practical use to enjoy what he had at the moment. There were certain advantages to being a vampire: preternatural strength and swiftness, the ability to cast a glamour over those he wished to influence. Indeed, he had enjoyed these talents when he had first discovered them, and a heady sense of power had filled him when he had first exercised these gifts.

But it had soon palled, and it was not enough for him. He never was one to exult in an advantage unless it was intellectual. Now, even that advantage he was beginning to question. Never had he thought that the enjoyment of one's physical senses fed the intellect, but now he was certain it did. He wondered how far into madness one could slip without the daily sensory sustenance the mind needed. If the woman who had made him a vampire had known or had cared to know, certainly she had had no wish to tell him. He grimaced, not wanting to know the answer. She had disappeared long ago, and he would not find out from her.

St. Vire sighed and pulled the cloth over the mirror again. He did not know why he bothered to ponder these things, why it made him want to smash the mirror and anything else inanimate—

Ah, but who was he trying to fool? Of course he knew why. He was not at all sure he would ever be fully alive again, regardless of his plans, not sure that he could escape the madness he was sure would overcome him at some time. One tended to wonder and fear, hate and deny when one's plans had small hope of success. But there was hope, at least.

St. Vire went to the window and noted the first faint lightening of the sky. The dawn was but a few minutes away. He had stayed up too late; he could feel the sharp tingling on his skin that promised pain if he did not protect himself from the sunlight. Almost, almost, he was tempted to keep the curtains open just a little longer. The pain would be real, and there was no blandness about it. He did this from time to time, just to prove to himself he was truly alive.

The tingling sharpened even more, and he pulled the heavy curtains across the window, making sure there was no place for light to come through. He did the same for the equally heavy curtains around his bed once he climbed into it. He lay down upon the cool sheets, pulled the covers over him, and sighed once more. Perhaps he would not dream this time, he thought, as he closed his eyes. He never knew what to make of his dreams, for sometimes they were full of portent, and sometimes only shifting images.

A brief picture of Leonore flitted through his mind as he drowsed. He wondered if she would hate him when she found out. But the thought faded into sleep.

Chapter 5

It must be, reflected Leonore cynically, the glamour of near-nobility that made her acquaintance so desirable now. She sat in the drawing room of her father's house, hoping she could maintain her smile for one more guest, glad her father had left for his club, and wishing her mother had not retired with yet another headache.

Once her betrothal had been announced in the *Gazette*, she achieved instant popularity. Five invitations to balls and routs had come to her within the week, and the callers she had received today had given her more. She was no fool, however; it was St. Vire they were curious about, and then secondarily herself as someone who had snared a most intriguing and eccentric, if not mysterious, man.

She smiled politely at Lady Brunsmire, a widow still young enough to look pretty in the frivolous dress she wore. The lady looked around the Farleighs' shabby drawing room with curiosity. No doubt she is wondering what it was that attracted St. Vire to someone like me, Leonore thought.

"Lord St. Vire is such an intriguing man, I vow, and so handsome!" Lady Brunsmire was saying. She looked toward the door expectantly and then glanced at the mirror near it, tucking a lock of her red hair back beneath her headband. The lady brought her gaze back to Leonore. "I have tried to invite him to my alfresco luncheon, but he says he cannot come." Clearly, the woman was hoping St. Vire would appear, and that Leonore would persuade him to go to the luncheon.

"I am sorry, my lady. But Lord St. Vire does not go out during the day. Not even with me."

The lady's eyebrows rose. "Surely he . . . You are his betrothed! Certainly you could persuade him."

"No, I doubt Lord St. Vire will change his ways. It quite amuses him to live as he does."

"Perhaps you have not been . . . persuasive enough. Few men are proof against a lady's charm." Lady Brunsmire looked at her pityingly as if to say that Leonore had no charm at all.

Leonore smiled slightly. "Oh, but you must admit he is quite out of the ordinary, certainly an original. And an original, especially such a charming one as St. Vire, should be allowed his little fancies, should he not? Why should he attend the usual common activities that everyone else does?"

Lady Brunsmire shot her a sharp glance, but Leonore kept her face politely bland. The lady's glance took in the worn furniture and rugs in the room, and she smiled, apparently deciding that Leonore was too gauche to have meant anything by her words.

"So true, Miss Farleigh. St. Vire is a clever man, is he not? He kept me so very amused a few evenings ago." A complacent smile came over the woman's face.

A sharp pang shot through Leonore's heart. Was infidelity the thing she must bear when she married him, just as her mother bore Father's rages? At least it would not be drunkenness . . . but somehow this did not comfort her. She made herself smile.

"Yes, he is a terrible flirt, is he not?" Leonore laughed lightly. "You must beware he does not break your heart, my lady! No one can take his compliments literally. You must know what a rogue he can be. Why, I have had all of four ladies admit to me this afternoon that he has quite stolen their hearts!"

The look of chagrin that flitted over Lady Brunsmire's face almost made Leonore laugh aloud. But enough was enough. This would be the last caller, she promised herself. She smiled politely and attempted to bring the call to a close, but Lady Brunsmire leaned forward in a confidential manner toward Leonore.

"But tell me, Miss Farleigh, how did you meet—"

Fortunately, Simpson, the butler, entered the parlor once again, interrupting Lady Brunsmire's question. Leonore sighed, resigned to more company.

" 'Tis Lady Jersey to see you, Miss Leonore," Simpson announced, clearly impressed, and opened the door wide.

Leonore rose hurriedly, as did Lady Brunsmire. She had not expected Lady Jersey to call upon her! St. Vire had surely been teasing that night at the opera. He could not have persuaded a patroness of Almack's to condescend to visit a relatively unknown young woman. It wasn't done!

But Lady Jersey it was. She smiled kindly at Leonore as she entered the drawing room, then turned to Lady Brunsmire. "I am so sorry to have broken into your farewells!" she said brightly. "Please do not let my presence keep you from any appointments you might have, Lady Brunsmire." She smiled and inclined her head regally.

Chagrin was writ clear now on Lady Brunsmire's face. "Of course, Lady Jersey! I was just taking my leave." She threw a slightly angry look at Leonore. "I hope to see you at some time in the near future, Miss Farleigh."

Leonore nodded politely. The door shut behind the widow, and she turned to find that Lady Jersey was looking at her with approval.

"Nasty woman!" she said. "I cannot abide her. You dealt well with her, and with good address, too."

Lady Jersey must have been eavesdropping at the door. Leonore suppressed a smile at the thought. It was not something she would have thought someone of supposed strict propriety would do.

"I think Lady Brunsmire was merely curious about Lord St. Vire."

Lady Jersey laughed and waved her hand dismissively. She took a seat near the fireplace. "Oh, you must be prepared for the curious, Miss Farleigh. Your betrothed is a singularly handsome man and eminently eligible, and he affects an intriguing mysteriousness as well. But it is just as well he does; if he wishes to be known, he must have a few affectations."

"Very true, my lady. St. Vire does like to amuse and be amused." Leonore silently congratulated him on making his need to avoid the sunlight into an asset. How clever he was! She wondered how long it would be before it was revealed as a symptom of his illness, rather than a fashionable whim. But clearly the mysteriousness with which St. Vire had surrounded himself made Lady Jersey curious enough to call upon Leonore. She relaxed at the thought.

"*You* do not have affectations, do you?" Lady Jersey asked.

"No, I hope I do not." Leonore smiled wryly. "I do not aspire to compete with St. Vire. I merely follow in his wake."

"The silent and devoted bride, Miss Farleigh?" Lady Jersey cast her an assessing glance.

"Oh, most certainly, my lady," replied Leonore, and her smile turned mischievous.

Lady Jersey laughed again and rose from her chair. "Oh, now I see why it was St. Vire settled upon you for his betrothed! I should have known he would not choose an insipid miss." Her own smile turned wry. "Well, I have promised St. Vire I would call upon you, however irregular it is, and so I have."

A shock went through Leonore, though she inclined her head gravely as she rose also. "And I am very honored that you have condescended to do so."

The older lady turned to the door, then hesitated. "Why *is* it that St. Vire refuses to attend functions during the day?" she asked.

"I am afraid I cannot say, Lady Jersey."

The lady's gaze turned sharp. "Then you know."

Though Leonore gave her an apologetic look, she said nothing.

An expression of discontent crossed Lady Jersey's face, then she chuckled. "Oh, that odious man! I vow he has half the *ton* wondering about him. Very well then! I know he wished me to send you vouchers for Almack's, but I could not do so until I called upon you—those are the rules, after all! Well, I have seen you, and just as he wished, I have approved. There now! You can expect the vouchers within the week."

Leonore felt a little dizzy. "I? Vouchers?"

This time Lady Jersey's smile was kind. "Yes, Miss Far-leigh. You did not expect them, did you?"

"No . . . of course not."

"Good." The patroness's smile grew wider. "I never send vouchers to people who expect them." She nodded and ex-tended her hand to Leonore in farewell. "And do make sure St. Vire attends with you. I have given him vouchers as well, but he has not come. It is to keep us all in suspense, I am sure!" With a last smile, she left the room.

Leonore sat down abruptly, then absently rang for Simpson to refuse any further callers. She thought St. Vire had been teasing when he had mentioned getting vouchers for Al-mack's. However, he had not only procured some for himself, but had persuaded Lady Jersey to call upon her so that she could have them as well.

She had not expected this when she had agreed to marry him. He had said he would help her family, but she did not think it would extend to launching her into society. Once she received the vouchers, she, herself, could approach one of the patronesses to call upon her again and perhaps offer some for Susan. Then she could see to Susan's welfare and see her well established in a good marriage.

She did not know quite what to think of St. Vire. Certainly he was extraordinarily handsome, and he had promised that he would treat her well. And so he had. More than that, he had gone to great lengths to please her, going so far as to insinuate himself into Lady Jersey's good graces to procure vouchers. He had an occasionally frivolous manner, had a clever tongue, and was even a little vain at times. Clearly he took great care over his clothes, for he dressed with impeccable taste. And . . . he liked her. Or so he seemed to imply by his wish to hold her hand and in the way he complimented her.

Leonore pushed the thought aside. No doubt he treated all ladies the same. Did he not manage to make Lady Jersey do as he wished? She smiled wryly. She was sure he had used the same wiles upon Lady Jersey as he had upon herself. He was a wicked flirt, to be sure!

And yet, there was something else. . . . Perhaps it was his illness that caused him to seem a little sad, made him seem as if he were a little on the edge of . . . Of what? Leonore was not sure.

Most certainly, sadness. She had seen it herself, flickering across his countenance from time to time when he did not know she was watching him. An answering sadness crept into her heart at the thought, and then a growing warmth. He had been kind to her, and even to Susan, which she felt sure he did either from the kindness of his heart or to gain her approval. What had she offered him in return? Surely, at the very least, she should give him her trust. He had asked nothing of her so far, except to hold her hand that once in the theatre.

She blushed, remembering it. That was all he had done, but it had been as intimate as a kiss. She had not known what to think of it at first, but she understood that certain intimacies were allowed between betrothed couples, and even more between married ones. Her mind went back further, to when Susan had left them alone in the parlor, how he had stepped close to her and had leaned forward as if he had been thinking about kissing her.

Leonore wet her dry lips at the thought. She had not liked the kisses that some former employers or employers' sons had tried to press upon her when they had caught her alone. She had rightfully repulsed them. But this, now, was different. It was not a forbidden thing to kiss one's betrothed.

She shook her head at her thoughts. What nonsense! Did she truly know that St. Vire had wanted to kiss her that evening before the opera? No, she did not. Most certainly, she did not know if he had wanted to do so lately. He had been the soul of courtesy and propriety each time he called upon her after the opera.

A glance at the clock made her rise hurriedly from her chair. It was late in the afternoon, and if she was to ready herself for Lady Bennington's ball, she had to start now.

St. Vire glanced up at the clock from the ancient *grimoire* he was reading. It wanted but an hour and a half until the start

of Lady Bennington's ball, and he was not at all sure if he
wanted to go. He had replied to the invitation tentatively, saying he might have to attend to some business at that time. He
gazed again at the book of spells he had been studying for the
last hour. His sleep had been full of shifting images, and he
did not know if any of them held a clue to his fate, but the *grimoire* had instructed that he take note of his dreams. He was
almost certain he was very close to finding the additional in-
formation he needed. Impatience flickered through his mind at
the thought of delaying the gathering of knowledge by yet another day, just so he could make an appearance at a ball.

Yet, Leonore would be there. He felt an unfamiliar eager-
ness at the thought, and his smile became crooked. She had become the icon of his restoration to humanity. In reality, it was
his research and knowledge of the magical arts that would re-
store the full use of his physical senses to him and stem the onslaught of madness. But somehow he had come to look upon
Leonore as the embodiment of all his hopes.

Well, it was true after all that he could not do it without her
willing participation. With luck, he'd be able to effect the
transformation without her knowledge of his true nature, and
so elicit her willingness all the more easily.

But of course, it would not happen if he stayed away from
her. With Leonore, it seemed that gentle attention from him
softened her to him more and more. If he stopped now, it was
wholly possible he might lose ground with her. He would,
therefore, go to Lady Bennington's ball. Marking his place in
his *grimoire*, he closed it.

St. Vire sighed and after a long look around the room, grimaced. He would have to tidy the place soon himself, as he
never let servants into his study. Some tiny shards of glass still
sprinked the floor from the time he had smashed the single
mirror that had hung above the mantelpiece many years ago. It
did not bother him, as he knew where they were and avoided
them, but from time to time it irritated his sense of order. He'd
tried sweeping them up before, but he always seemed to find
some slivers of glass scattered across the rug.

He shrugged. He would deal with cleaning later. A sense of

anticipation grew in him as he thought of the ball. He had not told Leonore he would attend, so perhaps she would be surprised. It occurred to him that he had not danced with her yet, as this was the first ball Leonore had attended since their betrothal. Leaving his study, he smiled slightly. He imagined her in his arms in a waltz—his hand on her waist, his legs brushing hers. It would be amusing to see how she reacted to such a public embrace. He chuckled to himself. It would be even more amusing to see how she reacted to a private one.

It was Leonore's fifth social function, but she was not accustomed to the brilliant lights, the laughter, and the gaiety she found amongst the *ton*. Most of all, she was not used to the attention. She had not thought about it when she first agreed to marry St. Vire, that she would have to make a change in attitude, different from the governess's diffident manner she had acquired. Regardless, she must now do her duty and present the best face she had to the world; she could not shame her betrothed after all he'd done for her so far, and that before they even wed.

As she and her mother descended from their coach and ascended the steps to Lady Bennington's house, Leonore smiled reassuringly at her mother. Mrs. Farleigh had been invited as well, as chaperon to her daughter. The change in status was difficult for her mother, who was more used to seclusion than Leonore. As a result, Leonore had to deal with the brunt of the attention. Her father had declined to attend any of these social functions, and she was thankful for it. He disliked balls and routs, and preferred to keep to his gaming hells and his taverns. She was ashamed of her relief when he told her this. What was worse was that she knew she'd be more ashamed if he decided to accompany her and her mother.

Leonore shook off these thoughts. Castigating herself over it was useless. She was used to her father's habits and had steeled herself against the humiliation he heaped upon her. He had once been the cause of her dismissal from a governess's post, banging at her employer's door and in his drunkenness demanding to see his daughter. But her life was changing now, and she would not have to bear the humiliation of being dismissed again.

The chandeliers within Lady Bennington's house sparkled as if hung with diamonds instead of glass. The jewels on the guests were as bright, and the laughter brighter. Leonore could feel people's attention upon her as she entered and saw a few guests whisper to each other. She raised her chin in defiance and smiled at Lady Bennington, who welcomed her and her mother warmly.

"Mrs. Farleigh, Miss Farleigh, I am so pleased to see you here," Lady Bennington said. "Please do partake of the refreshments, and there is a retiring room should either of you feel fatigued after dancing."

Mrs. Farleigh murmured a few polite though awkward words, but Leonore noticed her mother looked less anxious at the mention of a retiring room. Her mother would probably not stay in the ballroom for very long, and so she'd best resign herself to either finding a friendly guest to whom she could talk, or wearing her slippers thin from dancing all night.

Lady Bennington leaned toward Leonore a little. "I was wondering . . . will Lord St. Vire be attending? I sent him an invitation, but he had only replied that he might."

"I am sorry, my lady, but St. Vire has not informed me whether he would or not." Leonore could see a flicker of disappointment in Lady Bennington's eyes, but that lady was too polite to let it show on her face. She smiled instead and introduced Leonore to a blond young man who seemed eager to dance with her. She noticed that her mother retreated immediately to another room, and Leonore resigned herself to dancing most of the evening.

Leonore enjoyed the first dance and went from one partner to another for the next three dances. A part of her, nevertheless, kept wondering if St. Vire would appear after all.

An hour passed, and she mentally shrugged. No doubt he had decided not to come. Disappointment rose within her at the thought, surprising her. After all, she had not come to the ball expecting to see him. Yet, she wished he had come. She wanted to thank him for persuading Lady Jersey to call upon her and offer vouchers for tickets to Almack's assembly rooms. As she sat, resting between dance partners, she fingered the light blue silk crepe of her dress and smiled to herself. She may not have expected to see St. Vire, but she had hoped to. Her gown was of the latest fashion, and she had dressed with care, just in case St. Vire might attend the ball. Well, it was not a wasted effort, for one should always look one's best, after all. She fanned herself lazily, for the ballroom was quite warm.

"May I have this dance?"

Leonore looked up, startled, and her heart began to beat wildly. "Lord St. Vire! I . . . I had not thought you would attend."

She had not heard him approach—of course she hadn't. The noise in the ballroom would have drowned out anyone's footsteps. He looked impeccably elegant. He was dressed all in black; the only color upon him was his green eyes, his chestnut-red hair, and the ruby he seemed to be so fond of, set within the folds of his neckcloth. In all, he was a singular figure, and it was no wonder that people turned to stare at him as he passed.

He gazed at her, smiling, and brought her hand to his lips. "My dear, do try to call me Nicholas. I hear 'Lord St. Vire' from everyone, and I *am* fond of variety." He pulled at her hand gently, and she stood. "And of course I had to attend. I realized I did not know whether you danced well or not. I thought perhaps I should find out."

Leonore's breath became short. He was looking at her, and his smile was intimate . . . or so it seemed to her. "Of course, my lord," she said and went with him to the dance floor. She chided herself. She was sure he looked so at all women—it was nothing, really, just his usual manner.

A shock went through her when she felt his hand upon her back. It was a waltz! Heavens, but she should not be dancing the waltz, not now, before one of Almack's patronesses gave approval for her to do so. She stared, alarmed, at St. Vire. "My lord—"

"Hush, Leonore, and simply enjoy the dance." His smile

turned mischievous as they moved to the music. "Mrs. Drummond-Burrell is here, and I asked if I might dance the waltz with you; she allowed that it was proper for me to do so. I am your betrothed, after all."

Of course he would ask; he was a gentleman after all. She relaxed, and an answering smile turned up the corners of her mouth. "Do you *always* get your way, my lord?"

"Except when I ask my affianced wife to call me by my Christian name."

Wife. Her smile left her; she gazed into his eyes, his handsome face, then looked away. She knew she was not yet ready to wed this man, for the idea of herself being anyone's wife still seemed a foreign one. The idea of being a governess forever still had some hold on her.

"If you wish to call off the betrothal, you know you may do so," St. Vire said before she could speak. She thought a tight, bereft look crossed his face before it became pleasantly cordial again.

"I— No," she said firmly. Perhaps he truly did wish to marry her, perhaps for herself, for here he was clearly giving her a choice in the matter. A warmth rose within her at the thought and caused her to smile at him. "No. I do wish to wed you . . . Nicholas. You have been so very kind to me and my family. How could I not wish to wed a man like you?"

An expression of ironic amusement came upon his face. She felt his hands tighten upon her back and hand. "You need not feel obligated to me, Leonore. I am not as good as you think."

"Well, then, if you will not be complimented, then I shall be obliging enough not to do so," she replied. "Besides, I know you are not a saint."

"No?" He put on an expression of extreme chagrin.

She chuckled. "I think you are a terrible flirt and a little vain, also."

"Am I? How so?"

"Why, I know you flirt because half the ladies in London profess to be in love with you."

"And how do you know this?"

"Half the ladies in London have come calling at my house, inquiring after you, and all of them have said it."

He grinned widely, then his eyes half closed, assessing her. His hand shifted to her waist, caressing it lightly. "And to which half do you belong, Leonore?"

She felt a shiver pass over her as his hand moved up from her waist and his thumb made little circles upon her ribs. She gazed at him, and her breath came a little short, for his eyes held a caressing warmth. She firmly gathered her scattered thoughts together and raised her eyebrows. "Oh, I will not tell you that."

"And why not?"

"I have already shown that you are a flirt, and telling you would only inflate your vanity."

St. Vire laughed. "Well, that cannot be, for I am sure you would prick it with your words and it would burst."

"Alas, I fear my words would have little effect on you, as you fence so well with your own," she replied.

He gave her a wide smile and drew her a little closer to him. "You underestimate your effect on me, my dear."

The dance ended, and Leonore fanned herself, glad that she had the excuse of a vigorous dance to explain her heated face. They had ended their dance near some windows that opened to the terrace. Fanning helped her gain some measure of composure, though she thought her face must still be quite pink.

"A trifle warm, are you?" St. Vire asked solicitously.

She shot him a suspicious glance, but his expression was smoothly polite. "Yes; the dance was a particularly spirited one."

"Perhaps a short walk outside on the terrace would refresh you."

The ballroom was indeed oppressively hot, and the thought of a cool breeze was very tempting. She gave a little nod, and St. Vire left her briefly to fetch her shawl, which she had left draped over a chair.

The air was cool outside, and Leonore shivered slightly at the first brush of a breeze. She felt a light caress upon her arms; it was St. Vire drawing her shawl about her shoulders.

He smiled down at her, then took her hand and placed it upon
his arm. The noise and music of the ballroom faded behind
them as they walked a little upon the terrace. They said nothing for a while, but there was no awkwardness between them.
It was as if St. Vire was content to be silent, demanding nothing of her. They came to the low stone wall that separated the
terrace from the gardens below, and he drew her to it.

She gazed at him, seeing how the moonlight outlined each
of his features precisely so that his pale profile seemed etched
upon the darkness of the sky. The night suited him, she
thought, for night was full of contrasts, when all things seen
were either black or white. He, also, was full of contrasts; at
once kind and vain, generous while he protested he was
wholly selfish.

He leaned against the stone wall, looking over it to the gardens. He breathed in deeply, and an odd expression, a mix of
longing and frustration, crossed his features. He breathed out
again in a quick rush of air.

"Is there something the matter, Nicholas?" She moved toward him and touched his sleeve.

He turned and smiled at her. "No. I was merely thinking it
has been a long time since I have been in a garden."

A sudden sadness and strange warmth curled around
Leonore's heart. Of course it would be unlikely he'd venture
into a garden. It was a thing best seen during the day, and
Nicholas could only come out at night. He could not see the
open faces of flowers or breathe in the full perfume that
scented the air only during the day. Their colors would be var-
ied shades of gray under the moon, and never the rich panoply
of hues that would show so clearly under the sun. A wild impulse moved her to tug at his arm.

"Come," she said and pulled him away from the terrace
wall.

St. Vire's smile turned quizzical, but he followed nevertheless. He watched her step quick and light upon the terrace
steps to the garden. Moonbeams touched her form, and her
dress shimmered as she walked, clinging and releasing, hinting
at feminine curves beneath. Only the faint strains of music

reached his ears now instead of the murmur of voices and instruments combined. His feet soon touched earth instead of stone, and his legs brushed low shrubbery.

His eyebrows rose. He had not expected this, that Leonore would bring him here to the garden. He had thought her somewhat staid, for she had been all that was proper with him, never giving into any impulse. But now they were in the middle of the garden, the moon illuminated the clearing, and roses surrounded them. Their scent was not strong, or rather, he could barely smell them. But then an abrupt, sharp fragrance filled his nostrils, for Leonore had plucked a rose and brushed his cheek with it.

"I will give you this," she said, and she gazed intently into his eyes. "You have given me and my sister much, and I do not know how to return it. But when we are wed, I will give you roses, fill the house with them, and you will see their color even in the night."

Nicholas's breath left him suddenly as he looked into her eyes. They were no longer wary, but looked upon him with trust and even warmth. The light from the waxing moon shone upon her elfin face and silvered her blond hair, and the silk of her dress as she breathed shimmered upon her breasts like water. He had dreamed this today, of Leonore and the moonlight, fairylike and unreal. Even the scent of roses had come sharply to him, as it had in his dreams, as they never had since his change into a vampire. He took her hand, and then reached up and gently touched her cheek with his finger.

"Dance with me," he said.

She said nothing, but put her hand in his. The faint, lilting sounds of a waltz reached them from the ballroom. Slowly they moved and began to dance.

This time there was no proper distance between them, for he could feel the brush of her legs against his own through her skirts. He drew her close to him, sliding his hand from her waist to her hip, and she did not pull away. Instead, she looked at him, saying nothing, as if her whole concentration was upon him, trying to penetrate to his soul. Her head tipped back to look at him, exposing the long column of her throat.

The bloodlust caught him, almost making him gasp.

No. Not now, and not Leonore. His life would sink further into unreality if he gave into it now. He shuddered, and the thirst receded.

"What is wrong, Nicholas?" Leonore asked. The distant music from the ballroom faded, and their steps slowed, then stopped.

"A chill." He gazed at her, at her eyes and lips sculpted by the light of the moon and the shadows of the dark. Her body was still pressed against him, her legs almost entwined with his through her gown's thin silk cloth. A different sort of lust overtook him. He bent his head, and his lips seized hers in a fierce kiss.

At first Leonore froze. Then his kiss softened, and she moved into his embrace. It was proper, he was her betrothed, she told herself, and then all rationality fled. No one had ever held her so close, and the closeness was suddenly a thing to be cherished. For all that it was foreign, it was also rare, and a hunger rose in her for it.

He must have sipped Lady Bennington's champagne before their dance, for his lips tasted of wine. Beneath the scent of bay rum was a wilder tang, like a forest in autumn, and it mixed with the scent of the roses and the night. She moved her hands to his shoulders, and her hand came up behind his neck to touch the thick curls at the nape. His hair was soft and flowed between her fingers like silk.

"Nicholas . . ." she murmured against his lips, wanting to hear the sound of the name she'd said over and over again in her mind, but hadn't willingly allowed herself to say aloud.

In answer, his lips came down upon hers again in a deeper kiss. His hands caressed her hips, pressing her hard against him. Heat flared there, and Leonore trembled and sighed a low moan. His mouth moved across her cheek to where her hair curled around her ear.

"God, Leonore, how I want you. . . ." His whisper ended in a husky laugh, and his kisses trickled just below her ear down to her shoulder. He hesitated at her neck, and his tongue flickered out briefly to touch her there, before his lips descended further.

Her skin tasted sweet and salt to his tongue, and the agony of denying himself more than this taste transmuted into hot desire. He wanted to pull Leonore down to the grass and take her there, but he could not if he were to save himself from madness, and he groaned in frustration. It was madness itself, his desire for her: an amalgam of bloodlust and the abrupt hyperacuity the thirst always brought to him. Now he could feel her breasts and thighs against him, as if her silk dress and his own clothes were nothing but mist. The heady scent of roses and lavender water made him dizzy; the music of her sighs seized his heart and made him want to weep. It was ten times the agony, for he knew once the thirst faded, he'd sink into the mind-killing dullness of the senses again.

One more taste of her, he thought, once more before I stop. He pushed aside the gathers of fine silk crepe that covered her breasts and kissed the revealed skin. Her breath came fast, and her hands clutched his shoulders tightly.

"Nicholas . . . I don't . . . I want . . ." Her voice came out in a breathless sob.

He turned his face so that his cheek rested on her breast and, taking a deep breath, briefly closed his eyes. He pushed himself away from her, and though he tried to keep his hands steady, they trembled as he gently pulled up her bodice again. He did not want to look at her face, for he felt perhaps she would see his shame at his lack of control. The shame surprised him, for he had not felt it with other women—women whom he had seduced in the past. It was, no doubt, because he had not had to control himself with them, and anything that he took from them was amply paid for in coin or sensual pleasure.

"Nicholas . . ." He felt her warm fingers touch his cheek, the sensation already dulled, for the bloodlust had faded. It was as if a transparent cloth had formed itself about his body and muffled all his senses. He looked down into her eyes at last. A light dwelt within, and her mouth smiled, still soft with passion.

"Kiss me again," she said.

A husky laugh erupted from him, and he gently did so. She responded eagerly, and Nicholas pushed her from him after a moment. "No, Leonore. You don't know—" He stopped, then sighed. "You are altogether too tempting. And I am sure we are causing something of a scandal, for though I am certain we have not been seen, we have been gone long enough from the ballroom for people to notice."

"Oh, heavens." Leonore's hands went to her face, covering her mouth, and she stared at him, obviously embarrassed. She had apparently not thought of the possible consequences of being alone with him outside. "I didn't mean—"

He grinned. "I know. Let us hope our betrothal makes our absence more acceptable than it normally would."

A distressed expression crossed her face. "They will know that we— How can they not guess when they see my blushes? For I do not think I will be able to look at anyone without doing so."

Nicholas bent and picked up her shawl, which had fallen to the ground, and shook it out. Gently he placed it around her shoulders. "Never mind. We need not enter the ballroom again. It is late, and I can simply make an excuse for you to Lady Bennington, find your mother, and have you return home."

She looked gratefully at him. "Yes, thank you." He put her hand upon his arm and they walked around the house to the entrance.

He signaled a footman to fetch the coach and felt Leonore press his arm. "Please . . ." She glanced away, wet her lips, and then looked up at him again. "I hope you didn't think I was—I am usually very much in control of myself and do not do improper things. . . ."

Nicholas chuckled and caressed her cheek with a finger. "My dear, sometimes it is a pleasant thing to lose control." He raised her hand to his lips, helped her into the coach that had just arrived, then went into the house to find her mother.

Chapter 6

Some thought it was scandalous, but most smiled indulgently. Clearly, it was a love match between Lord St. Vire and Miss Leonore Farleigh. For though no one had ever *seen* them in any sort of compromising situation, many noted they disappeared together at times, and when they were seen together, each glance they exchanged was as intimate as a private embrace.

It was worse than that, thought Leonore, if anyone really knew. Even thinking of it brought a heat to her cheeks. She brought her fan up to cool her face and tried to train her mind upon the musicians who were tuning up for the next piece—and failed miserably. She hoped none of Lady Rothwick's guests would glance her way and see how discomposed she was.

She felt almost helpless against the onslaught of St. Vire's—Nicholas's—attentions. She could not even continue to keep a formal and mental distance from him by calling him St. Vire, for he was Nicholas to her now. It was unnerving how her gaze would inadvertently follow him about a room, how her hands seemed unable to keep from touching his hand, his sleeve, or his arm. Or how, when she would glance at him, she'd find him watching her, whether it was from across the room or beside her.

And Nicholas was expert at finding secluded places for their kisses—and not so secluded. That was the danger of it, what made it at once frightening and infinitely exciting. She never knew when he would draw her aside and kiss her, how long it would last, or if anyone would discover them. Every sense was

achingly on edge because of that uncertainty, and when he
touched her, even so much as a hand on her elbow, she felt her
body begin to tingle in readiness for a possible caress.

Yet, he confused her, for he'd call her "sweet" and all manner of endearments, but surely he could not be in love with her
in less than two months. And his attentions had a flavor of
wooing. But for what reason? They were already betrothed,
after all.

Did she take joy in it? A small part of Leonore's heart was
not certain. When he looked at other women, he might be admiring, and a mischievous light might enter his eyes. But
never did he look on other women as he did her, as if she were
wholly desirable. He never said he loved her, and she told herself again it was not something she expected.

There was nothing to dislike in Nicholas, and much to ad-
mire. She should be content with that, she knew. More than his
looks and charm, were his cleverness, intelligence, and undeniable kindness and generosity toward her. He refused any
thanks for his little gifts to her, or the large account he had
with Madame Etoile's dressmaking establishment, laughingly
saying that he was vain enough to want his wife-to-be to be
dressed as well as he. But there was no need for him to extend
his kindness to Susan. Leonore's heart warmed to him for this.
At first she'd been suspicious, for Susan was a pretty girl, and
Leonore trusted no one. But it was clear even to her that his attention was wholly upon herself, and his kindness to Susan
disinterested. For it was Leonore whom he watched, and he
seemed to glance only reluctantly at others when she was near
him.

And heaven only knew she was highly attracted to him
. . . almost obsessed. That was the word with no bark on it. She
knew if she so much as shook her head at his advances, he'd
stop. She had managed to do it once, and he had ceased his
kisses immediately. But just as immediately she felt bereft and
shamelessly sought them again.

Even now, as she sat at Lady Rothwick's musicale, she felt
intensely aware of Nicholas's thigh pressed against hers as he
sat on the chair next to her. She wet her dry lips and tried to

focus on the music. She was partially successful: Lady Roth-wick had engaged superb musicians, and they played the Mozart divertimento excellently. She could not help herself; she wanted to see what he thought of the music. Turning to look up at him, she saw he was already looking at her. You wanted to ask him about the music, she told herself. But then his gaze lingered on her lips, and a slow smile grew on his own, as if he were thinking of kissing her.

"The music," she blurted.

Nicholas's eyebrows rose. "Yes?"

"Do . . . do you like it?"

He turned his eyes to the musicians, and Leonore felt she was able to breathe again.

"They are very competent." His voice sounded indifferent, however, and she remembered he had been equally blasé about the opera they had attended. She frowned, thinking.

"You are not very musically inclined, are you?"

"No," he replied.

"Why do you bother to come to the musicale, then?"

"To see you, of course."

"Nonsense," Leonore said testily, though she blushed. "You have seen me five times this week, and you need not come to a musicale for that. Why *do* you come?"

Nicholas gazed at her, and she thought she saw indecision in his eyes. Then he said, "I used to appreciate music very well. I cannot seem to do so now. Sometimes I come, hoping I can remember what it was like." He still smiled as he had a moment ago, and she could almost think he was joking, but something in his eyes told her he spoke the truth.

"I see," she said.

"You believe me?" His voice held a note of surprise.

"Yes."

"Why?" The word seemed to come involuntarily from him.

She said, looking up at him, "Because I've come to trust you."

Oddly, she knew it was true. She did not know quite how it had happened, or why she should, but she did trust Nicholas. Though he had teased her and was sometimes oblique in manner, he had—so far as she could see—never lied to her. When he stated a thing, he made sure it was so, time and time again. More than anything, he was the only man who did as he promised. Perhaps it was not saying much, for the men she had encountered at her students' houses—fathers, brothers, guests—promised only things they could not give, each hoping to make her his mistress. She'd refused them all, for she was no fool and no harlot.

His face showed incredulity mixed with gratitude, and strangely, regret. "You should not trust me, you know," he said.

"No, I should not, for in general I do not trust anyone except perhaps Susan. But I do, nevertheless."

Nicholas stared at her, then looked away. "I thank you," he said, and his voice sounded strained, even to himself. "But again, you should not. You know little of me, after all." A curious feeling, warm and aching, twisted through his chest. He had intended to seduce her, slowly and carefully, and he had expected she'd succumb to it—as she had, so far. But trust? He had not expected it, had not thought of it, really. In truth, he did not want it. It was better she be a conduit for his goal, only a part—needed part, to be sure—of his cure.

Yet, he felt compelled to warn her . . . of what? He was being foolish. She would never know, for if she did she would never come to him willingly. Of course, that was it—if he told her a little bit of the truth, even warn her, and she still wanted to marry him, then it only proved how willing she was.

The musicians ended their piece, and the guests rose to exchange greetings and walk about a little. After nodding and smiling to a few new acquaintances, Leonore gave him a wry smile. "It is true. You do not reveal much of yourself—in words. But the very fact that you would warn me against you, shows me you are not as untrustworthy as you would make yourself out to be." They also rose, and Nicholas took her hand and placed it on his arm.

He gazed at her coolly. "Beware, Leonore. Ours will be a marriage of convenience. I hope you are not falling in love with me." *I cannot afford to return it. If the magic does not work, your short life will have no place in mine.* He thrust away the confused emotions that accompanied the thought. Better to train his attention on the moment.

"How very vain you are, to be sure!" Leonore replied lightly. "Have I said it?"

He grinned, relieved at her tone. "No, you have not, and you have caught me out again." He brought her hand to his lips. Though she smiled, he could see the guardedness in her eyes again. He felt satisfaction at it but also regret, then almost grimaced at himself for being so contradictory. "You are very good for the state of my soul; I am sure when we are wed, you will improve me to sainthood."

"No fear of that, my lord." She looked about her, clearly startled, and Nicholas smiled to himself. He had taken her out of the conservatory, where the musicale was held, and down a long hall. She had apparently not noticed it. A fleeting uncertainty slowed his steps. Did she not notice because he had unconsciously put a glamour on her? Sometimes people did as he wished even when he did not purposely put a glamour upon them. What did it matter, after all? he thought impatiently.

He pushed open a door, and it opened to a small room, dark and apparently unused, for the moonlight streaming through the windows illuminated the Holland covers over the furniture. He reflected with a smile that it was certainly convenient he had been in most of the noble houses in London so many decades ago and knew the arrangement of the rooms well. He shut the door behind them.

The dim light showed her eyes, wide and vulnerable. He did not kiss her immediately, but cupped her chin in his hand, stroking her jaw with his thumb.

"You are quite right, my dear," he said lightly. "I am irredeemable, a very bad man. I am surprised you have not guessed it yet, for I have led you to the edge of scandal more than a few times. Do you really think you should marry me?"

He throat moved in a swallow. "I . . . have known of worse men."

"Have you? But you do not know me well—yet." He slid his fingers down onto her neck, feeling the pulse of blood at the base of it. He could put a glamour on her now, and she would never know if he drank of her. His hand tightened slightly as the bloodlust surged within him.

He looked down at her; Leonore did not move, but simply stared at him. She trusted him, or so she said. He had told her when they first met he would never hurt her, and she appeared to believe it, for he never had—yet. Would he go against his word? He searched her face. Never had he put a glamour on her, but he could see her breath came quickly as she stared at him, definitely in his thrall. Or was it her damned trust again?

"I . . . know you well enough—more than many betrothed couples might in an arranged marriage," she said. He saw her swallow again and felt the pulse quicken at her throat. "We have never gone over the edge of scandal, I think."

Moving his hand lower still, he pushed the small puffed sleeve from one shoulder and her bodice from one breast. He watched her, the way her teeth bit her lower lip, the way her eyes closed at his touch. Ah, but she was delectable! Desire for her rose in him, and he smiled. He was becoming quite good at controlling his bloodthirst now, so that it burned low and fused instead with his lust for her lips and breasts and thighs.

"And what if we did now?" He ran his fingers up to her collarbone and then back down beneath her breast.

She shivered, opened her eyes, and stared at him. "Then we should have to marry immediately, of course. It wants but two weeks to our wedding, after all. Whom else would you be able to get to wed you at this late date?"

Nicholas laughed softly at her practical answer and seized her lips with his own. " 'Would she could make of me a saint/Or I of her a sinner,' " he quoted in a whisper against her mouth.

"The poet . . . Congreve," she replied, her voice trembling now, obviously trying to retain some control over herself.

He laughed again, amused that she let it slip that she knew this poem. "*Such* a good governess you are!" He kissed her again below her ear, then down her neck to the pulse beating wildly there. Carefully he let his teeth run against her skin. He was on the edge of letting his thirst overcome him again, but he could not resist the tantalizing possibility, even though he knew he would keep himself from piercing her flesh. "You cannot make me a saint, Leonore. Shall I make you a sinner?"

"We are sinning *now*."

"Oh, no, only somewhat close to it. Trust me to know more of sin than you, sweet one." He moved her backward until they came to a chaise longue and pushed her gently down upon it.

"What . . . what are you going to do?"

"Make us come closer to sinning than we have done before," Nicholas replied and kissed her full and deeply on her mouth.

Leonore moaned, a despairing sound. He parted from her, ready to stop, but a wild look came into her eyes. She seized his face with her hands and brought him down again, kissing him just as deeply as he had her.

This time his husky laugh held a note of triumph. Her lips moved upon his as he had taught her; her tongue slipped within and touched his own as he had done to her before. Her fingers slid behind his head and pulled a little at his hair. The former governess was a good student, and he chuckled again at the thought. He dipped his hand between her breasts and freed the covered one from her bodice. One last time he kissed her deeply before descending to the skin of her neck, her shoulder, and then the tips of her breasts.

Leonore felt hot and cold and hot again, and a fine tingling brushed across her skin. Sinning. He had called it that, or said what they were doing was close to it. He had said he was a bad man, and though she did not think this was entirely true, every touch upon her body told her he was a rake and a seducer. But if he were bad, then so was she, for she did not want his seduction to stop. Despair mixed with her desire; she was certainly her father's daughter, for she drank of Nicholas's lips as uncontrollably as a drunkard took wine. Where was her control? She had little; Nicholas had it all.

His kisses were both sweet and fierce, his embraces tender, and because she received so little of either in her life, she had no head for them. Nicholas's caresses were a fine liqueur upon her body, pouring over her breasts and belly and thighs. The scent of him, full of wildness and spice, made her feel dizzy. She opened her eyes wide when she felt his hand on her bare hip and realized with a shock he had pushed up the hem of her gown. Her eyes met his own, watching her; his smile was gentle, and his eyes full of warm desire.

"Let me touch you here . . . and here. . . ." His fingers played over her, and he kissed her throat and chin, then took her lips once again. We are betrothed, Leonore told herself. It is only two weeks until we are wed. It does not matter. But it did, for even she knew what they did was not right, most certainly not before they were married, however much it might be mitigated by their betrothal.

For a moment she let him touch her as he willed, biting her lip as a shimmering heat rose from her secret places to course through the rest of her body. I must stop this, she told herself.

"Stop," she said aloud, but her voice came out as a whisper. But his caresses ceased, though he was still pressed against her, and he took one last long kiss.

"I would not have taken you, Leonore, before our wedding night." He moved from her, as if reluctant to do so.

Slowly she pushed herself upright upon the chaise longue and breathed deeply. Her legs felt odd and shaky, so she did not rise immediately. She glanced at him in the dimness, glad he could not see the color rising in her face. "I thought you *had* taken me," she blurted.

A husky chuckle came from him. "Oh, no. That truly would have been sinning."

Leonore swallowed. "There is more?" she asked. She should not be talking of this with him at all, but she blurted the words before she could stop herself.

Nicholas pulled her up from the chaise longue and drew her to him gently. "Yes, sweet one. Much more. Shall I tell you what will happen on our wedding night?"

She did not answer him, for he kissed her deeply before she could reply.

"I shall continue to do all I have done to your delectable body so far, until you cry out with the delight of it." He bent to kiss her neck, her ear, and then her lips again.

Drawing up all her resolve, she pushed against him and stared at his face. His gaze was still hot upon her, and she knew he would kiss her again if she let him. "I do not think I want to do that. It does not sound proper." She felt foolish saying it, for she really did not know what was proper within the confines of marriage, but saying it brought a measure of control over herself. Putting on an air of briskness, she pulled up her bodice and adjusted it as well as she could.

He laughed softly. "Oh, but you will. And it is not proper at all. I told you I was a bad man, did I not?"

Chapter 7

He was becoming obsessed with Leonore.

St. Vire did not know if this was a good thing. He had enough control over himself so that he did not take her blood, but each time he tamped down the urge, the sensitivity that came with it changed the bloodlust into a lust for the touch of her skin, the sound of her sighs, and the scent of her perfume.

It was something he could not separate from his vampirism, and so seemed tainted somehow. Tainted. He smiled wryly to himself. Was she making him yearn for sainthood, turning him from being a contented sinner? He remembered their encounter at the Rothwicks' musicale, how she had allowed him to touch her intimately and how she had pulled him down for a kiss. His smile turned into a wide grin. Oh, he doubted he'd become a saint.

Looking in the mirror in his chambers, St. Vire adjusted his neckcloth with care, frowning a little until he achieved the precise folds he wished. He glanced up at his face and dared smile into the mirror, showing his sharp teeth. His reflection did not seem so repulsive to him now; he had refrained from drinking blood two months before the consummation of his wedding, as the spell required. Now it was his wedding day—or rather, wedding evening—and at least he could slake one kind of thirst. It had been, he admitted, somewhat frustrating seducing Leonore into willingness. His smile turned rueful. No, loin-twisting agony came closer to it. He could not even take any recourse with whores, either, for the spell did not allow it.

He took the hat his valet held out to him, set it at a rakish angle, then descended the stairs from his room. Sometimes he wondered if all this saintly abstinence was worth the cure.

Perhaps it was easier in ancient times to find a willing virgin who would give herself for a year. These days it was impossible without searching for one in a well-born family, woo the girl, and then marry her. The thought of being wed had almost made him give it up, for he'd always seen marriage as a nuisance. He remembered, however, the madness he'd seen long ago in another vampire's eyes before St. Vire was forced to kill him. He shuddered at the memory, and he decided it was worth it.

On the other hand, there was the church. St. Vire wondered how long he was going to be able to bear being inside one while he said his marriage vows. His mouth went dry at the thought. The spell in the *grimoire* had said if he had done everything correctly, he would survive it. But he'd seen what had happened when he had locked that other vampire into the church: It was how he had killed him. Thankfully, the church in which he was going to be wed was a different one, so he would not have to be reminded much of the unnerving incident while he said his vows.

As he climbed into the coach that would take him to the church, St. Vire became aware of the tension in his body and made himself relax. Perhaps he could pretend his apprehension was merely wedding nerves. He rolled his eyes at the thought. He was the furthest thing from a trembling virgin he could think of. God, but he was becoming ridiculous over it all.

The coach stopped in front of the church at last, and he hesitated before descending. He could sense the odor of sanctity emanating from the church even from the carriage, a sweet and bitter scent. Go to it, man! he said to himself. I might die, said another part of his mind. But I am undead; what, after all, is the difference? he told himself wryly. It was that or madness—and he would never choose madness.

He climbed up the steps to the church's open doors. The wedding company was small, for only Leonore's family would attend, and his few new friends. It was an odd thing to think of having friends; all the ones from his youth were dead. Thankfully, it was not the fashion now to have large weddings, and Leonore had not wanted a large one, either. St. Vire looked at the altar, at the lines of the beams and arches leading the eye upward to the cross near the roof. He took in a deep breath and stepped within.

The sharp tingling that coursed through his body started as soon as he put his foot upon the marble floor of the church. He made himself ignore it and stared at the altar instead. The vicar there eyed him sourly, for an evening wedding was quite irregular. However, once he knew that Leonore's family approved, and once the very large contribution from St. Vire's bank was in his hands, the vicar had agreed to do it.

His bride. St. Vire turned his gaze to the doorway at the sound of carriages. The tingling now became a slight sizzling pain, and in order to block it out he concentrated on the figures coming toward him. He wished he could better appreciate Leonore's loveliness as she came up the aisle on her father's arm. He could not feel the pleasure he normally would looking at her, for the pain increased with each minute he stood before the altar. Her sister, Susan, sat next to her mother in one of the pews, but he barely noticed. He spared one glance for her father, glad for her sake that he was sober for once.

At last Leonore was beside him, and St. Vire turned to the vicar. "Hurry," he whispered to the man and put a glamour upon him so that he would obey. Even so, the ceremony lasted longer than he ever thought it could, for the pain that seemed to burn his flesh seeped within until his lungs felt as if they were on fire. He wanted to cry out, but he did not have the breath to do so. His vision blurred, and he blinked to clear it.

"I do," he heard himself say, but he was not sure to what he agreed, for his mind now burned as well. *God help me,* he thought, *I must stay upon my feet.* But the red-streaked darkness descended upon him, and his knees hit the marble floor. . . .

A faint voice: "He needs air and quiet, I am sure. None of you need stay, for I will attend him. I am sure he will recover soon." A door shut—too loudly.

Cool air. Silk upon his cheek. Something wet upon his

brow. The scent of lavender came to him. It reminded him of someone . . . Leonore. He opened his eyes, and it was indeed she. She drew in her breath, and the tight, tense look in her eyes faded.

"Oh heavens, Nicholas! I thought . . . I thought . . ." A confused expression of anger and fear crossed her face, and she seized his face in her hands and kissed him fiercely. "Do not ever, ever do that again!"

"I assure you, I did not do it on purpose," he whispered when she released him, and closed his eyes. His lungs still burned a little, and coughing, he groped for the handkerchief he usually had in his coat pocket. His coat had disappeared, and he was in his shirtsleeves.

"Here." He felt a handkerchief thrust into his hand.

He coughed fully into it, and the sharp tang of blood came to his tongue, but he felt too tired to do anything about it. A sharp gasp burst in the air above him. He opened his eyes again and shifted his head; smooth silk rubbed against his hair. It seemed his head was resting upon Leonore's lap. How pleasant.

A small, distressed moan came from Leonore. "You *are* ill, then! I had wondered . . . I shall call for a doctor immediately." She eased herself from under his head, but he grasped her arm.

"No. I am merely thirsty . . . water, please. . . ."

"Nicholas, you stained the handkerchief with blood when you coughed into it," Leonore said, her voice impatient, but reached to a table beside her and poured him a glass from a ewer nearby. He drank it, washing the blood from his mouth.

"I shall be well presently." He pushed himself upright to prove it. He was in an unfamiliar room, plain and utilitarian. "Where is this place?"

"They—the vicar and the curate—brought you to the vicar's sitting room. You collapsed at the very end of our wedding ceremony."

"How embarrassing," he said lightly. "We are, however, married?"

A light blush suffused Leonore's cheeks, and she smiled. "Yes."

"Good. I think we should proceed to the wedding supper—unless I have been unconscious for too long?"

"No, it has been only a quarter of an hour—but you must let me find a doctor!"

"Nonsense, my dear; you see I am quite recovered." He stood up and was relieved to find he did not feel at all as weak as he had when he awakened. He looked about the room. "My coat?"

She gave it to him reluctantly. "Nicholas . . . you have consumption, do you not?" Her voice was tense.

He gazed at her face; it was as strained as her voice. He smiled crookedly. "No, not consumption. It is not something a doctor can cure, believe me." He put on his coat and spied a mirror. His neckcloth was creased inappropriately, and he ran a thumb under a fold.

He found his arm seized, and Leonore pulled him around to face her, her expression one of angry fear. "You vain, stupid man! You collapse at the altar, you cough blood, and now you say you are well and must adjust your neckcloth!"

"I can hardly greet the wedding guests with a badly tied one, my dear."

"The *devil* take your neckcloth!" Her face flamed at her own words and at Nicholas's raised eyebrows. "How long—How ill are you? How long will you live?" He heard aching desperation in her voice, and her words stumbled from her lips.

Surprise and troubled tenderness curled around Nicholas's heart. He touched her cheek softly. "You care how long I might live?"

She turned her face and pressed her cheek against his hand, closing her eyes briefly. "Yes. Yes, of course."

"You are very sweet, Leonore." He pulled her to him and kissed her softly.

Her lips moved hungrily against his, then parted from him by only a hairsbreadth. "Tell me, Nicholas. How long?" she asked.

"Mmm . . ." Nicholas could feel his strength returning steadily, and with it, desire. He kissed her again, deeply.

Leonore pushed him away, gasping a little. "Tell me."

He gazed at the clear desperation and longing in her eyes, and a curious ache grew within him. "I do not know. A year . . . or I could live forever. . . ."

"A year!" The word came out from her in a sob, and she bit her lip.

"Don't—" He took her in his arms again. "Don't cry." He stroked her hair and pressed a kiss upon it.

"I am not crying," she said, her voice muffled against his chest.

"Good." He chuckled. "I mean what I say. I could live forever." He thought about stopping the course of the spell and remaining a vampire, living forever. Leonore could even be by his side, also a vampire and his eternal consort. Just a very little he was tempted. . . . The image of Leonore rose before his eyes, her face moon-pale and twisted with the bloodthirst, going slowly insane. God, no. He shuddered.

"Nonsense! No one lives forever." Leonore the governess was back again. She moved away from him, her lips pressed together in a disapproving line. He reached out and ran his thumb over her lips.

"Smile for me, Leonore. Perhaps I will not live forever, but I could live for a very, very long time—as long as any man might. I shall know by the end of the year."

She grasped his hand and held it hard. "How will you know?"

He felt his smile turn crooked. "I shall be alive," he said simply.

"That is not enough! A doctor—"

"Can do nothing." He made his voice stern. "Enough! We have wedding guests to attend to." He glanced at the clock on the mantelpiece. "Another quarter hour has passed while we argued. I have given our guests enough to think about for now. If we delay more, I am sure they will wonder if they should turn the wedding supper into a funeral feast."

A bitter smile came to Leonore's lips. "A little early for that, I think."

"*Much* too early." He kissed her once more. "Come, come, Leonore! It is not as bad as you think." He caressed her cheek with his finger. "Besides, I am sure it is no less than I deserve. After a year, you may well wish to be rid of me. I am, no doubt, not at all easy to live with, with all my bad habits," he said lightly.

This time she gave a reluctant laugh. "No doubt!" was her dry reply before she took his hand and led him out of the vicar's sitting room.

How could anyone laugh and drink when the groom at a wedding party was to die in a year? Leonore made herself smile and nod cordially to another guest, then sipped her wine. It was acrid on her tongue, though she knew the wine was of the best vintage, for Nicholas prided himself on his cellar. She set down the glass with a snap on the table next to her. But of course, no one knew how ill Nicholas was, and she would not tell anyone.

Everyone had retired to the large drawing room in Nicholas's house after the wedding supper. It was a merry group, composed mostly of his friends, and of course Leonore's family. Even Susan came out of her shell a little, smiling shyly at Nicholas's jokes and the admiration she received from the gentlemen.

Nicholas was clearly enjoying the company. Leonore smiled wryly. He liked to be in a crowd, preferably in the center of it. It would destroy all his pleasure if she were to let anyone know he was so ill. He made a joke of it; even now he grinned as someone twitted him about the incident at the ceremony.

"I never thought you would come to the altar as nervous and fainting as a schoolroom chit, St. Vire," said Lord Eldon, whom Leonore remembered was one of Nicholas's friends.

"Not I!" Nicholas replied. "It was the prospect of ending my bachelorhood and deserting all my dear . . . companions." He eyed the ladies with exaggerated lasciviousness. They all blushed or hid their giggles behind their hands. As one they seemed to look at him with longing and regret, which made Leonore laugh in spite of herself. Incorrigible! She supposed he would never stop being a flirt.

He sighed theatrically. "I suppose my poor wife will now have to bear the brunt of my attentions." Suddenly he seized her around the waist and pulled her to him.

"Nicholas! Really!" she hissed, her face flaming hot. Nicholas wiggled his eyebrows at the guests like a villian in a bad farce, and their chuckles turned to laughter. "For heaven's sake! Do let me go!" she protested, half laughing and pushing her hands against his chest.

"A kiss first," he said.

"I— No, stop, oh surely you— Nicholas—"

"A kiss, a kiss!" cried the guests, laughing.

She looked helplessly at them, and then at Nicholas. "Oh, very well then!" She primly pursed her lips.

He grinned at her. "None of that, my lady," he said, and his lips came down over hers, kissing her until she gave in and kissed him in return.

Cheers came from the gentlemen, and Leonore could hear envious sighs from the ladies as well. She broke away at last, covering her heated cheeks with her hands, unable to look at anything but her feet. She felt a hand caress her chin, and she gazed up into Nicholas's amused eyes.

"Come, my dear. Surely it was not so bad."

She eyed him sternly. "You, my lord, are a shameless rogue."

"Yes, I know. I depend on you to reform me."

"I think it may be far beyond my powers to do so," she retorted.

"You can but try," he said and put on an innocent, hopeful look. The guests broke out in laughter again, and Leonore gave a reluctant smile. She wanted to laugh along with the others, but a heaviness in her chest weighed her down every time she looked at Nicholas. He smiled at her, then his attention was taken by another guest. She felt suddenly cold and alone, despite the smile she kept on her face.

Leonore did not want him to die. The heaviness became an ache, and she drew in a slow breath. When he died, she would be alone, more so than she had ever been in her life. In the short space of time she'd come to know him, her days had been filled; filled with his laughter, his touch, his kisses. When he held her, she felt comforted of much of the pain of her life, the loneliness.

She understood, suddenly, that she had been lonely all her life. There was Susan, but Leonore was the older sister and Susan's support, the strong one. She rarely revealed her thoughts and feelings to anyone, including her sister. No one really knew her, knew what was inside of her. She'd taken pride in her invulnerability; it was a thing that protected her heart, like a hothouse sheltering a rare rose. And yet, Nicholas had encouraged her to talk and listened to her, had opened a door and let in the wind. Sometimes the wind was warm, and sometimes it was chillingly cold; Leonore did not know if her heart would survive being exposed to such extremes. She had protected it so very carefully.

But now her gaze followed Nicholas around the room; she noted how he chuckled at a guest's gibe, how he looked mischievously into a lady's eyes as he kissed her hand. Should she close the door and protect herself once again?

He may die in a year. Leonore closed her eyes briefly, then made herself smile and nod at a gentleman who congratulated her on her marriage. What would she have after Nicholas was gone?—a title, and if he continued to be generous, funds enough so that she might live in luxury. A shudder went through her, a cold current of grief. These things seemed meaningless somehow. Nicholas looked up from his conversation with Lord Eldon and smiled at her from across the room. Leonore smiled in return, then bit her lip, for bleak desolation threatened to overwhelm her. She would give up the title and all the riches in the world if it would keep him alive.

She loved him. The thought startled her. Impossible! she said to herself. Her father had sold her to Nicholas; it was a marriage of convenience. But that argument and the resentment that had always accompanied it were long expired. A rising panic made Leonore's hands clench in her lap. What would she do? What *could* she do? She felt exposed and vulnerable and weak.

It came to her then, that her weakness was none of Nicholas's doing. It was she, herself, who had caused it. Protecting her heart from all the pain in the world had weakened it, for she had risked nothing, had not become strong from the exercise of risk. She'd never let herself receive any tender gesture, denied she had need of it. She had even refused to acknowledge the hopeful and proper approach of a gentleman at a student's house, and she had known at the time he would have meant honorably by her. But she could have been wrong, was her thought at the time, and it was not proper that a governess marry any man of the house in which she taught.

There had been nothing proper about Nicholas's advances toward her, however, though they had occurred within the bounds of their betrothal. He had wanted *her*, and he had made it clear that it was herself alone he wanted. He had spoken no word of love, and she'd not expected it. But he had treated her with—yes—respect. Her wishes had some value to him. Even his improper caresses had ceased when she had said no. And when she had inadvertently shown distress at his illness, he had taken her in his arms to comfort her. She was sure, in his own way, in some slight way, that he cared for her.

And all this would be taken away from her in a year. The pain of it almost made her groan aloud, but she swallowed it down. No, no, surely it was not "would" but only "could."

The sound of music startled Leonore from her thoughts. She looked for the source of it and found to her surprise that Susan had come to the pianoforte and was playing a dance tune. Some guests were already standing up for a set. She felt a touch on her shoulder and looked up to see Nicholas at her side.

"Dance with me," he said, an echo of his words that time they danced in the moonlit garden at the Benningtons' house. Wordlessly, she took his hand and stood up.

She had no occasion to dwell on her feelings, for the country dance was a sprightly one, and it took all her breath and attention to keep up. Even when she was not looking at him, she could feel Nicholas's eyes upon her, and even when the figures of the dance caused them to part. He looked at her as if studying her, as if he was trying to make a decision. Of course she could not ask him, for the dance kept them apart too much of the time. Later, she thought. Later I will ask.

The dancing continued, and even Susan blushingly agreed to dance while her mother or another lady played the piano. A quadrille came to an end, and a few yawns were suppressed here and there amongst the company, and Leonore looked at the ormolu clock upon the mantelpiece. It was not very late according to the hours society generally kept—only eleven o'clock. She looked at a few of the people who had yawned and caught laughing looks from them. Heat rose in her cheeks, for she suspected they had some notions about leaving the newlywed couple alone.

The room became thin of company then, for the guests began to leave. Leonore's family was the last to depart, and she dutifully allowed her mother to kiss her cheek and shook her father's hand. Then she smiled and held out her hands to Susan, who rushed into her arms and gave her a fierce hug.

"Oh, Leonore, I am so glad for you! Lord St. Vire has been so kind to us all! I am convinced you cannot be anything but happy you have married him."

"Of course I am happy," she replied and swallowed a small lump in her throat. "How can I not be?" Nicholas moved closer to her side and placed his hand on her shoulder. She looked up at him and gave him a slight, uncertain smile. Turning back to Susan, she said, "I would like you to visit me often—promise me, now!"

Susan looked uncertainly at Nicholas. "I . . . if it is permitted. . . ."

"Of course, Miss Susan, you are always welcome here," Nicholas said. "You may visit your sister whenever you wish."

Susan blushed shyly. "You are too good, my lord."

Nicholas grinned at her. "You must call me Nicholas, as you are my sister now, are you not?" He bent and kissed Susan briefly on her cheek. The girl's face blushed fiery red, and she put her hands to her cheeks.

"Yes, sir . . . that is, Nicholas." Susan looked shyly down at her feet.

Leonore gave her a hug and whispered loudly in her ear—loudly enough for Nicholas to hear. "You must not heed him, Susan, for he is a terrible flirt and delights in discomposing everyone about him."

Susan looked up and grinned. "That *is* true, isn't it? He did kiss you in front of everyone, didn't he?"

This time it was Leonore's turn to blush, and Nicholas laughed. "Touché! Leonore, your sister catches you out!"

Leonore turned an ironic eye to him. "I think it was you she caught out, not I!"

"Susan!" Mr. Farleigh called from the doorway. Susan looked hurriedly back at her father.

"I must go! But I will see you soon!" She gave Leonore one last hug and left.

The door shut behind her, and Leonore breathed out a long breath. It echoed in the now empty room . . . empty except for herself and Nicholas. His hand was still upon her shoulder, and now his thumb was caressing the skin of her neck. She gave him a tentative look.

"Are you glad, Leonore?" he asked, gazing at her intently.

"Glad of what?"

"That you married me." His thumb continued tracing a line up and down her shoulder and throat. She swallowed and looked away from him.

"Of course I am," she said. "You have been all that is kind to me." There was silence, and she glanced up at him. He was watching her, his eyes speculative.

"Shall we retire, then?"

She nodded and turned toward the door. Then she stopped and looked at him. "But you sleep only during the day."

"True."

"Oh!"

"Yes, 'oh!' " His smile turned into a grin, and he kissed her. She could not help kissing him in return for a moment, then gently pushed him away from her. She felt suddenly afraid, for what her mother had told her—in a vague, furtive manner—seemed a terribly intimate thing, and her emotions were almost too raw this evening to consider it. She gazed at his face, serious now, and touched the pale skin of his cheek, then let her fingers brush his lips. He has perhaps a year to live, she thought. He took her hand and kissed it.

"You are frightened, yes?" he asked.

"Yes," she said.

"I will be gentle with you, Leonore, I promise it."

She looked at him, surprised, then realized that he meant he would be so to her in the marriage bed. Her mother had told her it would hurt and that she should think of the clothes she would buy when next she went to the dressmaker's shop. But she did not want to think of clothes, for she knew the pain she'd feel when he was gone would be woven in with regret if she did not let herself know him fully. Then she could always remember and never wonder "if" later. She did not want to regret anything.

Abruptly, Leonore tugged his hand, and pulled him toward the door. His brows rose, but he said nothing, and only followed her.

They went up the stairs, and Leonore finally stopped in front of a chamber door, which earlier a maid had told her was her own room. She turned to Nicholas then and put her hands behind his neck to pull him down in a kiss, fierce and passionate. He was still for an instant, then brought her close to him. After a moment, she pushed him from her and stared into his eyes.

"Come to me. Soon." Her face flamed red in the candlelight at her brazenness. She turned, went into her room, and quickly shut the door.

Chapter 8

St. Vire stared at the closed door, then let out a quiet, triumphant laugh. She was willing—more than willing. Leonore wanted him. Everything was in place now; he needed only to take action.

He went next door to his room, where the conscientious but yawning Edmonds waited to help him remove his clothes. Perhaps his valet thought he had to help his master to bed this night. St. Vire gave him a quick smile and waved him away after removing his jacket. "You need not change your routine, Edmonds. I will not need you this evening."

"Very well, your lordship." Edmonds gave him a grateful look, bowed, and left.

Taking off his waistcoat, St. Vire glanced at the clock on the wall. It was almost eleven o'clock, midsummer night. He smiled in satisfaction. Each part of his plan had fallen into place, all on the schedule the spell indicated. He frowned. That was the thing . . . the spell indicated, but rarely stated. Then, too, the spell book was old and the words faded. He had abstained from both blood and whores prior to his wedding, enticed a virgin to the point of desiring his embrace, and married her in a church on midsummer night. Now he would bed her. The sign that he had succeeded so far was that he had survived in the church. The next step, however, told of releasing the maiden's blood . . . and this could either mean taking her virginity or her lifeblood, or even both.

To his surprise, his hand clenched into a fist. His whole body had tensed. He made himself relax and smiled wryly. He was acting as if he were the virgin, not Leonore.

But what if it was indeed her lifeblood that he needed to take? One would think, after all the austerities the spell had demanded, that it meant the lesser of the two, the taking of her maidenhead. What would happen, then, if it were not? What if he must draw her blood from her veins? Oh, God. If he did not do the right one, he would have no other chance to avoid the madness that was sure to come. He had already stepped upon the path by marrying Leonore. There was no going back.

And would she come to hate him if he drank her blood?

Why should he care if she did? She was just the means to cease the march toward insanity, after all. He could drink of her blood every week, and she would have no power to refuse, for Leonore was his wife. An image of her came to his mind's eye, her face filled with revulsion, flinching from his touch where she had sought it before. His breath left him suddenly. No, no, she had to be willing—that was what the spell required. It would ruin everything if she were not, and he much preferred her willing. Yes, that was it. It was better that way; it would be awkward otherwise, and he always did prefer finesse in all things.

His fingers became suddenly clumsy, and his neckcloth tangled in his hands; he tore it off and threw it on the floor. He was tired of this dance, this mincing around and about the spell. It made him feel things he did not want to feel, made him think he wanted Leonore's regard, made him obsessed with her. Why look at him! He'd been wondering *if* and *when* and *how* about the marriage bed as if he'd never eased his lust upon a woman before. He sneered. How stupid he'd become, all because of a spell . . . and a woman. He was more than eighty years old now. Perhaps he was coming into senility. What was more repulsive was that he, as old as he was, lusted after a woman sixty years younger than himself.

A laugh broke from him, at once exhilarated and angry. But he was not old, was he, after all? His mirror could show him that. He turned, thrust aside the curtain he had put over it, and stared at himself—stared at the face smooth of any sign of aging. Not even laugh lines showed around his eyes, though he laughed much. God, he was still young. He'd seen his friends die of old age—no, only noted they had died when he read their obituaries, for he could not let them see him after the years had scored their faces with lines but had left his alone. No one was still alive who knew him when he first was turned into a vampire. No one knew what he was, who the real Nicholas St. Vire was.

He knew, of course. He could see it in the old eyes that stared back at him, the colorless skin, the canine teeth long and sharp. And why could not anyone else see it? What did he, in truth, look like to others? He let out an impatient breath. He should be dead, for what was the use of living when all who once knew you were dead?

Stupid, stupid! This was old ground—he had walked this path before in his thoughts. A fire heated his mind, and he paced the floor, glancing at the mirror from time to time. He shouldn't have a mirror in his room, not at all. What he saw was all a lie, anyway. His whole damned, immortal life was a lie. Why should his mirror tell him anything different? He stopped before the mirror and laughed again, angrily. What was truth, after all, and what was reality? His fist shot out, and the sound of shattering glass and the crash of the mirror upon the floor pierced the night's silence.

He stared at the pieces of glass scattered upon the rug, his breath still coming quick and harsh. The fiery mist receded from his mind, leaving him feeling dull and slow. The scent of his own blood came to his nose. It sharpened his senses, and pain spread across the knuckles of his hand. He sighed and shook his head. He had broken another mirror. Really, he should not have put one in his room to begin with. And yet, how was he to tie his neckcloth properly without one?

"Nicholas! Nicholas, what has happened?"

Leonore . . . her voice sounded frantic with worry. St. Vire stared bleakly at the connecting door he usually kept locked, at the mirror, and then at his hand. His hand was oozing blood . . . he should do something about it. He shook his head, trying to clear his mind of the fog that had settled in it.

"Nicholas! Open this door!"

She cared for him. He could tell by the anxiety in her voice, and she had said she cared if he lived or died.

"Nicholas!" The doorknob rattled, and he could hear Leonore pounding her hand on the door.

He blinked and shook his head again. He had broken the mirror. He let out a shuddering breath. What a fool he was. The madness had not seized him for a while, and he thought perhaps he had controlled it totally. Of course, he had not. He supposed he should be glad he had not gone on to destroying other furniture, as he had done before. Or destroying people, for that matter, as he'd seen that other vampire do long ago. He took another deep breath, and it seemed to clear his mind.

"Please, Nicholas, open the door, or I shall call for Edmonds!"

Abruptly, he strode to the door and opened it. There Leonore stood, her hair disheveled and her eyes wild. "Yes?" he said calmly.

Fear and anger burned in her eyes, and she thumped his chest with her fist. "Is this all you can say? I thought you were ill again, and you would not answer! For all I know you could have died, and then what would I have done?"

He smiled slightly. "Why, then you would have been a rich woman and could choose another husband at your leisure."

She pushed at him, and he caught her hands. "I do not *want* to be rich!" Her breath caught in a sob. "I want *you*, Nicholas, only you, and— Oh, heavens, your hand is bleeding!" He saw her bite her lip to control its trembling.

"Never mind . . . it is nothing." He drew her close and kissed her, but she pushed him away again.

"Nonsense! You must tell me what happened."

"I . . . tripped and grasped the mirror—it fell and broke upon my hand."

Shooting him a skeptical look, she pulled him to her turned-down bed and made him sit.

"I was not ill again, Leonore."

"Hmm," she said. He watched her while she wet a handkerchief from the washstand. She wore a thin white wrap drawn over her breasts and tied with a single ribbon. The cloth shifted, outlining her limbs as she moved, and he could see her form, lithe and graceful, as she passed in front of the candles and the fireplace. His breath quickened. He wanted to touch her then, untie the ribbon and push away the bodice of her gown. He put out his hand toward her, but stopped himself, for it was yet another obsession, a little madness like the one he'd experienced just minutes ago, and he was not sure he was fully in control of himself yet.

She brought a brace of candles and set it upon the table next to the bed. A smooth spiral of her hair dropped forward from her shoulder as she leaned over his hand, and his other hand closed tight against the feeling that he must follow the line of the curl to where it lay upon her breast. She pulled with care a fragment of glass from between his knuckles and wiped away the blood. She began to wrap the handkerchief around his hand, but he stopped her.

"You need not bind it. It is but a small cut, after all."

She looked at his hand and raised her brows; it had indeed stopped oozing blood. She brought his hand to her lips and pressed a kiss upon it, then gave him a wavering smile. "There, then. Perhaps that will help if you do not want me to bind it."

"Yes, I am sure it will." He returned her smile and drew her to him, down to the bedsheets.

Now, now he pulled the ribbon and the robe fell open, now he slipped the gown from her shoulders, now he kissed her lips softly, tasting them. A salty tang was upon her lips, the faint residue of his own blood from when she kissed his hand, and he drew in his breath at the desire that rose in him, hot and feral.

"The candles—" She struggled up and reached toward them.

He grasped her hand and brought it down again. "No. I want to see you. All of you." His gaze went over what he had exposed so far: her shoulders and her breasts, round and full. He sighed deeply at the sight of it. He had been very good, bearing his abstinence with great fortitude, he believed. Damned saintly, in fact. He pulled the robe from her. Slowly he unbuttoned her gown from bodice to hem, kissing the skin he exposed as each button came undone. A glance at her when he released the last fastening made him smile. Her face was blushing, and her eyes were squeezed shut.

"Look at me, Leonore."

She opened her eyes and stared at him.

"You need not be afraid. You are familiar already with some of what I will do with you," he said and slid his hand up to her breast. She let out a long sigh, and he felt her body relax a little.

"I suppose I should think of the clothes I shall buy."

St. Vire let out a soft chuckle. "Is that what your mother told you?"

She smiled a little at him. "Yes."

He shifted atop her and kissed her. "Sweet one, very soon you will not be able to think of clothes at all," he murmured against her lips.

It was true. Leonore could not think of anything except his hands caressing her as they had before in the moonlit garden, in the Holland-covered room at the Rothwicks' house, in the many secluded places he had found to draw her close to him. She did not *want* to think of anything but how his lips tasted of wine and how his hands stroked her. She had thought too much already of his illness, the possibility that he would be gone from her someday. A fierce grief and tenderness overcame her, and she pressed her face into his shoulder to hide her emotions. The feelings almost banished the tingling that coursed over her body, but they merged with the sensation into a bitter longing, an aching passion to give him whatever he wished, whatever she could give him.

She put her arms around his neck and kissed him as he had taught her all those times, wanting to please him, but Nicholas's caresses caused her to moan and close her eyes, kissing him as she pleased—wildly, and with all the love she had and all the heat that rose in her body. Briefly, he parted from her, and then she felt him unclothed against her. She dared run her hand upon his bare flesh, her eyes still closed, feeling now the coolness of his skin warmed under her touch. His breath came short and she was glad, for perhaps he also felt as she did.

"I can make you . . . feel, as well," she whispered.

His lips slanted across her cheek and down her neck where his tongue touched her throat. "Yes. God, yes."

His touch brought a trembling upon her body that caused her to press herself to him, and his words brought an exhilaration that burned in her soul. She could give him back touch for touch, kiss for kiss, give him the heat and the joy she herself felt.

I love you, I love you, she said to him in her mind and her heart, said it with the passion she put into her kiss. She could not say it aloud, not now. Those words would die if she spoke them, for they were brief things that would hang between them only a moment. Better than she impress her love through her body's movements upon his body and her lips upon his lips, for these things were real and not mere breaths upon the air. Then, she was sure, he would remember it until the end. *I love you, Nicholas,* she murmured in her heart, and the pain of silence made her moan and kiss him fiercely. She slid her hands along his body. He gasped and kissed her cheek, then moved his lips and teeth against her neck.

He was on the edge of the bloodthirst, of the urge to drink of her from where his tongue lay against the pulse on her neck. He did not, relying on the practiced control he had exercised each time he had kissed and touched her before. Relief washed over him. He was not in the madness now, for the thirst's acute sensitivity brought him alive once again. The smooth contours of her shoulders and breasts were like silk to his fingers; her lips were sweet and hot against his own. Her hair flowed over his hands like a pale gold river, and her eyes were the color of slate. He breathed in her woman's scent and the silvery scent of lavender.

The onslaught of sensation at first overwhelmed him, but he controlled it, just pressing his mouth to her neck, and drawing back to put his tongue against the faint blue line that pulsed just under her skin. He pushed down the desire for blood, and it resurfaced as desire for her, as it had before. This desire was a common thing, he told himself. It was allowed, they could do this, and he would make another step away from the madness. He wanted to sink another part of himself into her and take her warmth into himself. But he could not hurry her, for he needed her to be willing.

Yet, he did not need to slow his pace at all. Leonore pressed herself against him without hesitation or shame and kissed him with passion. He parted from her to gaze into her eyes and threaded his fingers through her hair. She said nothing, but stared back at him, a soft smile upon her lips, her eyes tender and warm. Her hand came up, and she traced his brow and his cheek with her fingers until they rested upon his lips. A tightness in his chest made him draw in his breath.

"Do you . . . care for me?" he could not help asking. He felt as if the words had been pulled from him, as if she had put a glamour upon him and willed him to say it. *Say no*, he pleaded inside of himself, then, *say yes*.

Leonore's smile grew wider, and she put her hand behind his neck and drew him down to her. She kissed him full on the mouth, and he felt afire as her lips moved upon him, as her body moved beneath him.

"Yes," she said, parting from him for a moment. "Yes, and yes, and yes." Nicholas felt her hands slide down his back, and he pressed himself between her thighs in response. Her eyes widened, and she released her breath in a rush.

His laugh had a hint of triumph in it. It was as before, during all the times when they had been private together. He could make her respond as he wished, make her want him. Moving his lips across her cheek to her ear, he whispered, "Do you remember, at the musicale, what I told you?" He moved a little aside and brushed his fingers along her hip. Leonore shivered, but did not reply. "I said that I shall do all I have done to you so far, until you cry out with the delight of it. Do you remember?" Her head nodded slowly next to his, and a sighing moan came from her when he moved his hand between her legs.

"I lied," he said, sliding his lips from her neck to between her breasts and then to her belly. "I will do . . . so . . . much . . . more."

She closed her eyes and clutched at his shoulders, and her breath came short. The sound of it made him feel wild. Nicholas kissed and stroked her until he could not stand it, could not stand her sinuous movements beneath him without release. He thought he'd be in control, but that was a lie, also, for he was not. A madness descended upon him, a fine madness of the flesh instead of the mind, and he wanted to feel all of her, inside and out.

"Nicholas—" Leonore sobbed, and he could hear the dawn of heaven in her voice. *She wants me*, he thought, *she cares for me*. The knowledge was the thrust of a knife into him; he groaned as if on the edge of death, closing his eyes as he pushed inside of her. Her cry of mingled pain and ecstasy, the pulse within her, made him breathe in sharply.

The scent of blood—the maiden's blood. It seized him and shook him and rattled him until his soul was no longer his. She cried out in pure pleasure again, and it was music and torture for him. He thrust into her until his mind and body burst into a flash of light and darkness, then sighed and sank his teeth into the fine skin of her neck.

No. No. No. The pain was fierce as he drank of her, the pain of a man dying of thirst in a desert and given his first mouthful of water. A flood of power came into him, and his senses surged into a keen, tingling receptivity.

No. The word echoed in his mind more strongly, forced a semblance of rationality into him. His mouth was against Leonore's neck, the metallic taste of blood upon his tongue. She was tense beneath him, he could feel it. *No*. A leaden feeling pressed into his chest, pushing an abrupt groan from him. Quickly he cast a glamour upon her. "Forget," he whispered in her ear. "Forget the pain, and the . . . bite."

She put her arms around him then, and Nicholas drew her to him so that they lay on their sides. He closed his eyes and stroked her hair, then moved his fingers to the small wound upon her neck. He remembered a spell for speedy healing he had learned decades ago. Only a bruise would show in the morning.

He felt her fingers upon his cheek, and he opened his eyes. Leonore was gazing at him, a sleepy smile on her face.

"Thank you," she said.

"You are welcome. At any time, in fact." Nicholas made himself grin in return and kissed her forehead, then rested his chin on her hair. His smile faded. The heaviness was still within him, an unfamiliar emotion. He did not know what made him want to name it instead of pushing it away. Perhaps it was the oddly comforting sensation of Leonore pressed against him and the even sound of her sleeping breath that lulled him into it.

He had never been an introspective man. His mind had always delved into things outside himself, esoteric though these things might be. It had led him into rituals and practices both light and dark, but never had he been touched by them. He had even been amused by the fervor of others and was usually the onlooker, sometimes a detached participant. The most satanic of meetings and the most sublime of angel invocations had not moved him, for they were of only intellectual interest to him, and made him want to seek further and strip away yet another veil between himself and the essence of all magics.

But now the heaviness within him felt close to regret—he who regretted little or nothing in his life. More than regret, in fact, for as Leonore moved to curl herself into him in her sleep, the heaviness became an ache only somewhat assuaged when he held her close to him. He breathed in the scent of lavender that emanated from her, and the faint scent of roses came to him as well. He glanced up and saw a vase of roses near the bed. He had not noticed them when he had entered Leonore's room, for all his attention had been on her alone.

He remembered he had asked his servants to put flowers in her room, for she seemed to like them that time they had danced in Lord and Lady Bennington's garden. He had done it on impulse; all his actions regarding Leonore these days seemed to be sudden and without thought, he reflected wryly. He examined the impulse the way he examined ancient texts for hidden meanings—turning it over and over in his mind, seeking patterns. The patterns were there: He desired Leonore, whether she was near or not; he enjoyed her presence; she seemed . . . *real* to him, more so than other people seemed. What man would not feel so? She was a lovely woman, after all. And yet, he felt dissatisfaction with his conclusion.

What else was there? He acknowledged that he felt regret. He wished he had not taken the blood from Leonore, but he had no choice about it if he were to keep the madness away. Then, too, the thirst had caught him suddenly; it was at present his nature to take blood after all. It was no use regretting it. Would it have been different had it been another woman? He let out a quick breath. He wished it had not been Leonore— anyone else, but not Leonore. He had not thought she'd come to care for him, wished she hadn't, but would not have her change now that she did.

Fully asleep now, Leonore moved a little apart and onto her back, and Nicholas gazed at her profile. She had a sweet countenance, kind and a little sad when she slept. It was different from the careful neutrality of expression she usually wore. A small quiver went through her. She woke and turned toward him again, her smile sleepy and warm.

Nicholas could not help himself. He moved over her again, kissing her softly, and then with more heat. The heaviness within him made his chest feel tight; he felt as if he were breaking. It was no use searching his thoughts for the reasons behind the things he wished to do for Leonore, for the answer was not in his mind.

He feared it was in his heart.

Chapter 9

Warmth stroked Leonore's face, and she fancied it was Nicholas's fingers upon her until she opened her eyes and admitted to herself it was only the morning sun. She ran her hand across the sheets next to her, then rolled into the slight depression there, as if she could take that last evidence of his presence into herself somehow.

It was all foolishness, of course. He would not be in the bed beside her, for he could not have the sun upon him. Still, she burrowed into the sheets that had been under him and breathed the faint scent of bay rum from the pillow. The warm summer sun was persistent, however, and conspired with her growling stomach to move her from the bed.

"Oh, very well, then!" she said in a cross voice. She pulled on her robe, pushed aside the bed curtains, and went to the washstand. To her surprise, the water in the pitcher was lukewarm, probably from standing in the sun. She glanced at the clock on the mantelpiece. Good heavens! It was already past noon. She had never slept so late in her life. An image came to her of Nicholas smiling down at her in bed. Well, she supposed she had a good reason for her late awakening. He had been intimate with her three times last night. Her face grew hot. She'd been wanton, totally uncontrolled. His touch had done that to her.

No, she had to take the blame as well. She had not cared to exert any control upon her behavior, had touched and kissed and opened herself to him. Leonore pressed a wet cloth against her face, hoping to cool her blushes. It did, a little, but did nothing to cool the heat that stirred in the pit of her stomach at the thought of Nicholas. She bit her lip at the sensation, trying to quash it, but the memory of his touch and his kisses were too sharp and clear for her to banish.

For goodness sake, she could not forever be thinking of him; other things needed to be done. She must dress, put away all thoughts of him, and try to occupy herself until she saw him again. Leonore pulled the bell rope to summon a maid. First, she would speak with the servants and learn their names and their function. Then she would look about the house and see if she might do something to while away her time. Perhaps she might be useful, and when next she saw Nicholas, he would be pleased with her, pleased enough to take her in his arms and—

She groaned, despising herself for thinking such slavish thoughts. Never would she be like her mother, cringing or cautiously happy at whatever glance Father cared to throw her way. Leonore had never shrunk from her father, no matter that he raised his hand to her. She had taken pride in that.

But she could not stop thinking of Nicholas and wished he were here now so that she might curl herself into him and hold him close. It was what she craved most of all: the way he held her, stroked her hair, and soothed her after the almost unbearable shock of heat and light that came upon her at the end of their joining. The loneliness she'd always had within her would disappear then, and the sensation was like the warmth of the sun after a long, hard winter.

Her mother had not told her of this, that she would feel such things for Nicholas. She thought over the rage and the fear that was ever-present between her parents, and thought perhaps her mother could not tell what she did not know. Her observations of her parents' marriage did her, Leonore, little good, however. They gave her no clue to what she must do about it, if what she felt for Nicholas—both in her body and her heart— were what she should feel, and if it were proper.

A knock at the door startled her.

"It's me, Betty, my lady."

"Come in."

A pink-cheeked, round-faced girl peeped timidly in. "I was

hopin' you was awake, my lady," said the maid. "I'd like to do my best fer you, ma'am, this bein' the first time I've been a lady's maid, and all." The girl blushed.

Leonore smiled at her. "Do come in, I'll not bite." Betty smiled widely and entered the room. "I will need some break-fast—something hearty, for I am quite hungry—and I wish to dress."

"Yes, my lady." Betty gave a curtsy and hurried to the bell rope. She rang it vigorously. When another maid appeared, Betty said in a whisper quite loud enough for Leonore to hear, "Sal, you go tell Cook to fix up some victuals for m'lady, and be sharp about it! Good stuff, rib-stickers, like. And no skimp-ing, mind, or I'll skin yer silly arse for yer." Sal nodded quickly and ran off, while Betty beamed proudly at her new mistress.

Leonore winced. The girl would definitely need some train-ing in deportment. She hoped the rest of the servants were more refined. She smiled at the maid and said, "Let's see if my clothes have arrived in good order, shall we?" Betty nodded eagerly and opened the wardrobe door.

The dresses looked nothing like what Leonore had bought in the past few weeks. They were beautiful creations done in the latest style or in innovative designs, bold pieces of cloth she'd never dreamed she'd ever wear, or even dare to.

"Oh, heavens!" she said. "These cannot be mine. I am sure I did not order them."

A worried frown crossed Betty's face. " 'Tis what his lord-ship ordered, my lady. Who else would it be for?"

A courtesan, a woman of pleasure, thought Leonore as she gazed at one dress she had pulled out of the wardrobe. It was a diaphanous thing of stars and moonlight and the bodice but a whisper of silk and gauze. And yet no one could say it was gaudy or vulgar, for the shifting colors of deep blue, white, and pale pink were subtle and elegant. A vision of herself in the dress came to her, of Nicholas seeing her in it and smiling his seductive smile, of him taking her in his arms, kissing her. . . .

She could feel her face heat with blushes and hastily shoved the dress back into the wardrobe. "Well," she said and took a deep breath. "Well. That is obviously not a morning dress, or, or even an afternoon dress, so of course I cannot wear it now."

"Yes, my lady," Betty said, her face a picture of concentration. Leonore could not help smiling. Her maid was obviously trying her best to learn. Leonore hoped the rest of her gowns were not so daring, or the maid would have a difficult time selecting appropriate clothes should she ever go on to another mistress.

She went through one dress after another and finally picked a relatively plain, high-necked gown. Even so, it fit with precision around her body, making the best of any asset she had. She looked in the mirror and did not feel like herself at all; she was used to thinking of herself as practical and sensible, and this dress was impractical and frivolous to boot. It made the gowns she had selected in the weeks before seem drab in comparison. She was used to wearing cottons and sturdy woolen cloth. This dress slid over her limbs like warm water, a sensuous thing that made her think of Nicholas's hands upon her body. Leonore let out a swift, impatient breath. *Stop it*, she told herself. *Stop. You are obsessed with him, and this cannot be right, even though he is your husband.*

"My lady?"

Startled out of her thoughts, Leonore turned to look at her maid.

"My lady, is anything wrong?" Betty's face was anxious.

"No . . . no, you have done quite well." Leonore smiled at her. "We need only to put up my hair—simply, please—and I shall go down to my breakfast."

"Yes, my lady."

Betty did a credible job with Leonore's hair, and she smiled at her maid in approval. The girl blushed and grinned, then left, leaving the door of her chamber ajar. Leonore shook her head and closed the door.

She hesitated, thinking that she should go down to breakfast, but as she passed the connecting door to Nicholas's room, she could not help gazing at it curiously. She wondered if he rested well, or if he had any recurrence of his illness. Perhaps

. . . perhaps she should look in on him. She turned the door-knob and pushed open the door.

The room was dark as night, for the curtains were drawn tightly against the windows, allowing no light to pass through. Of course, Leonore remembered, the sunlight made Nicholas ill. She retreated to her room, found a tinderbox, and lit a lamp. Making sure to close the door behind her, she approached the bed.

Only her footsteps made any noise in the room, and that was only a soft padding sound upon the rug. She stopped and heard nothing, not even the sound of breathing. Her heart beat quickly, anxiously, for the silence almost made her think there was no one else in the room—or perhaps that Nicholas's illness had overtaken him. She touched the bed curtains surrounding the bed and castigated herself for her worries. The cloth was thick and heavy; any soft sound would find it impenetrable.

Slowly, Leonore drew aside the curtains and sighed. Nicholas was indeed within, and she felt foolish for thinking he had not been there at all. She lifted her lamp, and its light shone softly down upon him. His face was turned toward her, his eyes closed. He did not move at all, and a sudden fear seized her. Quickly, she put her hand out to him, hesitated, then laid it over his heart.

His skin was cool and this alarmed her, but then she felt a slight, steady pulse, the small rise and fall of his chest, barely perceptible. She felt almost dizzy with relief. Perhaps it was his illness that made him so, or perhaps he took some medicine that made him sleep this way. Feeling a little bold, she kept her hand upon his chest, for he did not wake or even stir, and seemed very heavily asleep.

She had not thought to touch him last night as he had touched her. She marveled at the way he felt, his skin softer than she thought it would be, the light curling hair upon his chest like feathers upon her fingers. His skin had warmed under her touch, and slowly she moved her hand up to his neck and cheek, then smoothed the tousled hair from his forehead.

He moved and Leonore jumped back, almost upsetting the

lamp in her hand. But still he did not wake, merely lifting his chin as if trying to feel her hand again. How silly she was! He had been so still, his movement had startled her.

Lingering was useless, she told herself. Nicholas certainly needed his rest, and she would not disturb him. She closed the curtains about the bed. It was time, anyway, for her to have her breakfast. Staring at her husband while he slept accomplished nothing, after all.

She looked at the clock hanging on the wall. It would be almost eight hours until twilight when her husband would awaken. Husband. She'd always thought—when she thought of the vague possibility—that if she should ever marry, she'd marry a staid, placid man. Once in a while, she let herself fancy such a thing and imagined a pretty cottage in the country, a simple life with an undemanding man, perhaps a scholar of some sort who would be busy with his own interests. She'd go about her own business, and they'd live together in peace and quiet.

Impossible to have had that, she knew. She knew she had to marry to advantage, so that her sister would have a better life than she did. She gave a soft, incredulous laugh. What she had now was the furthest thing from any idyllic dream or practical imaginings. Yes, she had married to advantage; yes, Nicholas demanded little from her. But placidity? Nicholas, staid? Heavens, no. Leonore shook her head and went down to the breakfast parlor.

A footman came in with her breakfast. The food was well prepared, and she ate hungrily of the coddled egg, ham, and toast. Finally, she sat back and sipped her tea, feeling refreshed. Perhaps after she met all the servants, she would explore this house a little, perhaps claim a sitting room for herself. Nicholas had said she could arrange things as she liked in the house. It would at least, she thought, give her something to do.

When she arose from the table, she rang for the butler, Samuels, and requested he bring the servants before her. She knew Nicholas thought well of Samuels and Edmonds, the valet, but beyond that she was not sure he was aware of the rest of the staff.

Cook was a clean and competent-looking woman, but the maids looked young and inexperienced, and Leonore was certain she smelled liquor on the housekeeper's breath. That would not do, she thought, but she would not say anything unless she saw signs of neglect in the house. So she merely smiled at the housekeeper and requested the keys to the house.

The house was probably one of the largest on Pall Mall, for it had many rooms and three floors, not counting the attic rooms. The housekeeping was uneven—some rooms were well kept and others quite dusty. Leonore breathed a relieved sigh. She would have some occupation during the day and not just spend her days in idle pleasure. The thought that she would have nothing to do had made her feel oddly anxious, though she had thought otherwise before she was married. She could distract herself from thoughts of Nicholas by taking Susan out and about town and keeping house as well . . . until she saw her husband again in the evening.

She was almost done with her tour of the house and had selected a particularly pretty room—unused, she saw, and full of light once the curtains were drawn—for her own sitting room. She had memorized which key went to which room, but one key remained that did not seem to go to any room at all. She had not gone into the attics, however; perhaps the key fit something there. Leonore shrugged and almost put the keys away, but the thought of the long time until twilight and Nicholas's presence made her pull them out again. She found and lit a lantern, for she was sure the place would be ill-lit, and turned in the direction of the attic.

Grimacing, Leonore brushed at the dust and cobwebs that clung to her skirts as she ascended the stairs to the attic. The middle of the steps themselves were relatively clear of dust, which told her the attic was occasionally used. If so, the maids had little excuse for leaving the railing and the banister so dusty and dirty. She frowned and resolved to speak with the housekeeper about it.

The door to the attic opened to a short hall, and on either

side was a door. One had no lock at all and opened easily. She peered in, holding her lantern high, and sneezed, for the room was quite dusty. Pieces of old furniture and trunks were stacked within. She went in and looked about her and discovered some old aprons, fabric, and other clothing within the trunks. She wished she had discovered the aprons earlier, for her dress was becoming quite dirty. Nevertheless, she pulled one apron from the trunk and put it on. Better late than never, thought Leonore. She noted a few promising pieces of furniture, which she might have brought down to grace her sitting room.

She came into the hall again and tried the other door. It was locked. Well, now, she thought, this must be the door that goes with the last key. She took the key from her pocket and turned it in the keyhole. She heard a click, and the door opened.

The room was larger than she supposed it would be and surprisingly well apportioned. A large, thick rug lay on the floor, and thick curtains hung over the windows so that one would almost think it was night, for no light showed through. She was glad she had thought to bring her lantern, for it kept her from walking into furniture. She went to the windows and thrust aside the curtains.

The action made her sneeze again, for the curtains were obviously dusty; dust motes swirled in the beams of sunlight that weakly streamed through the dirty windows. And yet, the room had obviously been used, and that, recently. A rag lay on a table next to a used candle, and a line marked the rag's progress across the table, as if someone had made a half-hearted attempt at dusting. The room contained a large armchair and a daybed next to a small fireplace. Dust lined only the top of the armchair and not the arms or the seat. Someone had sat there not long ago.

Obviously, this was no servant's room. Nicholas . . . this must be his room, she thought, and her puzzlement grew. Why did he choose an attic room when there were better rooms below?

A tall bookshelf lined one wall, and these had little dust on them, as if the books had been taken out and read recently.

Some of the books were very old, held together in their bind-ings with pieces of string. She ran her fingers over the book spines; she could not read the titles, for they seemed to be in Latin or some other language she did not know, and in badly faded lettering, at that. It seemed as if Nicholas was a scholar, perhaps a collector of antique books. She wondered why he had never mentioned it before; she, herself, enjoyed books im-mensely and would have been interested in anything he cared to mention about his collection.

One book seemed newer than the others, and she pulled it out, opening it at random. "Ministrations and Communion with Angels," it read at the top of one chapter. Leonore raised her brows. Did Nicholas collect religious works, then? An image of him rose in her mind, of all the times he'd been scan-dalously alone with her before they were married. A burst of laughter escaped her. Good heavens, but she never would have thought him religious! She covered her mouth, trying to stiffle her giggles, but it only caused tears of laughter to come to her eyes.

Finally, she sighed and dabbed her eyes with her apron. Heavens, but she was becoming irreverent. Certainly, Nicholas could be devout if he wished . . . although she felt the chances of that were small. That he was not a churchgoer was probably what he meant when he had told her he was a bad man. Well, she thought, perhaps it was only old and rare books in general that he collected. She pulled out another volume—*An Histori-cal, Physiological and Theological Treatise of Spirits* by John Beaumont. Another religious book, it seemed. She shook her head and took down a very old book, then opened it carefully.

"*Discoverie of Witchcraft,*" Leonore read. An uneasy feel-ing rose within her. This was certainly not a religious work. She shrugged her shoulders and pressed her lips together firmly, dispelling her uneasiness. Nicholas obviously collected unusual books, that was all. Besides, witchcraft is not real, and neither is magic, she told herself and smiled. What nonsense! Perhaps she would tease him about it when next she saw him, for he deserved a little teasing; he all too often won their ver-bal fencing, and she never would have thought he'd take an interest in such superstitious nonsense as witchcraft. She turned to leave the room, determined to ask Nicholas about the books and to do something about tidying the room.

"Ahh!" A sharp pain in her foot surprised her, and Leonore hobbled to a chair. She brought her foot up and examined it. A thin sliver of glass pierced through her slipper, and gingerly she removed it. The cut was somewhat deep, but not bad; she needed only to put a salve on it and bind it, and she was sure it would be well. She looked about her for a cloth to stanch the blood, but all she could see was the dusty rag, which she would rather not use. Grimacing, she pressed a clean corner of the rag to the cut. It stanched the bleeding a little, but not much. Well, she'd best get downstairs as quickly as possible so that she could find something better with which to bind it.

Leaving the rag upon the table, Leonore left the room and locked it. Surely, Nicholas could not object to having the room cleaned a little. She would have to see to it that any slivers of glass on the rug or floor be swept up so that no others would cut their feet on it. She shook her head. Nicholas should have had it done long ago. Perhaps he did not mind the dust much, although she would not have thought it of him. He was always so impeccably dressed and tidy, it did not seem quite like him to let this room be such a mess.

St. Vire did not dream this time. Or at least, he did not remember his dreams when he woke, but retained only a sensation of warmth and comfort that seemed to center in his chest. Perhaps this was a sign that the spell was beginning to work; he did not know, for the ancient *grimoire* said little of changes he might encounter as he went through the course of the spell. He only knew that he was glad he did not wake to watching images dancing before his open eyes, wondering whether these were real or not, or if he was still asleep or not.

He hesitated before he drew aside the bed curtains. Would it be daylight, then? Would the success of his actions last night make it so that he would be able to see the sun a little during the course of the spell? Briefly, he clenched his hand, then thrust open the draperies around his bed. He went to the heavy curtains at the windows and pushed them aside.

A frustrated sigh escaped him. It was night and quite dark. He would not see the sun yet, it seemed. A faint hope persisted, however; his room faced away from the setting sun, and it could very well be that if he went to a room with a western exposure, he would see it. His attic room faced the west—perhaps he could go there.

Quickly he pulled on a dressing gown, ascended the steps to the attic, then unlocked the door. A faint scent came to him as he entered the room and his senses sharpened, but he ignored it. He went to the windows and thrust aside the curtains.

Dark. The windows were dirty, however, and perhaps . . . perhaps . . . Nicholas hesitated again, then with an exasperated breath, he pushed the windows open and searched above the buildings in front of him to the horizon.

He did not feel the usual tingling across his skin when in the presence of the slightest bit of sunlight, because he could see no light. It seemed he had missed the setting of the sun. His shoulders slumped. He put his hand upon the window latch to close it again, then his eyes caught a faint color at the horizon. He was imagining it, surely, for he had seen no color in the sky but the blackness of the night and the whiteness of the moon and stars. Could he even remember what a sunset looked like? He stared hard at the horizon again. It was there, the last bit of light and color reflected upon the clouds from the sun setting below them, a thing he had not been able to see for sixty years without at least the beginning of pain.

St. Vire turned away from it, his hands clutching the window ledge. Perhaps he was imagining it. Had he not experienced some of the madness just the night before? He did not want to assume that what he saw was real. How could he tell, then?

Leonore. Leonore could tell him. He strode swiftly to the door, then let out a breathless laugh and stopped before he came to the door. Of course it was too late to do that, for no hint of light colored the sky now, and he would not importune her to stay up until dawn. Or, perhaps he could ask her. . . . He was not sure she would indulge him in this, waking just before dawn to watch the sunrise. He thought of the night before, of the way she had reacted to his caresses, and smiled. Perhaps he could wake her in a way that would make her more inclined to accede to his request.

His smile faded. He had taken blood from her and put a glamour upon her so that she would not remember it. He shivered. Going to the fireplace, he placed some wood in it. His hands shook a little as he used the tinderbox and failed to make a spark. He let out an impatient sigh, and gesturing with his hand, he murmured a few words. A little salamander of flame lit within his palm, and he emptied it into the kindling. He shifted the wood with the poker until the fire burned steadily. He twisted his lips ruefully. He did not know why he persisted in lighting fires the old way when he could do it with a few words.

Perhaps it was because it tied him to humanity still. All the vampires he had met feared fire and could not have it around them. Perhaps the warding spell he had put upon himself before he became a vampire had given a little twist to his condition and left him this last human attribute.

Finally, a vigorous fire burned in the hearth. The work of building a fire brought him some composure, and he smiled again. He'd been too eager to see the transformative spell succeed, and he knew it would take a year from midsummer before he was totally changed. Apparently the transformation would be gradual. He sat in a nearby chair. Really, he had no reason to regret that he had put the glamour upon Leonore. It was for her own protection, after all.

Staring into the flames that licked at the wood, he grimaced. No, it was not for Leonore's protection, it was for his own. He had not known whether he had to take her blood or merely her maidenhood and so had done both to ensure he would not descend into madness. It was beginning to work, too. Did he not see a bit of the sunset this evening? And, he realized, he had felt the night's cold, enough to start a fire in the fireplace, a thing he had not needed to do for a long while.

He'd done what he had to, that was all. He had needed her

willing in bed, and what woman would want to lay willingly with one such as himself—one who might drink of her blood from time to time? None, he was sure, unless he offered money.

You are a coward, Nicholas, admit it. He pressed his hands upon his closed eyes, rubbing them wearily, and sighed. He did not want her to know what he was. The thought of her cringing from him brought the tightness of the night before to his chest. It felt as if something were expanding from the inside, and it hurt him. He did not like it, for it was foreign to him, and he preferred the familiar when it came to the emotions. Such things were uncomfortable when he encountered them in himself or in others, for that matter.

And such musings were useless. There was nothing he could do about it, after all. Much more to the point was getting proof of his perceptions from Leonore. Perhaps if he pleased her in some way, she would do this for him. What would she like? A trinket of some sort? She had not spoken of any interest in jewelry to him; indeed, she did not wear much jewelry at all, even though he had given her some very fine necklaces as a wedding present. St. Vire frowned. She had asked nothing of him, really; nothing for herself, only for her family or for her sister. He put his hand on the small table beside him, tapping his fingers upon it impatiently. Was there nothing she wished for? His fingers touched the rag he had left on the table some days ago, and the scent he had encountered when entering the room came to him again.

Blood. Blood was near, recently shed. Someone had come into this room within the last day and had cut himself, perhaps on the shards of glass that were still scattered on the floor. He clenched his teeth in anger. No one should be here but himself, for he had told his servants that he did not want anyone to disturb anything in the attic. Whatever servant had disobeyed him would be out on the streets this night.

The books he had were valuable, and he'd had a devil of a time finding them; he trusted no one with them. And the implements he'd collected when he'd experimented with the more elaborate spells—many of them were of strange and foreign construction. While he cultivated his eccentric reputation, he could not let anyone come close to realizing his vampiric nature. It was hard enough to attend to daily business matters during the night without that.

He drew in his breath and found that the scent came from the rag. Smoothing it out, he found a large, dark spot upon it. Apparently whoever had come into this room had stanched the wound with the rag. Well, the culprit would be easy to find, then. Anyone who showed a cut would be suspect. St. Vire rose from his chair. He would find out as soon as he dressed.

Chapter 10

It was past twilight. Leonore cast another glance at the parlor clock as she turned the page of her book. Nicholas must appear soon. She brought her attention back to her book, then realized she did not remember what she had read for the last half hour. Sighing impatiently, she closed it with a snap. This was useless! Surely Nicholas would not think her forward if she went up to his chambers to see if he was up and about yet. Perhaps he had forgotten that they were to go to the theatre tonight, or overslept. She rose from her chair.

You are being quite silly, Leonore told herself as she ascended the stairs to his room. Nicholas would come to see her in good time, and he had promised they would go to the theatre. Had he not kept all his promises to her so far? There was no reason why he shouldn't keep this one. Her footsteps slowed, then halted. She smoothed her hand over the deep blue silk of her evening gown; she had dressed in one of the gowns Nicholas had bought for her. It was beautiful, but she felt awkward wearing it, for it was not in a style she had thought would suit her. She shook her head. Perhaps Nicholas thought fine clothes would make her look pretty; but peacock feathers on a sparrow did not make the sparrow a peacock.

But he had bought it to please her, as he did with other things he had given her and her family, and she didn't want to slight his generosity. He had asked nothing of her except that she marry him, and she supposed by implication, that she bear him an heir. The least she could do was show her appreciation for his gifts. She stepped quickly up the remaining stairs to his room and knocked at the door.

"Enter!"

Leonore opened the door and peered in. The room had no mirror in it now; she could see the imprint of the mirror's base upon the thick rug. Only the fire in the hearth and one brace of candles lit the room. Nicholas was looking into a small hand mirror that Edmonds was holding up for him. Leonore said nothing while he carefully tied his cravat and pressed his chin gently down upon its folds. She smiled to herself. How vain he was! But it was his only fault, and one which she found quite amusing. She wondered, too, if it was just one more piece of playacting that he performed, for she often had the distinct feeling he thought his own vanity amusing as well.

Finally, with a last glance at the mirror, Nicholas dismissed Edmonds and turned to her, smiling as the door shut behind the valet. His gaze went slowly from her face to her dress, as if he measured the gown upon her body with his eyes.

Leonore's face grew warm, and she turned away, blurting the first thing that came to her: "My, Nicholas, but you keep your room quite dim, even though it is night. I know candlelight doesn't hurt you, so there is no reason for so little of it." It was a stupid thing to say, she thought, but she felt she couldn't look at him without remembering last night and what they had done in her bed.

It was useless trying to avoid the thought, for Nicholas's arm went around her waist, and he cupped her chin with his hand so that she could not help looking at him. He was still smiling at her, but there was an assessing look in his eyes.

"And a good evening to you, too, Leonore," he replied.

A chuckle bubbled out of her, and she felt more at ease. "*Good evening,*" she said. "There, have I retrieved myself?" His measuring expression disappeared and he grinned.

"No. Lack of courtesy is anathema to me, and I exact a stiff penalty for it." He pulled her closer to him, and a fine anticipatory tingling came over her skin.

"Oh? And what is this penalty?" she managed to say.

"A kiss," he replied and moved his lips upon hers. "Or perhaps two . . . or three. . . ." He kissed her eyes, then her mouth again. "No, four is better." His lips moved down to her neck.

"Five is *much* better, actually. Or, no, six," he whispered at the edge of her décolletage. She gave a gasping laugh.

"Heavens, Nicholas, do stop!" He moved a little away from her; she was blushing furiously, she was certain, and her breath came quickly now. "I . . . I thought we were to go to the symphony tonight, you had said. . . ."

He grinned at her. "I suppose I did say that. But I can be persuaded otherwise if you wish for some other . . . activity."

"Yes, no, that is— Oh, for goodness sake, Nicholas, how you tease!" She felt her face grow hotter and put her hand to her cheek. She had forgotten another fault of his: He somehow always managed to get the last word. She pressed her lips together, trying to gather her thoughts together for a stinging reply.

"I? Tease?" He put a wounded expression on his face. "I live only to serve you, my dear," he said and bowed low.

"Nonsense!" Leonore said and tried to look stern. "How odious you are, to be sure! For that, we shall go to the theatre, where you will have to behave yourself."

"I suppose I will . . . ," he said, but the look he gave her was totally unrepentant.

"Besides, you are dressed for the theatre, so you cannot tell me you had forgotten it."

He looked down at his clothes in mock dismay. "Alas! Betrayed by my own vanity."

Leonore burst into laughter, for his grin made him look like a naughty boy.

A knock at the door interrupted her. "The servants are assembled, my lord," came Edmond's voice.

Nicholas's expression cooled to ice as he glanced at the door. "Very good. I shall be down directly," he said. An odd, uncertain feeling came over Leonore at that look. She had mostly seen him in a pleasant mood, but now her watchfulness came to the fore again.

"I hope you are not gathering them so as to introduce me. I have met them already; I needed occupation this afternoon and thought I might meet them myself." She watched him. He still smiled, but his body seemed tense.

He turned to her, and his smile grew a little warmer. "You did well. I am seeing them about a matter of discipline. One of the servants has gone into a private room of mine, a thing I have forbidden." He turned toward the door.

A chill went through Leonore. "I . . . Is it one of the attic rooms?"

His foot seemed to catch upon the rug, and he steadied himself with his hand upon the closed door. "Yes," he said, though he did not turn around.

"I . . . I am sorry if you don't like it, Nicholas, but I took the housekeeper's keys and toured the house. I thought I might find something useful in the attic, and I found some furniture I could use for the sitting room." She was babbling, and she hated how her voice sounded nervous even to herself, but the words kept tumbling from her lips. "There was a key—you didn't say you had a room up there—I thought perhaps I would find more furniture. I never knew you had . . . had . . ." Her words trailed off, for he had turned and stared at her, his eyes remote.

"Had what?" His voice was sharp and wary.

"So many books!" Leonore blurted. "You never told me you were a scholar."

He let out a sigh and smiled, though his eyes were still cool. "Yes, I am, and have been for a long time."

"And a collector, too. Although I never would have thought you would have collected religious works."

Nicholas laughed, and his eyes lost their remoteness. "No, I suppose not, considering. . . ." His gaze lingered at her lips, and she was sure he was not thinking of religion.

Leonore blushed again. Her shoulders relaxed; she had not been aware that she had tensed them. She returned his smile, but the disturbance within her did not leave. She had felt, for a moment, threatened. Perhaps she was so used to her father's rages that her fear had come over her, but Nicholas had promised he'd never raise his hand to her. He had kept all his promises to her, and more, since the time they were betrothed.

"Yes, especially *considering*," she replied and felt her composure returning. She held out her hand to Nicholas. "No more nonsense, now! Shall we go to the theatre before the concert ends?"

Nicholas brought her hand to his lips. "As you wish, my dear," he said, and this time his smile was warm.

And yet, thought Leonore as they left the room and descended the stairs to the carriage, she felt uneasy. It was not his nearness that gave her discomfort—that had disappeared after she had admitted her love for him last night at the wedding party. It was something else quite familiar that she had experienced before she had come to know him.

Nicholas smiled at her as he helped her into the carriage, and she returned it. While they rode to the theatre, she was glad the carriage's interior was dim. For though he took her into his arms again and kissed her until they arrived at their destination, she was conscious that a wall had arisen tonight. She knew Nicholas never told her everything of himself; she had believed it didn't matter. But there was something of import he did not want anyone to know, more than his illness, she was sure.

For when she had told him she had entered the attic library, there had been an emotion she hadn't thought to see in his eyes: fear. She'd seen it before, but had ascribed it to his fear of his illness. This time it had nothing to do with the illness, she was sure, but something about the attic room. Why else would his eyes reveal his feelings thus when she talked about it?

Though his kisses were intoxicating, a small part of her mind was still clear, holding the puzzle secure to examine later. When they parted at last, Leonore looked into her husband's eyes as if it were possible to see into him. But though they were penetrating and smilingly seductive, she found only desire there.

The carriage stopped in front of the theatre, and the groom opened the door to let them out. An ache grew in her chest, and Leonore sighed as she descended the carriage steps. Once more she felt her defenses rise. It hurt to put them up, for she had become accustomed to openness with him. Now, it seemed, there was to be none of that, or perhaps there never had been. No doubt she had been indulging in a fantasy the whole time.

As the concert began, she looked at Nicholas once more. A frown crossed his brow, then it cleared as he caught her gaze, and turned into concern instead.

"Is anything the matter, Leonore?" he asked.

She was silent for a moment, then shook her head. "No, Nicholas. Let's listen to the music. It is a very fine rendition of Mozart's last symphony."

Nicholas nodded and turned his attention to the orchestra. Leonore looked at him one last time, then transferred her gaze to the pit as well. No, something was, indeed, the matter, but she would discover what it was in time. She had taken down the walls around her heart, and though her defenses had risen once again, she knew they were useless, for she knew they made her weak. She would find out what made that flicker of fear appear in her husband's eyes. At least she could do that for him and help him with whatever he feared, and never again would he look at her so remotely as he had this evening. She would make sure of it.

Nicholas hadn't precisely forbidden her to enter the attic library, and Leonore believed the best approach was to go boldly into it and proceed to tidy it. Though she wanted to find what it was that disturbed her husband so, she also found a simple comfort in the activity.

She was dusting a table when Nicholas entered. When he caught sight of her, he stopped in the threshold. He said nothing, but merely stared. She could not discern anything from his expression; he seemed indecisive, for he hesitated before he stepped farther into the room.

She said lightly, "Since you won't allow the servants in to clean this room, I thought I should do so. I cannot see how you can go about your studies in such a dusty, dirty place. You are such a tidy person yourself, I was astonished to see this room in such a state."

A reluctant smile touched his lips, and a twinkle entered his eyes. He went to the fireplace and held up his hands toward the fire. He glanced about the room. "It does look better than it did before," he said.

"Thank you. I have not got to the books, however. Many of them are sadly dirty and in disrepair."

"You needn't attend to them, I assure you."

She looked at him carefully, for his voice seemed to have cooled. He still smiled at her, but though his face was half in shadow, she saw his hand tense briefly. The books, then. The books held a clue to his fear. If so, there would be little good in denying she had looked at them; he was too perceptive to be fooled. She made herself smile and laugh lightly.

"Are you afraid that I shall damage them further? I assure you, I am good at restoring books. The ones in my father's library would have been in worse condition than yours if I hadn't taken the time to mend and clean them. I have examined a few of your books and can repair them with little trouble."

Nicholas walked over to her and put his hand under her chin so that she looked him in the eyes. "Is that all you are interested in, Leonore?" he said softly. "Being the consummate housekeeper? Or is it that there is something you wish to know about me that you think to find in here?"

So, he was going to be direct about it. Very well, then. Leonore made herself stare into his eyes. "Yes. I do wish to find out more about you. You may call me nosy if you like, but I . . . I care for you, Nicholas, and there is something you fear. I wish you would tell me."

He released her chin. "I? Fear?" He chuckled. "I think not." He kissed her gently, then more with more passion. "There is little you could do that would make me afraid, Leonore."

For a moment she moved into his kiss, then pushed against him. "No, Nicholas. You won't seduce me away from finding out. You may not wish to tell me everything, but someday I will know what it is that frightens you."

He moved away from her impatiently. "There is nothing, I assure you. I wish you would stop prying, my dear, for you would find little of use to you. And if you did, what would you do with it?"

Leonore gazed at him as he looked into his reflection in one of the windows to adjust a fold in his neckcloth. His voice was nonchalant—almost. She had spoken only about some unspecified fear that he might have, not one that she could cause. *He* had voiced the possibility, not herself. She played a part, then, in the thing he feared. A familiar feeling—cold loneliness—filled the pit of her stomach. But she would never hurt him! And why did he marry her if he thought so? She went to him and laid her hand upon his arm, making him look at her.

"Nicholas, I would never do anything to hurt you. How could I? You've been kind and generous to me and my family. It would be unjust and cruel if I were to return all your goodness with anything painful to you. Haven't I said I care for you?" She touched his cheek with her fingers and at his uncertain look felt tears come to her eyes. She drew him down to her, kissing him so that he would not see them.

Nicholas's sigh sounded like a groan, and he pulled her to him hard, kissing her breathless. "Ah, God, Leonore, you don't know . . . you don't know . . . ," he murmured as he kissed her eyes and lips and throat. His hand came to her breast, and he pushed away her bodice, tearing the delicate fabric. She didn't care, for his touch was fire and life to her. He drew her down to the daybed, pressing himself against her. She felt his hands pull up her skirts, then felt him hard against the apex of her thighs, and she closed her eyes, shivering with the pleasure of it.

"You hurt me now, the way you make me feel," he said. His words made her put her hands against his chest and open her eyes again. He pressed himself against her, moving sensuously, and his eyes were closed tight, as if he were indeed in pain.

"I don't want to hurt you," she whispered, then gasped at the pleasurable ache he produced in her.

He looked at her, his eyes confused and lost. "When I hurt, I know I am alive," Nicholas said. "It is worth more to me than anything." He pushed himself into her, and she could not puzzle over his words, for she was lost in pleasure. He trembled as he thrust into her until she cried out twice, three times with the heat and ecstasy that burst within her. At last he groaned himself and thrust hard into her, breathing in sobbing gasps. "God, oh, God, Leonore, how you make me feel," he murmured against her ear. "Sometimes I cannot bear it."

Leonore sighed and relaxed, but said nothing. A still distrustful part of her mind wondered if he had seduced her once again for the purpose of distracting her. His arms came around her then and held her tightly; perhaps he had not meant to seduce her this time. She took some solace in the thought. In this, at least, he wanted her and seemed to take comfort in it as well.

But a still, lonely voice inside her heart mourned for him and for herself, for now she knew there was something in her that caused him fear, and she did not know what it was.

Chapter 11

St. Vire sat up with a gasp. His hands shook, and he pressed them to his eyes to suppress the images that had come to him—more vividly this time, as if to make up for their long absence. It had been months since he had dreamed anything; he had not dreamed since he was wed, and that was four months ago. This dream had a clarity that transported him sixty years to the night when he had been made a vampire.

In it, St. Vire had smiled at the whore who accosted him. The orgy—for that was what it was—was a farce, nothing more than men and Covent Garden ware dressed up as monks and nuns, profane and stupid with drink. Discarded bagwigs and buckram coats littered the floor of the abbey, and the scent of spilled wine made him grimace.

He absently stroked the woman's exposed breast as she cooed in his ear, and looked across the crowd at Sir Francis Dashwood, whose dissipated countenance was now fired with lust. Dashwood had said he'd knowledge of certain forbidden magical arts, and so lured Nicholas to this idiot's gathering.

The Hellfire Club. He should have known any group with true knowledge would not have let itself be advertised with such a flagrantly provocative title. A group with any knowledge of the magical arts would not have advertised itself at all. They had also called themselves the Amorous Knights of Wycombe, and he should have suspected the meetings were nothing but a debauch.

However, he was not averse to harmless diversion. He looked down at the woman pressed against him and this time noted with surprise that she was beautiful. She had black hair, unpowdered, contrasting with flawless white, translucent skin. Her eyes were black as well—large and heavy-lidded with impending seduction, and her lips were full and red as ripe plums. He smiled at her with growing interest and she returned it, her teeth white and delicately small.

A loud thumping at the center of the room took his attention. Sir Francis had seized a curiously shaped staff and brought it down forcefully once more on the ground.

"We have taken profound delight in our unholy gathering," Sir Francis intoned and paused. The noise quieted to just under a dull roar. "In thanks, let us send an invocation to our dear Lord of Darkness."

St. Vire felt bored and looked about him for an exit, but the woman pressed herself to him insistently.

"Stay," she said. "There is more to come . . . more delightful things, I assure you."

Her voice had an interesting lilt—foreign, though she spoke English clearly enough. He shrugged. She was beautiful, and she felt sinuously sleek against him. Why not?

She pulled him behind a pillar and dragged at his clothes, taking off his cravat and lace, kissing him hard upon the mouth. He heard Sir Francis's voice chanting some rhyme and calling upon infernal spirits. The hairs on the back of his neck rose at the sound. He ignored the sensation, for the woman pushed him down with surprising strength to the floor. She gazed into his eyes and smiled slowly, seductively.

"You want me. . . ." she murmured, her voice barely above a whisper. Yet, he heard her over the noise in the room, and he wanted her then, indeed—badly, savagely. He took her quickly, behind the pillar upon the floor. She moaned with pleasure, pressing her lips to his throat, and reaching her crisis faster than he'd thought she would despite the lack of caresses on his part. She laughed huskily. "You are mine, now," she said. "Always."

And she sank her teeth into his neck. The pain of her bite and the pleasure of his climax combined to make him cry out and clutch her arms in a bruising grip. Red darkness flooded his mind, and he felt as if he were dying, dying. . . .

Nicholas groaned and shook his head to dispel the images that rose up again before his eyes. It was only a memory now, but the memory of his foolishness made him wince. He had learned to be more cautious since that time, learned more than he ever had thought anyone could of magic, but it was too late. He'd been tricked and made into a vampire by that woman who took the opportunity when it presented itself.

Moving from the bed, St. Vire shrugged his robe over his shoulders, then pulled the bell rope for his valet. He had not thought of her for a long time. He did not know her name—not her real name, for she had changed it often, and lied easily. She had told him to call her Mercia, and after he'd got over his initial rage at her trickery, he'd been intrigued by all that she could tell him of his new powers. They'd traveled to Paris, where they had quarreled, and she'd left him for easier company. He had caught glimpses of her in his yearly travels to the rest of Europe, but they had avoided one another.

A knock on the door interrupted his thoughts. It was Edmonds, carrying freshly ironed neckcloths. St. Vire selected his clothes for the evening, a little less particularly, for the memory of his dream distracted him. He wondered what it meant, for surely a dream so vivid and occurring after months of no dreaming at all had some meaning. He hoped to God it did not mean he would see her again. Surely not now. Mercia had always said that next to Rome, she detested London.

St. Vire sighed and made one last adjustment to his neckcloth. The last time he had seen her, he had not been so caught up in discovering the extent of his powers or in his studies that he did not see the unrest that was the beginning of the French Revolution. He had left amidst Mercia's scornful laughter and retreated to his estates in Avebury to study and find the spell that would reverse his condition. He had heard or seen nothing of Mercia since that time, and in fact had rather hoped she had been done in by the French mobs for her association with the aristocracy.

He grimaced, thinking of her indiscretions, then shrugged. He would ponder the dream later, after he had his supper with

Leonore. He would much rather think of his wife, after all, than some vulgar woman he detested.

"Leonore, will you watch the dawn with me?" St. Vire asked abruptly. The sound of his voice echoed in the dining room, rattling the silence that had descended between him and Leonore often these days. He did not mean to ask her right then, for it was in the middle of supper, and he had thought he'd ask when he was giving her something, perhaps a necklace or a ring. He had put it off for four months—never finding exactly the right time, or at least the right time in which he felt comfortable. And how was he to ask it, after all? "Leonore, will you stay up so that I can confirm that I am not going mad?" Or, "Leonore, I need to see if I am going to stay a vampire for eternity?"

But she had smiled at him just then, her eyes warm and tender over the wineglass as she sipped. She looked beautiful, and he had been caught up in gazing at her, forgetting that he wanted to time his request at the right moment. He had simply opened his mouth and blurted out the words, graceless as a nervous schoolboy. He made himself look steadily at her and was, for once, glad he could not blush.

"The dawn?" Leonore's eyes widened, and her hand nervously twisted her pearl pendant. "I thought . . . I thought you could not have sunlight upon you."

Nicholas looked away from the clear concern and pity in her eyes and pressed his lips together in frustration. He did not want her pity, only her cooperation. He let out a breath, releasing an emotion that came too close to disappointment, and made himself smile at her. "I thought I might try to see if I could bear it this time." He could see her indecision, how her teeth worried her lower lip. "Please," he said.

She gazed at him and nodded slowly. "You must tell me if it hurts you, and I will close the bedroom curtains quickly."

He shook his head. "No, that room faces west, and I cannot see the dawn clearly from there. I would like to see it in the attic library if you would not mind."

"Of course," she replied and with a quick, uncertain smile lowered her gaze and returned to her supper again.

"Thank you," he said.

There it was again, her reticence. He had thought he'd eliminated it before they had wed, but it cropped up again and again since a few days after their wedding night. He was not sure what had made it appear. Did he not please her with his gifts, and did he not pleasure her in bed? He did not like her to act in this manner, alternately elusive and pitying. When she lay with him, she was not this way, but wholly herself—fierce and ardent, giving and receiving in equal measure. He had seen how tender and caring she was to those she held dear. Now, he only glimpsed that passion when they joined together, as well as that unrestrained naturalness of her laughter and tenderness when she protectively shepherded her sister Susan about to balls and assemblies.

Dissatisfaction made him tap his fingers impatiently upon the table. Leonore had carefully partitioned herself depending on whom she was with, and he knew he received a scrupulously dished out part of her attentions. He shook his head at himself. How greedy he was, to be sure! He did not need her regard, tenderness, or her passion to effect the completion of the spell, but he wanted it anyway. Well, he had been right when he had told her she'd prick any bubble of vanity he had left. She had told him he was vain, and now she showed him—not in so many words, it was true—that he was greedy. He wondered what other deadly sins in him she'd reveal and hold before his eyes, however unintentionally.

He grinned to himself as he let his gaze linger over the soft expanse of breast revealed by her low-cut evening gown. Certainly lust was another one of them, but it was not one he regretted. They were married, after all, and surely it was not a *deadly* sin to lust after one's own wife.

His grin turned wry. More foolishness! Here he was, concerning himself with the idea of sin when he never considered it much before—certainly not during his life as a vampire. It was a novelty to think on these things, however. He shrugged and sipped his wine.

Meanwhile there was Leonore . . . sweet and lovely and wholly desirable. He had thought her pretty when he first saw her, and now she was more beautiful to him with each night that passed. Indeed, as the weeks went by, it seemed his senses became slowly more acute, even when the bloodlust was not upon him. Surely, he had set his foot on the right path where the spell was concerned.

But with Leonore? He watched as she picked the sharp bones from the salmon on her plate. That was what she was when she was with him—careful, as if there were some hidden threat she might happen upon.

He looked down at his own plate then and pushed the vegetables about with his fork. There *was* a threat to her, and he did not want to think about it. Little chance she'd turn into a vampire, not without the proper rituals and circumstances. But once in a while, not more than once a month, when he lost himself in combined passion and bloodlust, he'd drink her blood at last. She could become weak from the lack of blood, and he knew it, and so he kept himself from slaking all of his thirst so that she would not become ill.

And truth be told, it disgusted him now. He had accepted the taking of blood as a necessary condition of his survival. Now it seemed it was not so. He'd always enjoyed being in control of any situation. Now that he was regaining his senses again, now that he felt the thirst with far less frequency than he had before, each time he drank from Leonore's veins, he . . . he . . .

He hated himself. He pushed his plate away and swallowed down bile. He took and took from her, and she asked nothing from him. *That* was why he had hesitated asking Leonore to watch the dawn with him for so long. *That* was why he offered her time and time again trinkets for which she thanked him, but in which she clearly had little interest. A short, mirthless laugh escaped him, and when he looked up, he encountered Leonore's questioning look.

"A joke, my dear," he said in explanation, and even he

could hear a tinge of bitterness in his voice. "A private joke that means little to anyone but myself."

Leonore nodded and looked away from him, down at her plate again. She seemed to shrink into herself.

"Stop it, Leonore."

She glanced at him again, her brows rising in question.

Nicholas let out an exasperated breath. He was making matters worse. How was he to bring her out again? He wanted her natural with him, not only in bed, but when they were in the same room, in the theatre, in the dining room, anywhere.

"What have I done to make you withdraw from me?" he asked.

"Nothing. And . . . I was not aware I was withdrawing from you. I am sorry."

"You have nothing to be sorry for, my dear." This was getting nowhere, Nicholas thought. He looked at her again and saw the loneliness in her eyes as she gazed back at him. Relief washed over him. That was it, certainly. She had little company during the day, especially since he was not available. She needed companionship. "Are you lonely, Leonore?" he asked.

A relieved expression crossed her face. "Yes . . . yes, that is it. I miss my sister, and I worry about her. I see her at assemblies and such, but there is no one to talk with when you are not here."

"Well, then, you must invite Susan to stay with you here—unless you feel she will not like it. You may even bring her out for the Little Season if you wish."

His reward was her wide, grateful smile and sparkling eyes, and he found himself smiling in return. "Oh, Nicholas— If it would not be an imposition, I would like it of all things!"

"Not at all," he said. "It displeases me to see you moped, that is all." He frowned. "Do you not have friends, then? I thought perhaps you might make some and accompany them to luncheons and such."

"Not really . . . I do not always know what to say to people."

"Oh? I had heard from Lady Jersey that you put Lady Brunsmire firmly to rout when she called upon you."

Leonore blushed lightly, but put up her chin. "I fear I manage to find my tongue when I lose my temper, and Lady Brunsmire made me do so."

"Did she? I shall be sure to give her the cut direct when next I see her, then."

"Oh, you need not do so," Leonore said hastily. "Lady Jersey gave her a set-down as well, so Lady Brunsmire has become quit amiable."

He felt a little disappointed and smiled ruefully at himself. Did he want to play the knight errant, now, as well?

"I am rather bookish, too," Leonore continued, and her smile grew crooked. "It is not popular thing to be, and it's difficult to strike up a conversation about the things that interest me."

"No, I suppose it is not popular, which is why I keep my bookish habits a secret, you see." It occurred to him that he had never asked her what she liked to read and knew only a little of her interests. He looked down at his plate again, and his smile turned ironic. He was wholly self-centered and selfish, too, in addition to being vain and greedy. Again, she did not say it and showed no hint of even thinking it. That she thought him generous and kind was clear. He knew he was not. The contrast between what she thought and what he knew threw his faults in his face as no accusation could have. Well, he knew he had no virtues; perhaps at least he could assume a few of them.

"Is that why you keep your library in the attic, then?" Leonore said, her gaze clearly curious.

The truth trembled on the tip of his tongue. He wanted to tell her everything, for he was tired of the secrecy, and a part of him wanted her to know everything. It would be a relief, even if it meant she would run from him in horror. But he would go mad if she left him, and he could not risk that.

"No," he blurted and felt a flash of irritation. How impulsive and graceless he was becoming! He'd tell part of the truth, then. Perhaps she would accept that. He poured himself a glass of wine and drained it. Glancing at the footman who came forward to take the empty bottle, Nicholas rose from his chair. "Perhaps we should remove ourselves to somewhere more comfortable than the dining room?"

Leonore nodded, clearly curious now, and stood up. "My sitting room, perhaps?" she said. He nodded and requested the footman to bring some refreshment to them there.

He went to her and put her hand on his arm as they left the dining room. She glanced at him, her eyes puzzled as they walked down the hall.

He had not been to her sitting room before, though she must have claimed it for her own for quite a few months already. An embroidery table was set next to a cozy-looking chair in front of the hearth. A cheerful fire played amongst the logs in the fireplace, and a folded, prettily embroidered fire screen leaned against one wall. It was a comfortable place, he noted with some surprise. He had not thought much about it, but it reflected what he glimpsed of Leonore when she let down her guard. He thought of his library in the attic. It was not comfortable at all, and he wished for the first time that it was. She gestured invitingly to a nearby plump chair that also faced the hearth.

"This is a restful place," he said as he sat. "Very pleasant."

"Thank you. I have always wanted a room for myself where I could have some quiet and do what I wished." She smiled gratefully at him. "You were generous to let me have one."

A pleasing warmth flowed over him. Here, then, was something he *had* given her, something she valued. He was glad of that. He waved his hand dismissively. "No, not generous at all. I have my own room, after all. Why should you not?"

Leonore frowned. "I do not know why yours should be in the attic, however. Would you not like a room like this one?"

He looked about him, at the fire and the ornaments upon the mantelpiece. The rug was soft beneath his feet, and the wing chair in which he sat held him snugly. It would be pleasant to have a room like this. But he shook his head.

"Not with the books I have," he said. "I do not collect just any ancient volume, however. They are books on arcane lore, on witchcraft, and magic."

Leonore leaned back in her chair and smiled. "Is that all

there is to it?" she said. "I cannot see that as a reason why you should keep them hidden away in the attic. Magic is not real, after all."

He felt his responding grin turn crooked. "Are you so sure?"

"*I* am not so superstitious. If magic were real, then why have I never seen it? Or anyone else, for that matter?"

"Have you never read fairy tales, Leonore, or ancient legends?"

"Oh, for heaven's sake, Nicholas! They are *only* fairy tales. I know the difference between fantasy and reality." She opened the table at her side, took out some embroidery, and began setting precise, even stitches. She gave him a derisive glance before attending to her needle again. "We live in the nineteenth century and are not uneducated serfs in fear of some sorcerer's curse or witch's evil eye. Magic? I think not." She said it firmly, as if she had once believed in it as a child, but would not believe any longer.

Should he show her otherwise? He grinned, thinking of how shocked out of her good sense she would be. Well, perhaps not now. She would no doubt prick her finger on the needle and ruin the embroidery she was stitching so diligently. "Many people are not as sensible as you are, Leonore," he said. "Our servants, for example. What will they think if they should come upon my books? They are not as educated as you or I."

"We will tell them not to be so foolish," Leonore said firmly.

"Really? And what are they to think of that, with my habit of waking only during the night?"

She bit her lower lip and lifted her eyes from her stitching. "Of course . . . you are right," she said. "Thoughtless of me. We never had many servants, so I am not used to having them about." She looked away from him, as if embarrassed by the admission.

Nicholas nodded, not commenting on her words, for he did not want to embarrass her further. A small porcelain figurine on the table beside him caught his eye. It was in the shape of a fairy, delicately made and painted, and its wings were those of a butterfly. He picked it up and turned it over, then looked at Leonore with a grin.

"So, you do not care for fairy tales, eh?"

She blushed lightly. "It was a gift from Susan, long ago. She fancied I would like it."

"Now, I wonder why?"

"If you must know, it is because I used to read her stories and legends at bedtime, when she was a little girl."

"And you thought fantasy was appropriate material for a young girl, oh Leonore-the-governess? On the other hand, I do seem to remember your fondness for the love poems of Congreve." Nicholas shook his head dolefully. "My, my. I am amazed your employers allowed you to teach such . . . provocative material."

"For goodness sake! Of course I did not teach these things to my pupils! How you tease!"

"Your sister, then?"

"I did *not* read any Congreve to Susan!"

He breathed a sigh of mock relief. "How thankful I am that you are not a corrupter of children," he said, then eyed her sternly. "But definitely fairy tales?"

Leonore primmed her lips, but a laugh broke from her nevertheless. "Have I not said it?"

St. Vire gently rolled the figurine about in the palm of his hand. "May I hope, then, that you once believed in them when you were a child? That sometimes you wished they were true?"

"I have grown up since then and know these things are fantasy only." Her hand came up to twist her necklace again.

"Really?" He put down the figurine on the table and reached over to caress her cheek. "Sometimes it is not a bad thing to dream and wish for things that seem impossible." He snapped his fingers, and a cool puff of air next to her cheek made her start.

"This is for you," he said. She stared at the red rosebud in his hand, and then at him.

"A trick," she said.

He grinned at her. "If you wish." He rose and went to her

embroidery table, selected a pin, and fastened the flower to the bodice of her dress. She gazed at him uncertainly, and he gave her a brief kiss before sitting down again.

"What do you like to read, then, Leonore?"

She looked a little relieved at this change of subject and said, "Oh, some philosophical works—"

"Like Congreve."

She burst out laughing. "Oh, for heaven's sake! That is not a philosophical work, as you well know!"

"What do you read for pleasure, then?"

Leonore's lips turned up in a smile. "Congreve, as you have so insistently pointed out. Keats, Byron, and Sir Walter Scott's works, as well as Jane Austen's."

He reached beside his chair and pulled up a book. "And Walpole's *The Castle of Otranto*, I see. Gothics, Leonore?"

"Where did you . . . I didn't . . . I thought I had returned that to the library—"

"So you admit you have a fondness for gothics, then, eh?"

"Well, yes."

"So do I. Shall I read for a while?"

She stared at him a moment, then nodded. He opened the book and began to read.

Leonore plied her needle while she listened. Her stitching slowed, for Nicholas read with such expression that she could almost imagine she was seeing the story as if she were in a theatre, watching a play. Occasionally he sipped the brandy that had been brought to the sitting room, but the pause in his reading did not disturb the pictures that were in her mind. Finally, he ceased reading, and she found she had stopped her needlework and was staring into the fire. She looked up at him, still in a haze from the sound of his voice and the lulling warmth of the fire in front of her.

Nicholas had the book open in his lap, his hand about to close it. "You seem tired . . . would you prefer to retire to your bed rather than go to Lady Russell's ball?" he asked.

"No . . . oh, I am a little tired, perhaps, but I am sure it is because of all the housework I have been doing. I would like to go out tonight, for I have been indoors all day and wish to do something different, but I don't wish to stay past eleven."

Was there disappointment in his eyes? But she thought she would please him by agreeing to go to the ball, for she knew how he liked to be in company. She almost retracted her words, but thought perhaps he felt disappointed because they would not be staying long at the ball, rather than that they were going at all. Well, they would go, and if he wished to stay past eleven, so be it.

She dressed in good time, but still in the most modest of gowns she had in her wardrobe. After all these months she would have thought she'd become used to the way her husband looked at her, but she was not. It made her think about him too much, a thing she had not resolved yet. She hadn't given in to the impulse to stay at home tonight, however, despite the thought that if she had retired to bed as he had suggested, it probably would have been with him in it. Perhaps she was regaining a measure of control over herself, after all.

But when she saw Nicholas downstairs ready to leave for Lady Russell's ball, his appearance a study in black, white, and red, she did not see how anyone could resist thinking of him. His coat was night black, and beneath it his waistcoat was black also, chased with silver designs. Pale knit breeches hugged his thighs so that she hastily looked away from them, blushing. Within the folds of his linen cravat winked his favorite ruby, the single touch of color in the chaste white cloth. The starkness of his dress made his face seem almost translucent, unearthly, as if he were some elemental spirit instead of a man, and the dark red of his hair and his vivid green eyes emphasized it all the more. He is all fire and air, thought Leonore, and then dismissed the thought firmly. She smiled ruefully to herself. Their talk of fairy tales and legends had made her think it.

Nicholas's smile turned into a grin as he watched her, and he spread out his arms. "I hope you approve?"

Leonore smiled primly at him. "*I* will not cater to your vanity," she said.

He shook his head morosely. "How grudging you are with

your praise! I am sunk in despondency, certain you think me a hideous beast."

"Oh, not hideous!"

"A beast, then?" He leered comically at her bosom.

"Silly man!" Leonore said, blushing. "If you must know, I think you quite beautiful, and a terrible beast for putting me to the blush. There, now! I have fed your vanity and there will be no bearing you for the next week I am sure."

"Beautiful?"

Leonore glanced at him and saw that his expression was just as astonished as his voice. "Why, yes. You have a mirror. Certainly you can see that for yourself."

"Well." He cleared his throat. "Well, I . . . I don't know what to say." There was a tremor of laughter in his voice. "It is not how I would describe myself, certainly."

"What you must say, is 'thank you kindly, ma'am,' and then take my hand and proceed to the carriage so that we may go to Lady Russell's ball." Leonore smiled triumphantly at him and could not help feeling a little gleeful that she had caught him short of words at last.

He laughed and took her hand, placing it on his arm. "Thank you kindly, ma'am," he said.

They reached the Russells' house in good time. Leonore danced a waltz with Nicholas, enjoying his gracefulness and the ease with which he led her around the ballroom. The dance ended, and she found herself next to Lord Bremer. He had been at her wedding, and she quite liked him and his wife, so she smiled at him.

He returned her smile, then looked at Nicholas. "Well, St. Vire, I hope you will not keep your wife all to yourself while at this ball." He looked at Leonore and bowed. "May I request a dance, my lady?"

Nicholas grinned at him. "I shall be watching with a jealous eye, Bremer, so do watch your step." He nodded at his friend and smiled at Leonore as Lord Bremer took her hand.

They danced a vigorous country dance, which left Leonore too breathless to make much conversation. She could not help glancing at Nicholas, who was also in the set, partnering a red-haired lady who was looking at him avidly. He caught her eye, and after sending Leonore a mischievous glance, gazed soulfully down at his partner, which nearly sent the lady swooning, if her dazed look and stumbling feet were any indication of her state of mind. Leonore bit her lip, trying to keep herself from laughing. If he did not know how handsome he was, certainly he knew how he affected the ladies and could use it to purpose.

"Beast!" she hissed at him as she passed him during the dance.

She caught Nicholas's innocent expression from across the circle of dancers as Lord Bremer led her around a turn and had to bite her lip again to keep from bursting into laughter. She became warm from the effort, then was glad when the dance came to an end and she was able to fan herself.

Lord Bremer smiled at her and bowed over her hand. "A pleasure to dance with you, Lady St. Vire. Perhaps I can be so bold as to ask for another— Good Lord!" he exclaimed and groped for his quizzing glass. He put it to his eye and looked past her shoulder.

It must have been something quite astonishing for the impeccably polite Lord Bremer to break off and stare in such a manner. Leonore turned and looked past the crowd to the door of the ballroom.

Half the guests must have held their breath for a moment, for she could hear a definite lull in the noise in the room—the male half of the guests, reflected Leonore wryly. For the vision who had stepped into the room was the most extraordinarily beautiful lady she had ever seen. Her hair was black and thick, curling around her pale face in a dark halo. Her eyes were large, her lips sensuously red. As she moved, her fashionably low-cut gown shimmered green and blue over her limbs, like the waters of a lake in summer. Her escort, a handsome, well-dressed young man, looked at no one but her, even when Lady Russell came to greet them. Leonore could not blame him. How could any man resist anyone like this lady?

"I wonder who she is," Leonore said, turning to Lord Bremer. But he had already left her and was wending his way

through the crowd to the lady. Leonore grimaced. She had
not thought Lord Bremer a ladies' man. Judging by the way
Lady Bremer was looking at him, Leonore was sure his lady
would have a thing or two to say to him once they went
home.

Leonore sighed and made her way to a chair at the side of
the ballroom. She wondered where Nicholas was. When the
country dance had ended, he had been directly across from her
and Lord Bremer in the set. The next dance was a waltz, and
though Nicholas had not requested it of her, he usually did not
dance it with anyone else.

Looking about her, she spied him at last, only three feet
away from her. She managed to catch his eye and smiled at
him, but Nicholas only looked at her gravely for a moment.
Then he, like Lord Bremer, looked across the room at the newcomer.

Suddenly, Leonore found that she could not look at her husband. She had seen him look at other women, beautiful
women, and it had not bothered her, since Nicholas did not
seem to take them very seriously. Now it was different. The
woman across the room was also beautiful, and Leonore assumed any man would want to look at her. And yet she felt as
if a hot, sharp knife had been thrust into her chest.

She wanted to run, pretend that she was not here, for the
sight of her husband staring at this woman tore at her, and
Leonore was horrified to find that she was jealous. An acquaintance paused for a moment beside her and said something cordial she did not hear, though she murmured—she
knew not what—in response. Stop it, Leonore, stop it! she
thought fiercely to herself. Nicholas has looked at other
women before, talked with them, danced with them, and you
never cared one whit. This is no different.

But she was not convinced. The expression on Nicholas's
face disturbed her, for there was recognition in his gaze. He
knew this woman, and his stare said that he took her presence
very seriously indeed.

Chapter 12

The nape of his neck tingled, as if the hairs upon it had risen in response to some threat. Nicholas looked up from the tittering redheaded lady at his side and searched the ballroom. There was nothing. He frowned.

"Oh, Lord St. Vire, I cannot think it is all that bad!" complained his partner. He looked at her blankly. Ah, yes. Mrs. Bradley.

"Not at all," he replied, not caring what it was he had missed in their conversation. "But I think perhaps some lemonade would refresh you. Allow me to procure you some." He moved away from her, ignoring her puzzled expression, and signaled a servant to bring a glass to his former dance partner.

Leonore was a few feet away from him, chatting with Lord Bremer, and he moved toward her. The tingling began again, and he hunched his shoulders to rid himself of it. He saw Lord Bremer start, his jaw dropping, and St. Vire followed his gaze. He froze.

Mercia had not changed at all. Of course she had not, despite the decades that had gone by. Her hair was still black, and Nicholas knew it was not from the dye pot. Her skin was as pale as his own, and her carmined lips as sensuous as he'd remembered them. She was still extraordinarily beautiful.

And no doubt just as dangerous.

He looked at Leonore for a moment, and then at the ballroom door. He was not sure if they could leave without drawing attention to themselves, for the door was across the room and the well-mannered Lady Russell would stop them with her long, polite good-byes. Damn! How could he be so stupid? The dream that had woken him this night had been a warning—he knew that now. He should have gathered up his belongings at once and taken himself and Leonore to his estates at Avebury, but all his thoughts had been on Leonore and the pleasure of her company.

Then Mercia looked away from her escort and saw him, and it was too late. She turned again to the young man at her side and laughed. St. Vire was conscious of her attention now, even though she did not look at him. He gave another glance at Leonore. The next dance was to be a waltz, and he preferred to dance it only with her, for she danced gracefully, and he liked the opportunity the dance gave him to touch her.

But to dance with Leonore would be a risk—perhaps even a risk to her life. He did not know why Mercia was in London, and he could not presume his presence would not attract her in some manner. She was unpredictable; she had told him she hated this town, but it had not prevented her from coming here. Until he knew Mercia's purpose, he should stay away from Leonore until they could escape the house. He saw Lord Eldon speak to Leonore. Perhaps he could depend on his friend's good nature to escort Leonore home while he, Nicholas, left the ball alone. Yet, he'd be a fool to think Mercia would never know that he had wed. He had no choice. Ignoring the hurt look in Leonore's eyes, he made his way toward Mercia.

The desire he had felt for her was decades gone, but he smiled charmingly at her. He let his eyes linger upon her half-exposed breasts, obscenely white and firm like those of a nubile maiden, before he lifted his gaze to her face.

"Why, I do believe it is Nicholas St. Vire!" Mercia exclaimed in her lilting voice and put her hand on her chest in apparent surprise. The gentlemen around her eyed him with envy.

"How fortunate I am that you remember me, Miss Mercia. . . ."

"Lazlo. I am Lady Lazlo now, can you believe it? But alas, my poor Constantin was not long for this world, and I am all alone in it now." Her lip trembled dolefully. A murmur of sympathy arose from those within hearing, and the young man at her side patted her hand.

Nicholas looked at her fine, diaphanous gown, at the jewels at her neck and wrists. A rising nausea made him press his lips together. Perhaps she had married; it mattered little. She was conducting herself as she always had. He did not doubt that she had lured some rich man to her bed, put a glamour upon him so that he lavished upon her all his worldly goods, and then killed him. It was her way, and always had been.

He bowed, lifting her hand to his lips. "My poor Mercia. I hope he did not leave you in dire straits."

She sighed and lifted a finger to her eye, as if to remove a tear. "Ah, my dear Constantin was always so generous! But I must have company, you know I must! I cannot bear to be lonely."

St. Vire's gaze passed innocuously over the group of gentlemen around her, then returned to her. "I cannot suppose you will be for long . . . as lovely as you are, my lady."

A slow, satisfied smile formed on her lips, and she hid it with her fan. "Charming as always, eh, Nicholas?"

"For you, always, Mercia." He still held her hand, and he put it on his arm, leading her away from the crowd she had gathered around her. "I see the musicians are starting up for the next dance. Dare I ask that you be my partner?"

A belated protest rose from the men behind him, and he grinned at them over his shoulder. Lady Lazlo tapped his arm with her fan.

"I should refuse . . . ," she murmured, then cast a seductive look at him. "But I will not, this once."

They stepped up to the line of dancers. Nicholas did not see Leonore amongst the guests sitting by the ballroom walls; he assumed she had also decided to dance. He hoped she would not approach them, that she would stay away after the dance, but it was a small hope, he knew.

Mercia was light in his arms, feather-light, as if she had little substance to her. He gazed into her eyes, wondering if the madness he had seen so long ago was still there. He did not see it now, but it meant nothing.

"I thought you did not like London, Mercia," he said, smiling at her.

"Oh, one changes, over the years," she said carelessly. "Perhaps I thought to renew some friendships . . . or make new ones. I grew bored with continental society."

They grew suspicious, is what you mean. Still preying on the aristocracy, and indiscreet as ever. He grinned and pulled her a fraction of an inch closer. "I am sure you will not be bored here," he said. He glanced at her escort, who was leaning against the wall, staring at them jealously. "Who is the young fire-eater who came with you?"

"Oh, that is Sir Adrian Hambly. Such a lovely boy, don't you think? And so . . . passionate." Mercia's eyelids drifted half-closed, as if remembering how passionate the young man was. "I do love passionate men." She gazed with wide eyes at Nicholas.

He almost grimaced, remembering how passionate he, himself, had been when she had first caught him in her web so long ago. The winter solstice was approaching, and he wondered whether she intended to turn Sir Adrian into a vampire at that time.

"But you know, my dear Nicholas, I came to London to see how you were faring." She smiled gaily up at him. "Yes, it's true! You didn't think I would visit after our unfortunate disagreement so long ago, but I am not one to hold grudges, you see."

"You don't know how delighted I am," he replied, even as his heart sank, leaden, to his shoes. It only needed this, he groaned inwardly. He'd have little chance of shaking her off now. The dance parted them for a moment, enough time for him to form a pleased smile upon his lips. "I am flattered, Mercia, but I cannot see the attraction, truly."

"So modest!" she murmured and cast down her eyes. "But you see, I still need a consort."

"There is young Sir Adrian, very willing, I am sure, to be at your side forever. As you said, he is so very passionate and, even better, is no doubt quite malleable."

She raised her head, and a flame of anger sparked in her eyes. "But there is no guarantee he would last as long as you, dear Nicholas. He might be like poor, dead Henri. I think you owe me a little consideration, truly I do."

Henri, who had gone mad, and whom he had killed. St. Vire placed a smug and gratified smile on his face. "You flatter my stamina, my dear."

The anger grew hot in her eyes, and he was sure she would have slapped him if he had not held her hand tightly.

"Ah, ah!" he chided. "What a scandal we should cause if you should strike me now. It would never do, for it would put off your admirers, and you would not want that."

The tension left her, and she gave him a resentful glance. "I can find more, I am sure."

"But in such refined company? I think not." The music ended with a flourish, and St. Vire released her hand and bowed. "A most . . . revealing . . . dance, Lady Lazlo. I thank you." He breathed a sigh of relief. *Now, now I will leave, and see what I can do about traveling to Avebury.*

It was a foolish hope. Before St. Vire could turn away, he felt a hand upon his sleeve—Leonore's hand. She smiled up at him uncertainly. He could not escape; St. Vire had no choice but to introduce them, especially with Lord Eldon at her side.

"My dear Leonore, and Lord Eldon, may I introduce you to Lady Lazlo? I met her long ago, when the Russian tsar came to visit England. Lady Lazlo, this is Lady St. Vire, my wife, and my friend, Lord Eldon." He made his voice cordial, and he continued to smile. He knew he must measure his words and tread a fine line between de-emphasizing Leonore's importance to him and letting Mercia know he would protect his wife.

The lady's eyes scanned Leonore's face and form, and she smiled lazily. "So Nicholas decided to wed! What a pretty little bride you have chosen, my dear. And quite young, too. I never would have thought it."

"There was something very appealing about the idea of

marital bliss, Mercia. A very convenient arrangement, as I am sure you know. I thought I should try it," replied Nicholas. He stepped close to Leonore and put his hand upon her shoulder. Leonore gave him a puzzled smile.

Lady Lazlo's gaze sharpened at the movement, then she turned and smiled at Lord Eldon. "And you, Lord Eldon? Have you thought of emulating your friend?"

Lord Eldon grinned. "Not I. I've not been so lucky as Nicholas here." He looked at her as if he hoped his luck would turn, and Lady Lazlo's smile widened. Taking her hand, he bowed over it. "Dare I hope that I am the next gentleman to ask for a dance?"

"You need not hope at all," Lady Lazlo said. "I would be very pleased to dance with you." She glanced at Nicholas and nodded. "Another time, my dear."

Nicholas's hand tightened on Leonore's shoulder, then he bowed. "Perhaps," he replied. He watched Lady Lazlo leave, her hand on his friend's arm, then let out a sigh and turned to Leonore.

"I hope you do not mind, but I believe we should leave. I think you said that you wished to return at eleven o'clock?"

"Yes, but if you wish to stay—"

"No," he said and smiled at her. "No, you must not sacrifice your own wishes for me, Leonore. You must allow me some respite from my selfishness. Otherwise I shall become a dead bore, and that would be a terrible blow to my self-consequence."

She smiled slightly. "Very well, then. I do wish to go home."

"Thank you. You have saved my vanity from a severe downfall."

Leonore chuckled—a reluctant one, it seemed to him. Nicholas was conscious of discontent, even disappointment. He had wanted her to laugh and realized he liked to make her do so. He took her hand; her body felt tense beside him, her hand tight upon his arm. Though she smiled and thanked Lady Russell very graciously, her eyes held no smile at all.

Leonore spoke little during the ride back to their home, replying cordially to any of his questions, but contributing almost nothing of her own. At last he gave it up, and they continued in silence until they stepped inside the house. She quickly moved past him in the direction of her sitting room. He hesitated, then followed. She pushed open the door, and he put his hand upon her arm, stopping her.

"Wait, Leonore." He lifted her chin with his fingers. "You are unhappy, are you not? Tell me what is wrong."

Her eyes were miserable."I . . . I can't. I am . . . I shouldn't . . . Oh, Nicholas, I am despicable!" She turned from him, stumbling into the room in her haste. He went after her, shutting the door behind him.

"What is this? You, despicable?" Her back was to him, her head bent. He turned her around and took her in his arms. "What have you done? Nothing criminal, I hope. I refuse to harbor criminals in my house, especially ones who weep upon my cravat."

"I am not weeping."

"No, of course you are not. You never weep. I am sure it is a leak in the roof, which I have neglected to repair." He led her to a sofa and sat down upon it. "Oddly enough, it seems to have followed us, even though we have moved."

She laughed aloud then, and raised her tear-filled eyes to his. "Very well then, I did cry, since you insist."

He kissed her gently. "Tell me why."

"Oh, Nicholas!" She heaved a large sigh and covered her face with her hands. "I . . . I was jealous." He opened his mouth to speak, but Leonore spoke hurriedly. "I know I should not be, for you looked at her—Lady Lazlo—and you danced with her, just as you would anyone else, but she looked at you in *such* a way, I thought she must have been—I should not have thought it, and after all, ours is a marriage of convenience, and I should expect at some time we would do as we pleased, whether apart or together, for people do. . . ."

Patiently, he let her talk on until her voice faded, until the ticking of the clock was the only sound in the room. He had not thought that she would be jealous of the attention he might pay to any woman. He felt absurdly pleased at the idea.

"Well, you need not look so happy about it!" she exclaimed indignantly.

Nicholas kissed her soundly. "Silly Leonore. Yes, Lady Lazlo used to be my mistress, but that was many, many years ago. I do not like her and did not even like her then."

"Do . . . do you like me?" Her voice became breathless as he kissed her just below the ear.

"Of course, sweet one," he said and returned his lips to hers. He parted from her and sighed. "It is late for you, Leonore, and you need to rest after all your work today."

"I don't—"

"No, go. I will come upstairs later. I need to attend to some business I had forgotten in the library."

She looked uncertainly at him, but nodded as they left her sitting room.

After they parted at her chamber door, St. Vire permitted himself to sigh deeply. While he had sat silent in the coach on the way home, he had thought of what he would do, now that Mercia had appeared. It was the middle of the Little Season in London, and he supposed he could remove Leonore and himself to Avebury. But now he was not sure it would be the wisest thing to do. He had implied to Mercia at the ball that he had married Leonore for the sake of convenience. Mercia, of course, would believe he had the same motives as hers—for riches, or at least an easy supply of blood. He sighed and pushed open the library door, and after lighting a fire in the fireplace, he sank into a chair.

To take Leonore away from London would show that she was not just a convenience to him, but rather a necessity. That would be dangerous, both to Leonore and to himself. Mercia wished him to be her consort once again, and she was a difficult woman to convince otherwise once her mind was set on anything. He supposed she still wanted him because he had not turned insane yet. It was useless to speculate on her reasons, for he knew she was insane herself, though her madness was subtle and cunning.

If Mercia knew why he had wed Leonore, how important his wife was to him, she would kill her. That was one of the few predictable things about Mercia. If someone was in her way, she thought nothing of killing and was extremely clever about it. She could even put a glamour upon people and convince them to do the work for her.

If, however, he could convince Mercia that Leonore meant little to him other than something from which he could slake his bloodthirst, that he was at least thinking of becoming Mercia's consort, the chances were good that she would leave Leonore alone. It would give him time to think of how he could rid himself of Mercia forever and make sure she would never be a threat to anyone again.

He thought, then, of how he would go about convincing Mercia of his supposed willingness to become her mate. An ache grew in his chest, and he grimaced. He was becoming very good at identifying these feelings now. It was anger and despondency this time, for he knew he'd have to hurt Leonore, and he did not want to.

She might leave him. Nicholas rose abruptly and cursed under his breath. What would he do, then? Leonore had to stay with him for a year or else he would slide into madness. And yet, if Mercia received even a hint of Leonore's importance to him, Leonore would surely die. He could not even put a glamour upon her to stay—he was riding over rough ground as it was when he used it to make her forget that he took her blood.

If he told her the truth, however . . . No, God no. She would leave him then, most certainly. He suppressed a groan. He'd worked for years trying to reverse his condition . . . and now it could be at the cost of Leonore's life.

Damn Mercia! If she had not come to London, it would have gone smoothly, he was certain. But this excuse did not satisfy him. He pushed away the feelings that rose in him—his anger at Mercia, his fear for himself and Leonore—and forced himself to look at his situation logically.

This time his sigh was very close to the groan he had suppressed earlier. All his actions could turn Leonore away from him, whether from death at Mercia's hand or from her own repugnance at his vampiric nature—if he told her the truth about himself—or because of his supposed infidelity. Regardless of what he did, she would become cold to him, he was sure.

He thought of the way Leonore had looked at him tonight, the way her eyes had told him she cared for him . . . perhaps even loved him, though she never said so. For a moment, he closed his eyes and swallowed. He did not want her to stop caring for him, for he had grown . . . used to it.

Abruptly, he strode from the library. He'd accomplish nothing here; he had only come here to think, and he hadn't even done that well. He wanted . . . he wanted to be with Leonore. Quickly he went down the stairs.

The sound of slow breathing told him she was asleep. Nicholas watched her, the rise and fall of her breasts, her sweet face. The ache he'd felt earlier in his chest expanded, and he let out a long, shaking breath.

None of his gifts would hold her to him, for she did not value the trinkets and dresses he had given her, though she always thanked him gratefully. He had thought the drunkenness and brutishness of Leonore's father would keep her from returning home . . . but he was not sure of that either, for her sister, Susan's, presence gave her some solace.

And because he had to pretend to be enamored of Mercia, he could not even tell Leonore that he loved her.

He closed his eyes against the leaden sensation in his chest. God help him. He had not wanted to love her. It was an awkward emotion, a stumbling block to his plans, a thing that made men into fools. But she had crept into him like a thief in the night, and his heart was lost to her now. He did not even know when she had done it, when his desire for her blood and body had transmuted into desire for her regard, her respect, and her love.

God. Oh God. What was he to do now? If Leonore died, he felt he would die, too. He would go mad immediately, knowing it was because of him that she died, and he'd much prefer to expose himself to the sizzling agony the morning sun would bring than fall into insanity. And if she left him, he would go mad anyway, only perhaps slowly. But then she would be alive, and perhaps . . . perhaps he could find a way to rid himself of Mercia. He would still be a vampire, but Leonore would stay alive.

Nicholas gazed at his wife and touched her cheek gently. Her skin was soft and warm from sleep. He could feel it with more sensitivity than he'd ever had since the beginning of his life as a vampire. He had progressed this far, and now he'd have to give it all up.

He bent and kissed her, running his hand around the fullness of her breast. Slowly Leonore woke and sleepily smiled at him, then reached out her arms for him. Once more he would make love to her, give her everything he could give her of himself now—now that he'd have to give her up, as well.

He would not ask her to watch the dawn with him, to see if he could bear the light of the sun. It would be useless. Regardless of whether his wife chose to stay with him or leave him, she would never again come willingly to his bed or gaze at him with tenderness.

He would stay a creature of the night, and except for when the bloodthirst was upon him, his senses would fade into dullness, and music would be noise in his ears. Tomorrow he would begin to court Mercia, and Leonore would begin to hate him.

And that was a living death, indeed.

Chapter 13

As the maid helped her dress for the masquerade three evenings after Lady Russell's ball, Leonore wondered again that Nicholas had not woken her up at dawn to see the sun rise the day after the ball. She felt relief and disappointment. She would have liked to have seen if his illness had receded; however, if they had stayed up, the sun might have made him ill. It was just as well that they had not, she supposed.

Leonore looked in the mirror, twirling to see how her spangled dress swirled in featherlike waves around her figure. She was dressed as the Elfin Queen Mab, in green silk with thin strips of silver gauze as the overskirt. The light gauze drifted around her as she moved, making her seem as if she floated instead of walked. A white domino draped over her shoulders, and her mask was silver. She smiled at her maid. "You have done very well, Betty. Thank you."

Betty blushed, bobbed a curtsy, and beamed at her mistress. "Thank *you*, my lady. I tries ter—That is, I *try* to do my best."

Leonore's smile grew wider. Her maid had, indeed, improved in the few months she had been in Leonore's employ. She complimented Betty once more and proceeded down the stairs. Nicholas was already waiting for her in the parlor, and he looked upon her dress with approval as he kissed her hand and put it upon his arm. He wore a black mask and domino, but was otherwise dressed in elegant evening clothes.

"You look lovely, as usual," he said and smiled.

"Thank you, Nicholas. I wish you had decided to wear a costume, too. It would have been quite amusing, I think. I wonder you did not."

His eyebrows rose. "But I *am* in costume, my dear."

"Oh, really? What is your disguise, then?" She held up her hand, then put her finger to her temple in thoughtful concentration. "Let me guess. . . . You are dressed all in somber black, except for your gloves, which are white . . . ah hah! I have it. You are a lowly shipping clerk."

Nicholas shuddered theatrically. "If so, then I cannot be all that lowly. Shipping clerks do not wear silk or impeccably tied linen neckcloths."

"What, then?"

He seemed to hesitate, then his smile turned wry.

> "But thou, false Infidel! shalt writhe
> Beneath avenging Monkir's scythe;
> And from its torment 'scape alone
> To wander round lost Eblis' throne;
> And fire unquench'd, unquenchable,
> Around, within, thy heart shall dwell. . . ."

"That is Byron's poem 'The Giaour,' " she said, puzzled. "I do not think you look at all like a Turk."

"Very good, Leonore. Do you remember the next few lines?" He seemed to watch her carefully, and this puzzled her further.

"Only vaguely. I think they say something about the tortures of hell, and then, oh, let's see . . . 'But first, on earth as Vampire sent, Thy corse shall from its tomb be rent—' The rest of it is quite distasteful. I never did care for that part of the poem." She stared at him, then burst into laughter. "Oh, heavens, Nicholas, a vampire? A 'livid living corse'? With 'gnashing tooth and haggard lip'?" Her giggles burst from behind her hand, and she wiped tears of laughter from her eyes beneath her mask. "I think you will have to find a more convincing costume than that. Yes, I admit I have read some gothics, and I am afraid you look nothing like the vampires depicted there."

Nicholas had grinned at her laughter and now smiled at her words. "And can you not conceive of a vampire who looks, well, as tidily dressed as I am?"

"Silly! Vampires are evil, ugly, ravenous creatures. That is the way they are in those stories. I am afraid you will have to resign yourself to either being an exalted sort of shipping clerk, or Nicholas St. Vire with a mask and domino."

His expression became somber. "I am afraid I cannot be the clerk. That, upon thinking of it, would have been very amusing."

"Then you will have to be Nicholas St. Vire with a mask, for you are certainly not evil, ugly, or ravenous."

He smiled again, slightly. "I suppose it makes no difference."

But something in his expression dampened Leonore's spirits, and she gazed into his eyes for a sign of what it was. He glanced away from her. "Shall we go?"

"Of course," Leonore replied. She looked away as well. The fear was there again in his eyes, and a terrible longing. She bit her lip. Just a little, it frightened her.

She did not understand it. She had found no clue to what it was he feared, even though she had perused the books in the attic library for something that would tell her. His books covered the whole scope between the sacred and the profane, with no emphasis on either. Even if he were superstitious enough to try any of the so-called magic in those books, she could not tell whether he practiced good or evil. It was just a comprehensive collection of ancient works. She shrugged to herself. She would question him later. Perhaps as time went by, he would trust her more and tell her.

She conversed easily with him in the coach, making Nicholas laugh a few times. His smiles reached his eyes then, and it seemed his mood lightened. It made their carriage ride short, and Leonore surprised herself by sighing in relief when they reached Lord and Lady Harlowe's house. She glanced at Nicholas. For one moment it seemed he stared angrily at the house, and then his face became smooth and unconcerned.

The Harlowe residence was not as well lit as Leonore would have supposed from their obvious wealth. It gave the rooms an intimate cast that made her feel uncomfortable. She did not know the Harlowes well at all, but Nicholas knew them. She glanced at him, and he smiled down at her. She felt herself blush, for it seemed his smile was seductive in the extreme . . . but perhaps it was only the light.

As soon as she stepped into the room in which the guests gathered, Leonore wished she had not come. She knew some of the people, and those she knew had reputations that bordered upon the scandalous. She looked at Nicholas, wondering why he had brought her here, for he had always escorted her to those events that contained only the most respectable of people.

Heavy drapes hung over the balcony windows, and though some of the windows opened to the air, the rooms were hot and humid. A quartet of musicians diligently played their instruments, and some people danced the waltz in a languid manner, many of them too close for propriety. The guests were lords and ladies—barely masked—and many of them were nowhere near their spouses. She noticed a Sir Jamison whispering in Mrs. Burlingame's ear, his hand caressing her neck as he spoke, while his wife walked out to the balcony with a man who draped his arm around her waist. She thought she saw Lord Eldon, as well, but he was far to the other side of the room and she could not be sure.

She turned to Nicholas to ask that they leave, but he was gone. Her teeth gritted in panicked anger. What could he have been thinking of? How dare he bring her to such a place! She searched the crowded room, but did not find him.

"Perhaps a dance, my Queen?" an unfamiliar voice whispered by her ear, and she turned quickly. A Harlequin leered at her from under his mask, and she took a step back.

"No, thank you, I do not wish to dance," she said.

"A walk out upon the terrace, then?"

"No." She turned away from the man, searching the room once more.

"You are unobliging, pretty one."

She felt a hand slide around her waist. Fury flared within her at the man's actions and at Nicholas's abandonment. Her hands turned into fists, and the sticks of her fan bit into one palm.

"I pray that you unhand me now, sir, or you will certainly

regret it," Leonore said between clenched teeth. The man only laughed and pulled her to him.

She did not think, only acted. Sheer anger propelled her fist around in a circle, and she drove the pointed end of her closed fan into his stomach.

"Oof!" The man fell with a decided thump to the floor.

Horrified at what she had done, she whirled to stare at the man who had fallen. He was gasping for breath and holding his stomach; his mask had come half off, affront writ large upon his face. Laughter broke out around her, and she raised her head with a jerk. Her face flamed hot. A crowd had gathered around her, obviously enjoying the scuffle. Their masked faces—amused Columbines, laughing cavaliers, leering pirates—seemed monstrous to her, and she ran blindly away from them, away from the heat and the suffocating humiliation.

Cool air struck her face and calmed her heated emotions a little as well. Leonore looked about her and found she had run out onto a balcony. She drew her domino close about her shoulders and leaned against the edge of the balcony, breathing deeply of the night air. She would go home as soon as she recovered herself and found Nicholas.

The night sky was black and dotted with the light of stars. Leonore looked up at the moon shining serenely as if nothing had happened only a few minutes before. Some calmness returned to her. She could hear the musicians inside the room still playing relentlessly, and the muted noise of the guests. Relative silence surrounded her, and she was glad of it. The murmur of voices, closer, came to her.

"Nicholas . . ."

Leonore froze, but did not turn around. She was sure the voices came from just below her where the door opened out to the terrace.

"Well, Mercia, you see I have arrived as I promised." Leonore closed her eyes. She knew Nicholas's voice very well.

"You wed her, my dear. I don't know if I can forgive that."

"Oh, come, my dear!" Nicholas said ironically. "Surely you

don't think it is any different from your own . . . marriage to your poor Constantin."

"She is well-born, however. I am sure she could not be living with you without your wedding her in a church. How did you manage it?" Leonore could hear suspicion in Lady Lazlo's voice.

"It was short, believe me. I have lasted longer than any of the others. Why shouldn't I be able to bear this, as well?"

"Then I was right to return here." Lady Lazlo's voice grew eager. "Look you, Nicholas, we shall be a powerful pair should we join together. We could rule here, take what we wish."

"I remember the last time you said that, Mercia. How will I know your indiscretions will not force you to hide once again?"

"I was never indiscreet!"

"So you say. Your depredations amongst society's best were always obvious to me."

"You—" Lady Lazlo's voice had risen, but she stopped herself. "Oh, come now, you know what I am. You are another one of my kind. Of course you'd notice my actions." Her voice was soft and seductive.

Leonore's hands closed into tight fists. *Please, Nicholas, please don't go to her.* She wanted to leave, but moved only to turn and look over the balcony. There she saw Nicholas, not quite facing the balcony; Lady Lazlo was turned toward him.

"Of course I would notice your actions, Mercia," Nicholas replied. "But so did the Parisians."

Lady Lazlo shrugged. "I merely convinced them I was helping their cause. They became very sympathetic after that."

A slow smile came to Nicholas's lips. "How very clever of you, my dear." Lady Lazlo stepped close enough for her to lay her head upon his chest.

"Dear Nicholas, will you join me?" Leonore could see Lady Lazlo's fingers trace a trail from Nicholas's coat lapel to his cheek. He did not move from her, but smiled.

A hot, sharp pain struck Leonore's chest, pushing a short groaning sigh from her. She covered her lips immediately and

shrank behind a pillar. For a moment she thought Nicholas's
eyes had shot to where she stood, but she could not be sure.

Nicholas was looking at Lady Lazlo now, however. He
brought his hand to her shoulder and caressed her neck. "I
have yet to hear anything to make it worth my while."

A low, husky laugh floated up from Lady Lazlo. "Kiss me,
and perhaps that will convince you."

Don't, don't! cried Leonore inwardly and pressed her hands
to her mouth. She watched, numb, while her husband slowly
bent and pressed his lips to Lady Lazlo's. Leonore turned then,
closing her eyes tightly, and bit her lip to keep herself from
crying out. The pain and the taste of blood brought her to a
semblance of control, and she swallowed the tears she felt rising within her.

"You will have to convince me more than that, Mercia."
Nicholas's voice was smooth, almost emotionless.

This time Lady Lazlo laughed complacently. "Come to me
tomorrow. I will do my best to persuade you then."

Leonore's feet unfroze in that instant, and she stumbled
from the balcony into the room again. She had to leave—now.
She could not stand the idea that Nicholas would go to that
woman when only a few days ago he had told Leonore he
liked her. Liked. That was not much, was it? Obviously, he felt
more than liking for Lady Lazlo.

Her feet sped her past the guests. Tears started to drop from
her eyes. She dashed her hand against her mask, dislodging it
so that it obscured her sight, and stumbled hard into a firm,
male body. Her arms were grasped, and she struggled wildly.

"Let me go! Please let me go!"

"I say, Lady St. Vire, what are you doing here?" came Lord
Eldon's voice from above her head. She pushed up her mask
and gazed into his concerned eyes. "Not quite the thing, you
know."

"Oh, Lord Eldon, please take me home! I—It was a terrible
mistake. "I . . . I have the headache, too." She pressed her hand
to her temple, for indeed a headache was beginning to form
there.

"Where is St. Vire? Surely *he* did not bring you here?" He took her hand and patted it comfortingly.

"No, no, he did not," she lied. "I came with some friends . . . I thought they were friends, but of course they are not." She let out a near-sobbing breath. "Please take me home."

"Of course, of course," said Lord Eldon. His voice was kind, and Leonore nearly burst into tears at the sound of it.

He hailed a hackney and made sure Leonore was comfortable in it before he entered it. Lord Eldon's light, inconsequential chatter calmed her so that by the time they reached the house, she was able to thank him for his assistance in a friendly way.

"Are you sure you do not wish me to see you to the door?" Lord Eldon said.

She smiled at him. "No, I assure you I will be better presently. I *am* much better now that I am gone from that place."

He nodded and tipped his hat to her. "Very well, then. But I shall wait until you have gone into the house."

Leonore waved to him when the footman opened the door, and she watched the carriage start off. Then she turned and entered the house.

Her nod to the footman was automatic, without her customary smile, and her steps to her room mechanical. She thought of the kindly Lord Eldon and wished she had married someone like him. She would not be so confused now, so filled with turbulent emotions that it made her feel ill. From the start Nicholas had confused her, had made her feel things she did not want to feel, and made her want more from this marriage than a marriage of convenience had to offer.

Her maid had stayed up to attend her. The girl smiled uncertainly, and Leonore made herself smile reassuringly.

"You are doing well, Betty. I am tired and have the headache. I only wish to sleep."

A relieved expression lightened Betty's features, and she bobbed a curtsy. "Yes, my lady. I'll be quick, then."

Betty was as good as her word, and Leonore was soon in bed. She gave a last smile at her maid as the door closed.

Then the wracking agony came.

"I will not cry. I will not cry," moaned Leonore into her pillow. It was a chant, a dirge that echoed in her dark, quiet room. She had held off the tears so long they would not come now, and she moaned as if she were gravely ill and in a fever. All her love, her loneliness, and her hopes she whispered into the pillow, all her rage and feelings of abandonment. It did not comfort her.

Above all, the thought that hurt her, that made a rising nausea lie heavy in her belly, was that Nicholas had lied to her. He had said he had not liked Lady Lazlo for years now. It could not be true, not from the way he'd kissed the woman. Leonore had trusted him as she had no one else, for he had never lied to her and had always kept his promises. She had even come to love him.

The thought made her groan aloud, a short, sharp sound. Anger fired her mind, and she was abruptly, fiercely glad she had never told Nicholas of her love. She had told him she cared for him. But she had not, at last, told him she loved him. She held close that thought, as if it were a buoy above her churning emotions. He would never know. She would never let him know.

"I will never let him know," she murmured into the night's silence. She said the words over and over again, and slowly her breath evened out. She was tired, very tired.

"I will never let Nicholas know," she whispered again, and the phrase became a mournful lullaby. At last she breathed a long sigh and fell asleep, her husband's name on her lips.

Nicholas glanced again at the balcony. Leonore had left at last. He gazed at Mercia and smiled at her.

How I hate you. He wished he could rid the world of her, for she was nothing but a monster . . . like himself. He almost grimaced at his newly born sense of ethics. Could he condemn her for the bloodthirst he, himself, had? But then, he never killed his victims unless they were in the process of killing others. Perhaps he could put some ward or spell upon her to render her harmless to those he held dear. He could not be sure he would find one, however. It would take time.

Regardless, she had to be handled carefully. She was dangerous, both to him and to Leonore—to anyone who came in her path, for that matter. Even now, as she twined her arms around his neck and pressed her body against his, he saw the subtle madness in her eyes, an almost animal cunning.

He grasped her arms and moved her away from him. "I thought you said you would try persuading me tomorrow."

Mercia looked at him with heavy-lidded eyes. "Oh, I suppose I could try persuading you now."

Nicholas gauged his words. "You have no sense of finesse, my dear. Everything must be 'now,' and 'soon,' and 'tonight' with you. Where is your sense of anticipation?"

"There is nothing wrong with doing what I want."

"There is, when more pleasure can be had when one waits."

Lady Lazlo seemed to consider this. "Very well. But don't bring your wife. I saw her inside earlier colliding with a Harlequin." She shook her head. "A clumsy wench. How you came to wed her, I do not know. You are so graceful yourself."

Biting back angry words, Nicholas shrugged. "It was convenient. I grew tired of hunting. I am a lazy fellow, after all."

She looked at him slyly. "Or, you could bring her and perhaps we might have some sport with her."

Hot rage and loathing shot through him, and it took all his control to keep from killing her where she stood. He made himself smile and shrug again, feeling ill from the effort. "Perhaps," he said. Even to himself his voice sounded strained. "But I am afraid it would shock the poor creature quite horribly, and she'd be useless for a long time afterward. She is a very good housekeeper. Finding a replacement would be tedious."

"Very well, then. We do not need her." She shot him an indecipherable look. "But you must rid yourself of her at some time, you know. Otherwise I will suspect you are not wholly committed to me."

St. Vire sighed in a bored fashion. "How you harp on that!

So you said during our dance at Lady Russell's ball. I will rid myself of Leonore when I am tired of her. I am not tired of her yet. Besides, I am not as indiscreet as you—*I* do not care to have Bow Street snapping at my heels. Do try to be a little more civilized, Mercia."

"How stupidly particular you are, Nicholas!" she said pettishly. "All these little concerns of yours." She took his face in her hands and pulled him down to a hard kiss. "There! That's to remember me by . . . and remember that if you do not get rid of her in a reasonable amount of time, I'll do it for you."

Fear for Leonore nearly caused him to shudder, but he made himself grin boyishly instead. "But I like my little pet! Can I not keep her a bit longer?"

Mercia burst out laughing. "Oh, very well! But mind what I have said!" She turned and took a few steps away from him, then paused to throw him a kiss before she left the terrace. For one minute he stared at the doorway through which she had gone.

The sharp sound of broken pottery cracked the air. His knuckles hurt, and he looked down at the dirt and shattered clay before him. He'd hit a large plant pot that had been sitting in a niche in the wall, but at least his emotions had calmed a little. For just one moment, it was Mercia who had been in front of him. For just one moment, he had rid the world of her.

St. Vire sighed. He had better look for Leonore. He'd seen her on the balcony. She must have heard most of the conversation between Mercia and himself. It was necessary, he told himself. Better Leonore hate him now. Mercia would then be more easily convinced that the marriage was merely one of convenience.

He entered the assembly room again, but did not find Leonore. Fear shot through him. Had Mercia—no, she couldn't have, not after their conversation. He wished he had never brought Leonore here, but he knew she'd question his absence, and he had not wanted to lie to her in this, at least. He had not realized the sort of people who would be here until after he had stepped into the house. He knew Harlowe was a bit of a rake, but he did not know Lady Harlowe and had assumed it would be a different sort of masquerade because of her presence. He had almost taken Leonore home, but then thought about what he must do. It was better she begin to hate him from tonight; postponing it was futile, for it would make no difference in the end.

Discreetly he questioned a few of the guests he knew and found to his profound relief that Leonore had left with Lord Eldon. He knew he had nothing to fear from his friend, as Eldon was a remarkably kind-hearted young man. He made a mental note to warn him away from Mercia. His friend did not deserve a liaison with her.

His carriage took him swiftly home. When he entered the house, his feet took him up the stairs two at a time. He realized what he was doing and stopped. Of course Leonore must be here; he could trust Eldon to bring her home safely. And yet . . . and yet . . .

Nicholas's hand shook as he opened Leonore's chamber door. The silence in the room was almost unbearable to him . . . surely she was sleeping. He went to her bed. The moon streamed through the window, outlining Leonore's sleeping form. She lay on her side, curled into a tight ball, her knees up to her stomach, her hands crossed over her chest.

A now familiar leaden sensation pressed into him, and the breath that came from him was almost a groan. He had seen people curled in this position before—in Paris when the victims of the Reign of Terror tried to escape the beatings of the mob, in the slums of London when poor drabs tried to protect themselves from a winter's night. He had made Leonore miserable, had hurt her—he who loved her.

St. Vire turned from her, gazing out the window to the moon-silvered street below. It was necessary, he told himself, not for him, but for Leonore. But who had gotten her into this situation in the first place? He had no one to blame but himself.

God, how I despise myself! He almost laughed aloud, bitterly. Leonore had not turned him into a saint, but she had shown him all his sins, shattering his image of himself. He'd been an arrogant fool to think he could simply pluck her from

her family and use her for his spell—as if she were some herb
in a dish served up for his liking.

"Nicholas . . ."

Turning swiftly, he saw she was still asleep. Even in her
dreams she thought of him—no doubt now with misery and
grief. He wished he could comfort her. He put out his hand
and stroked the hair from her face. She breathed a soft sigh
and turned her head so that her cheek fit into the palm of his
hand. An ache grew in his chest. Even with the way he had
treated her, some part of her seemed to seek his touch.

He removed his coat and neckcloth, draping them over a
chair. Just this once he would hold her in his arms and not
make love to her. She would not know, for she slept heavily,
and he could always move softly on the bed and never rouse
her.

The mattress was soft beneath him, and Leonore's form
softer still against him. He gathered her to him, her back to his
chest, his cheek upon her hair. She sighed, and her body
seemed to relax, uncurling slightly from her earlier position.

"I love you, Leonore," he whispered softly, knowing she
could not hear him. "You don't know it, but I do." His breath
caught in his throat. He wished he could have said it in a
clever, witty way . . . but it did not matter, for she was asleep.
"Your lovely face and form, your laugh and even the way you
tell me I am vain. But God, I must hurt you, and I wish I need
not."

He drew her closer, kissing the nape of her neck. She sighed
again and nestled into him, and he wished he could weep. But
he could not, for vampires had no tears.

"I love you, Leonore. . . ."

She turned and reached for Nicholas, but he was not there in
the bed beside her, and she knew it had been only a dream.
Leonore opened her eyes. The sunlight that streamed into her
room told her it was day; of course he could not be here.

The events of the night before rushed into her then, and she
closed her eyes, gasping as if in pain. He would be with Lady
Lazlo, most certainly. He had kissed her. Leonore had seen it.

With a low groan she rolled over in her bed and into a depression in the mattress. The faint scent of bay rum arose from the pillow beside her. It was the scent Nicholas always wore, and she was familiar with it.

Why had he come to her last night? He was enamored of Lady Lazlo, she was sure. And yet, he had certainly been in her room. He had not made love to her, but simply lain beside her.

She reached into her memories of last night, hoping to catch perhaps one moment she might have wakened during the night. All she remembered were turbulent dreams that faded into a vague, odd sense of comfort.

And Nicholas's soft whisper, "I love you, Leonore. . . ."

Leonore shook her head fiercely. No. No, he did not love her. She would not believe it, for she had shored up her heart again, and to let the thought in would surely tear her apart.

Pulling on her dressing gown, she rose and rang for her maid. Hers was a marriage of convenience. She had forgotten it and allowed herself to fall in love with Nicholas. It was too late to stop the emotion, but at least she would not let it show.

Betty entered the room and helped Leonore dress. She pushed down the shadows of rage and grief that had obscured her thoughts the night before. A proper wife turned her eyes away from her husband's indiscretions; her own mother had told her that. She would heed the advice, and her marriage would be as any other.

And yet, the soft dreamlike whisper she had remembered entered and nestled in one corner of her heart and stubbornly refused to leave.

Chapter 14

Leonore sat at the window seat, looking down at the London traffic below, her hand folding and unfolding the portion of her skirt she held between her fingers. She was hungry, but she had no appetite; she was thirsty, but she did not care to drink. She did not care about much these days, for a dullness had descended upon her mind, and her heart had frozen into ice.

The March sun shone brightly, doing its best to tempt her into going out. She closed her eyes against the light. She wished Nicholas was with her now, then pushed the wish away. It was daylight, and of course he would not appear. And when the night arrived, he would not be at her side, but would leave her to be with Lady Lazlo. Leonore had tried to bear it for months now.

It would have been bearable if she did not receive speculatives looks and sly questions from those who resented St. Vire's earlier infatuation with her.

The ice around her heart threatened to break, but she would not let it. She would weep if it disappeared. She sighed and rose from her seat at the window. There were things to do about the house, and then she would call upon her sister, Susan.

Leonore busied herself with various tasks, but knew she got in the servants' way. Well, she would go to see Susan and her mother. Her heart lifted, for she was sure of her sister's affectionate reception, and at least a smile from her mother.

She had not even reached the steps to her parents' house when the door burst open and Susan ran to her with her hands outstretched and a beaming smile upon her face.

"Oh, Leo! You must come and look! We have got a new pianoforte!"

Leonore laughed and gave her sister a brief, warm hug. "Only for a pianoforte would you be so excited as to rush out into the cold air without your pelisse." Her sister was beautiful, her guinea gold curls thick and healthy instead of lank and dull as they had been before Leonore had married. The girl's cheeks bloomed with health, no doubt because she had more food and less worry than in the past. "Is Mama in?"

"Oh, how you fuss, Leo! It is only a few steps into the house. And Mama is out shopping for a ribbon. Can you imagine? Her headaches have not been as bad as they used to be."

Susan's blue eyes danced, and she shook her head, making her curls float about her head like a halo. A passing gentleman stopped and stared at her sister before he collected himself and walked by reluctantly. She smiled with pride. Her sister had been attracting several eligible gentlemen's attention lately. Susan had bloomed under the approval she had received from those to whom Leonore had introduced her. Her painful shyness had faded; it became a sweet, innocent manner that, combined with her beauty, gained her popularity even from the sternest of dowagers.

"Do come look, Leo! It's beautiful." Susan seized Leonore's hand and pulled her into the house. Leonore laughed. It warmed her to see Susan so happy. For this, at least, Leonore was glad she had married Nicholas. The thought of him damped her spirits a little, but she dismissed it. No, she had married well. She now only needed to see Susan wed.

The pianoforte was indeed beautiful. It was imported; the workmanship marked it as from one of the finest instrument makers in Germany. Leonore ran her hand over the smooth, lacquered surface, admiring the way some artist had painted intricate gold designs on the edges and singing cherubs and angels on the inside surface of the lid. She looked at Susan's expectant face.

"Well?" Susan said, her voice eager. "What do you think?"

"Beautiful! Have you tried it yet?"

"Yes, of course! I had it tuned immediately when it arrived." Susan sat down upon the bench and laid her hands on the keyboard. A lilting melody—a waltz—sang sweet and pure from the instrument. "When we go to the ball tonight, I must thank Nicholas for buying it for me."

"Nicholas?"

Susan glanced at Leonore, her eyes laughing. "Of course, silly Leo! Who else would have been so generous? Father detests music and would never think of it, and Mama would not know how to go about ordering one."

"Of course," Leonore replied, giving a short laugh. "I suppose I am still not used to Nicholas's generosity." Two months ago she had mentioned in passing that she thought it a pity Susan had to play upon such a poor instrument. St. Vire had nodded absently, and they had talked of other things. And now here was the pianoforte in her parents' home.

Susan had stopped her playing and was looking at her sister anxiously. "Is there something wrong, Leo?"

Leonore shook her head. "No, not at all. I have been gadding about too much, is all, and I am a little tired. I would, however, like to rest and listen to you play a while." The girl smiled and began a sonata.

Leonore listened, but her mind turned to Nicholas again. She did not understand him. Each time they went to a ball or other social function, he would spend a large amount of time with Lady Lazlo if she was there. His attentions were just within the bounds of propriety. And though he was discreet, she noticed they'd disappear together for a short while each time.

Yet, he spent almost equal time with her, Leonore, and would also find time to be private with her. He never initiated conversation about Lady Lazlo. When Leonore would say her name, his lips would harden, and an angry, fearful light would flash in his eyes. Then he would turn the conversation to other things.

And still he would come to her bed at night when she retired, sometimes making love to her. Even when he kept to his room or had gone out with his friends, she could tell the next morning that he had lain at her side for a while. At first she did not want him in her bed at all. Yet, two weeks of his absence had set a yearning fire in her belly, and when he kissed her one evening she had abandoned herself to it and had given him back every kiss and caress. She despised herself for her weakness.

And now this, the gift of the pianoforte to Susan. He still showered gifts upon her and her family, though she told him it was not necessary. She needed only to wish it, and it would appear for her, however whimsical her wish. Once she had told him of a sweet lamb she had seen at a market, and the next day a toy lamb had appeared on her bed. She could almost think he cared for her, for when they were at home, he looked at her as if he desired her. Yet, the whispering about him and Lady Lazlo grew—and with it her own jealousy. She hated herself for it. It made her feel powerless, without control over herself.

The music had stopped, and she looked at Susan to find that her sister was gazing at her with concern.

"What is it, Susie?"

"There is something wrong, I know it. Tell me what it is."

Leonore made herself smile. "Nonsense, Susan! Do continue playing."

Susan frowned and rose from the pianoforte. She sat down next to Leonore and took her hand.

"Leo, there *is* something wrong. You never call me 'Susan' unless there is. Tell me." She hesitated. "I know you are my older sister, and I have confided everything in you since I was a baby. But I am your sister also, and it is not fair that you should carry all the burdens and tell no one."

"Oh, heavens, Susan, there is nothing—"

"Stop, Leonore! I have grown up—can you not see that?" Susan squeezed her hand. "I have always wanted to be like you, strong, brave, and loving. How can I do that if you don't let me? I cannot be protected forever. I do not say much, but I always listen and watch. And since my come-out, I have had many chances to learn." She nodded her head wisely, and Leonore almost wept to see the old look on her young face.

Years of watching for signs of her father's rages had put it there, she was sure.

"You have always been so good to me, Leo," Susan continued. "Perhaps I cannot help you directly, but at least let me know why you are so often sad these days." She gave Leonore a hug. "Please tell me."

A lump in Leonore's throat almost choked her, and she swallowed. She managed to put a smile on her face. "It is nothing. . . . I . . . I, oh Susie, I'm in love with Nicholas, and he is in love with Lady Lazlo!" she blurted. Horrified at her outburst, she covered her mouth with her hand, rose, and walked to the windows. She stared blindly out at the street, trying to control herself and not blather on. She failed. "Oh heavens! Never mind, Susan, it is nothing after all. We have a marriage of convenience. I am content, truly, and I am sure Nicholas is quite satisfied with the way things are. I . . . I am being stupid, for there is nothing anyone can do about it, surely—" She felt Susan's arm come around her in a hug.

"Yes, Leo, I think you *are* being stupid," Susan said gently.

"Susan!"

"Oh, Leonore, you need not look so . . . so older sisterish!" she said with a touch of impatience. "I am not ten years old any longer, but eighteen! I have eyes in my head, after all. I can see for myself that Nicholas is in love with you."

The ice around Leonore's heart threatened to crack. "Nonsense!" she said.

Susan let out an impatient breath. "For goodness sake! Can you deny how generous he is to you—to us, your family— when I know he needn't be? I don't know how many times I have seen him watch you when you were not looking. Or how he must like to touch you, for I have seen him almost reach for you but stop when he recollects he is in company. He takes every excuse to be near you. How can you not think he loves you?"

"But the gossip—Lady Lazlo—"

"Heavens, Leo! I am surprised you listen to such things."

Leonore felt a reluctant laugh bubble up inside of her—how

their roles had reversed! Susan sounded so very grown up. She shook her head, however.

"Susie . . . you will not let this go further, of course—" Leonore began. Her sister gave her a disgusted look, which caused Leonore to laugh. "Stupid of me. Of course you would not." She hesitated and wet her lips. "I saw, many months ago, him kissing her. And they talked as if they were considering a . . . a liaison." Susan's brow furrowed in thought.

"Perhaps that has some significance," Susan said slowly, and Leonore smiled at how grown-up her sister sounded. "But I cannot think it has much, for it seems gentlemen are very fond of kissing." A light blush appeared in Susan's cheeks, and she hurried on. "But still, I cannot think Nicholas is in love with Lady Lazlo, for I believe he quite hates her."

Leonore gave a short, bitter laugh. "How you can say that? I have seen with my own eyes how he dances a little too closely to her for propriety, and how he has disappeared with her from time to time. If he hates her, he would not have kissed her."

Susan shook her head. "I don't know why he kissed Lady Lazlo, but he doesn't like her. He looks angrily at her whenever she looks away from him, and his hands close into fists when she approaches. It is only for a moment, but I have seen it each time. I think if he were like Father, he would probably hit her." Susan sighed. "I've learned it is not right for gentlemen to do that, and I am certain Nicholas is a gentleman."

Her sister had grown up, indeed. Leonore did not know why she thought her protection had kept Susan from understanding what their parents were. It brought a bitter taste to her tongue. She had done Susan a disservice, thinking she could not see what was in front of her, or could be protected from ugliness. What arrogance! She had not protected her from much, it seemed.

"I don't know what to think, Susan, truly I do not. I have tried to broach the subject, but he grows cold and does not wish to speak of it."

Susan patted her hand. "I am certain he loves you, truly."

Leonore's smile was ironic. "Are you, Susie? How can you be certain when you have never been in love yourself?"

"I have so!" cried Susan indignantly. She stopped and blushed a beetroot color.

"Oh, my dear, I did not mean to tease!" Leonore took her sister's hands and squeezed them. "Perhaps you can tell me?"

"It . . . it is Jeremy Fordham, Lord Eldon's younger brother." Susan gazed at Leonore, her face alight. "He is so handsome and so kind to me, Leo! He makes me laugh, for he says the most comical things. And I am sure he loves me, too, for he has told me so, and he looks at me as I have seen Nicholas look at you."

"Oh, Susie! How happy I am for you!" Leonore hugged her tightly. Mr. Fordham did not have the title and wealth she had hoped for her sister, but she knew he was as kind as his brother, and would inherit a sizable legacy from an elderly uncle. Mr. Fordham had appeared at Susan's side nearly every ball or rout. Leonore remembered Susan's earlier words and almost smiled.

"I suppose he kissed you as well?" she said and made her voice somber. She reflected on the quality of her mother's chaperonage—it'd been easy to be alone with Nicholas before they had married. No doubt Mr. Fordham would have had ample opportunity to kiss Susan.

Susan blushed again. "It . . . it is not a bad thing, is it? I have not let anyone else kiss me, for I didn't think it proper, but somehow it seemed different with Jerem—Mr. Fordham. He told me he wishes to speak with Father, that he wishes to marry me. And, oh, when he kissed me I . . . I wanted it to go on forever, but he stopped and said we mustn't go any further until we were wed." She looked miserably down at her slippers. "Cassie Brighthelm looked at me in *such* a way when we came back inside from the gardens. It made me think I should not have, that I was . . ."

Leonore winced at her sister's innocently revealing words, thankful that Mr. Fordham was at least that much of a gentleman. Perhaps all men were easily lured into kissing a pretty woman, although Mr. Fordham meant honorably by Susan. "Never mind, Susie, it is not a terrible thing for him to kiss you. In fact, Nicholas and I—Well, some things are allowed between betrothed couples. Has he spoken with Father yet?"

"He said he would do so today and let me know immediately," Susan said, her expression relieved. She looked curiously at Leonore. "You and Nicholas kissed—"

"Yes, we did," said Leonore hastily, and it was her turn to blush. Heavens, she hoped Susan would not ask questions about what went on between Nicholas and herself before they married.

"And did you—"

A knock on the door interrupted Susan, and Leonore breathed a thankful sigh as the maid Annie opened it.

"It's Mr. Fordham, my lady, Miss Susan."

Leonore smiled. "Please show him in." She glanced at Susan's anxious face. "Don't worry, Susie. I am sure Father must have consented." She hoped Mr. Fordham had offered a large marriage settlement to her father, or else she was not at all sure that he would consent.

A tall young man strode through the door, running his hand through his blond hair and destroying what probably had been a windswept style. He spied Susan and took her hands in his.

"Susan, he said—"

Leonore cleared her throat, and he turned, startled, to her.

"Ah! Lady St. Vire. You must excuse me, I have been remiss. I take it you are well?" he said and bowed.

"Very well, thank you. I see you are looking quite happy." She glanced at Susan, who was anxiously shifting from one foot to another. "I daresay you have something to say to my sister?"

Mr. Fordham grinned. "Yes, I do." He turned to Susan and kissed her hand. "Miss Farleigh, will you marry me?"

"Oh . . . oh, Jeremy! Has he—" Susan's voice trembled, and her eyes suddenly filled with tears. Leonore could feel her own eyes become misty. "Oh, has Father consented?"

"Yes, sweet, silly girl." Mr. Fordham chucked Susan under the chin and looked very much as if he would like to kiss her. "Otherwise I wouldn't be asking you now."

"Yes! Oh, yes, Jeremy!" Susan exclaimed and flung herself into his arms in a fierce embrace.

It would not hurt, thought Leonore, to leave the two alone for they were betrothed now. Mr. Fordham, certainly, was not at all like Nicholas, who had gone out of his way to tell—even show—her that he was a "bad man" as he himself put it. She smiled at the pair, knowing they would not notice that she had left, and left the room, with the door of the drawing room slightly ajar.

She took a hackney back to her house, and once seated, gave a large sigh. Her sister had indeed grown up and would not need her anymore, for Mr. Fordham was fully capable of protecting her now. It would be his duty as Susan's husband.

The thought struck a chord in her. Leonore stared down at her hands in her lap, concentrating so as to bring forth the idea that had been roused in her mind. It seemed an important one, but she could not quite grasp it. She shook her head. Whatever it was, it would come to her in time.

It was an hour and a half to sunset by the time she arrived home. Nicholas would be up soon. She used to step into his room sometimes during the day to watch him sleep; she had not done that since Lady Lazlo had come to London. A strong urge to do so seized her, and she walked quickly up the stairs to her room. If she hurried, she would be able to watch him for a while and leave before he woke. Once in her chamber, she looked for the lamp she used when she went into his room. She could not find it—perhaps it had been taken away to be cleaned. She lit a candle and opened the connecting door to Nicholas's room.

As usual, it was dark, for the curtains were drawn against the light. She drew aside the bed curtains and gazed at her husband. He slept deeply, as he always did, barely breathing. One arm was flung up over his head, which was turned to the side, the lines of his profile like a bas-relief upon his pillow.

A warm, painful ache flowed into her heart, and she knew she would always love him. Perhaps Susan was right. Perhaps he did not like Lady Lazlo at all and had some other reason for kissing her. But that made no sense. A man did not pay large amounts of attention to a lady he did not like, she was certain of that.

She looked at Nicholas, who looked more boyish in repose than he did when he was awake. His lips looked soft in his slumber, and she wanted to kiss them. He was deep asleep; it was not yet dark, and he would not wake just yet. She had not initiated any kisses since Lady Lazlo had entered their lives. If she did it now, she could leave with Nicholas none the wiser.

Leonore leaned over and pressed her lips against Nicholas's. She could feel the slight breath that came from his mouth, soft and lax with sleep, and moved her own lips across his gently. Even in sleep he moved her, causing her to shiver.

She gasped, for hot wax poured from the candle onto her hand. She had forgotten she was carrying an uncovered candle instead of a lamp. Her hand shook from the pain, and more wax spattered from the candle. Another gasp, not her own, made her jerk her head to its source, and a strong hand grasped her wrist.

"What the devil are you doing here?" Cold green eyes stared into her own.

Leonore said nothing, at once frightened and embarrassed, merely staring back at Nicholas. He shifted himself until he sat up, and the bedclothes slid down around his hips. He wore no nightshirt as usual, only his underclothes.

"I hope you were not trying to burn me in my bed, my dear," he said, taking the candle from her hand. "That would be a foolish thing to do, for it would take the house down with me, and then what would you do?"

Anger flared within Leonore. "I . . . I was not trying to burn you at all!"

"No? And what is this?" He peeled a large piece of wax from his shoulder. Beneath it a red welt was forming, and Leonore blushed guiltily.

"I am sorry. I did not mean to do it. I forgot I was holding a candle, and my hand shook and spilled the wax. I spilled some on myself as well," she said and extended her hand.

"I wish you were more careful. It was a stupid thing to do, Leonore. You could have burned the curtains." His words were harsh, yet he took her hand in his. Nicholas peeled the wax quickly away, and she clenched her teeth against the pain. She, too, had red welts upon her hand. He whispered something under his breath as he worked, clearly irritated. Finally, he was done and grasped her hand tightly so that she could not escape.

"Now, tell me. What were you doing in my room?"

"I am your wife, Nicholas. I suppose I can enter your room as I see fit. You are ill with the condition you have, and I believe my duty is to see if you are well." She felt embarrassed that he had caught her here, but she had meant no harm, and he had no cause to question her. The thought brought a spurt of anger to her, which she suppressed.

He looked away from her. "Oh, really? Or was it to cause me more pain? You pushed the curtains away. I told you the sunlight makes me ill." He did not sneer, but his voice came close to it.

"How dare you! How *dare* you accuse me of wanting to hurt you, when it is you—yes, you—who has hurt me!" Leonore gritted her teeth together hard, for angry tears threatened to rise in her, and she would not allow it.

"I? How have I done that? Have I ever lifted my hand to you? Have I not given you every luxury you might want?"

This time it was Leonore who sneered. "And what is that to me? I have had a man's hand lifted against me most of my life—should I lick your boots and be grateful that you refrain? The jewels and the dresses you have given me you can take away, for they are yours by law, not mine."

Her hands clenched into fists, and she tore herself away from Nicholas's grasp. Her mind was afire with rage and humiliation, and she could not stop herself, though she knew her anger twisted her perceptions, whipping her into a rage. The image of Nicholas kissing Lady Lazlo rose in her mind again, and all her suppressed emotions flared into high heat. Her words tasted acid on her tongue, and she spat them out.

"No, Nicholas, it is you who has hurt me, for it is you who has betrayed our marriage."

He tossed the bedclothes from him and swung his legs over

the side of the bed. Leonore moved away from him, but in less than a breath he pulled her into his arms. He pushed up her chin so that she was forced to look at him. His eyes were amused.

"Jealous little cat! You know nothing about it."

She struggled and pushed at him, but he was too strong and she could not move.

"Do not patronize me!" Leonore cried. "I know what I *see*! And don't you think I hear the whispers about you and Lady Lazlo? No, not even whispers—I've been pitied and, yes, *commiserated* with on your new interest!" Her own words humiliated her, for she knew she was losing control, and this humiliated her further. The heat of her rage had melted the ice around her heart, and the pain of it made her want to cry out. She wanted to hurt him, as she had been hurt, and she would push and push at him until she did. If Lady Lazlo was his mistress, she wanted to cut her feelings from him quickly. Their marriage would be one of true convenience, with not even love on her part.

"Thank them for their interest, smile, and say you have nothing for which to be pitied," he said flippantly.

He did not care. That was obvious. Leonore's rage flared hot; she could barely think. "How I hate you!" she said, her voice low and shaking.

Nicholas released her, and instantly she regretted her words. It was not true—she loved him, and that was why she hurt so. She would not have cared otherwise. But she could not tell him, for he had turned his back to her—that and her own sudden fear that she had gone too far. He clutched a bedpost, and for one moment he leaned upon it. Finally, he turned to her, his face smooth and urbane.

"Go change your dress. We are to attend Lady Comstock's masquerade ball and cannot cry off now. Or, if you have the headache, I can make your excuses."

Leonore stared at him, unable to speak.

"Leave. Now," Nicholas said, and anger appeared in his eyes at last.

She turned abruptly and slammed the door after her. She did

not want to go to the ball. If anyone found Nicholas had gone without her, however, the *ton* would talk more than ever, especially if Lady Lazlo attended.

More than anything, she wanted to be alone. Leonore stared at the connecting door, imagining Nicholas intent on dressing for the evening, and a burning defiance made her leave her room. She would not dress right away, but would go to her sitting room.

It comforted her a little to be there. When she opened the door, the warmth from the fireplace and the room's familiar comfort was a balm to the confusion of her thoughts and emotions. She sat in her favorite chair and pressed her hands to her eyes, pressing back the tears she could feel behind them.

God help me. She wanted to leave. She did not want to see Nicholas at that moment, not for the next day at least. But she must keep up appearances.

"I do not want to go, do not want to!" Leonore whispered. She stared out the window, not seeing the sunset above the rooftops of the city. She was tired of the facade she must put up, and never be her own self, her true self, or lose the loneliness the facade must always bring. She seldom discarded that protection around her heart. It happened only when she was caught in the wordless passion of the body, when she and Nicholas discarded their clothes and met flesh to flesh; or when her emotions flared and made her discard words like a foolish gamester at cards.

She felt she did not belong to London society, for she did not know how to laugh lightly, as seemed to be required of all ladies. She wished she could flirt with anyone, not just when Nicholas teased her. She wished he had no effect on her at all.

But Lady St. Vire had an obligation to her station in life and to the name she had taken in church with the vows of her heart and soul. And the former Leonore Farleigh had an obligation to her sister, so that no breath of scandal touch Susan's impending marriage.

Leonore closed her eyes for a moment, then took a deep breath and stood up. She could take up the roles she must play now. It was necessary. She had vented her emotions in an improper way; she should never have done it and could not unsay the words. Now she must go forward as best she could, turning her eyes away from whatever Nicholas chose to do.

A sharp pang went through her heart at the thought, but she suppressed it. She needed to behave with dignity. She'd apologize to Nicholas for her outburst; she should not have done it, regardless of the truth. A niggling voice within her told her that she might be mistaken . . . well, that might be true. Susan had said something of the sort, and she was more perceptive than Leonore had thought.

As she went up the stairs again to her bedchamber, Leonore sighed. She was glad she had come down to her sitting room. It was hard to think around Nicholas, for he always managed to distract her somehow. She knew she had been foolish and had embarrassed herself. She had little excuse for her rage. True, she'd seen Nicholas kiss Lady Lazlo; true, he did spend a great deal of time with her. But it didn't mean she needed to act like a jealous wife . . . though that was precisely what she was, Leonore admitted to herself. She should not have mentioned it at all.

She was glad she had not taken him up on his offer to bring Susan to live with them for a while. Perhaps she could go home. Father was mostly gone from the house, and her mother, with her megrims, hardly ventured forth from her bedroom. There would only be herself and Susan, with Mr. Fordham and other friends calling from time to time.

And yet, as she pulled the bell rope to summon Betty, she knew that it wasn't that Nicholas had kissed Lady Lazlo. He was the only person—aside from Susan—she had allowed herself to trust. She had thought she'd found a firm foundation upon which to set her heart, but now knew she had not. The discovery was like having a leg kicked from under her, and she had stumbled badly this evening. She would not do so again.

Betty arrived with a pair of new gloves. Leonore reflected that it was a good thing the gloves would cover her hands and hide the welts she received from spilling the wax on herself. But as she drew on the gloves, she frowned. The welts had disappeared, and her hands were as smooth, white, and free of pain as if she had never burned them. She shook her head. No doubt she had not burned them as badly as she'd thought, and the pain had been heightened because of her agitation.

Leonore shrugged and focused her mind on the ball she was to attend. She would keep her wits about her and put on an unconcerned face if Nicholas went to Lady Lazlo's side. At least the mask she wore would help hide any slip she might make. She sighed. It was too bad she could not always wear a mask. At times her emotions crowded up within her so she was sure they showed for all to read. She looked in the mirror, then pulled up her gold mask and could see her eyes peering from the slits. She did not look like herself, and it made her feel at once free and oddly frightened. How easy it would be to pretend she was someone else while at the masquerade ball, someone whom Nicholas loved.

Again Leonore shook her head at herself. How nonsensical she was being! She dismissed the idea firmly, and it drifted down into a small, shadowed corner of her mind, convincing Leonore that she had indeed forgotten it.

Chapter 15

Nicholas stared at the door for a moment, then turned and wearily rubbed his hand over his face. Well, he had done it now, hadn't he? Leonore hated him—precisely what he meant for her to feel. And she had thrown his sins in his face once again. It was just as well. Perhaps she would decide to leave him and go back to her parents' house. He shivered and threw a log into the fireplace, not bothering with the tinderbox but summoning a fire-salamander, which he let loose upon the wood. It licked and crawled upon the dry wood until the fire shot up high, then merged with the flames it had created.

He had told Leonore he'd make her excuses if she chose not to go to Lady Comstock's ball, but it was he who wished he did not have to go. Mercia would be there, and she had been getting impatient. Well, he could tell her that Leonore was leaving him, and that should put an end to her impatience.

Pulling on his robe, Nicholas rang for his valet and sighed deeply. He had not been able to find the right spell to protect Leonore or keep Mercia from harming her. It had taken him years to find the one that would turn him mortal again. He was lucky Mercia had little interest in magic, or else she might be more suspicious than she already was . . . although who knew what she might have discovered during the decades she was gone. Certainly, she'd known enough of satanic rituals to create more vampires.

At least the warding he had put upon Leonore had made Mercia overlook her presence. It was not precisely invisibility, but it gave the illusion that he was neglecting Leonore more than he really was.

And that was just it—he could not stay away from her, could not help wanting to touch her and do things for her that would make her smile or laugh or sigh in pleasure. He was a weak coward, to be sure. If he were resolute, he would have made Leonore leave him long ago. Well, he was sure he'd done it now.

When Nicholas finished putting on his costume, he looked in the mirror and could not help laughing. He had selected the mask of a golden dragon, one he had found in China when he had traveled there many years ago. He'd gone to seek the dragon knowledge he'd read about in some of his books. It had been an uncomfortable trip, for his dark red hair and pale skin had frightened many of the people there. They believed him to be a demon . . . and they were not far from wrong, at that.

The only man who had not run from him in fear was an old Taoist priest, who had consented to speak with him of ancient magic. It was he who had shown him how to summon a fire-salamander—the little dragon—and it was he who had given him the mask. St. Vire understood dragons to signify wisdom to the Chinese and so was honored to have received it from the old priest, though he did not know why the man had decided to give it to him, a foreigner. The only thing the priest would say was that for St. Vire, it signified hope.

Perhaps that was why he selected the mask to wear tonight at the masquerade ball. He was not sure of what he hoped . . . or perhaps it was a farewell to hope. He pushed down the persistent despair that threatened to seep into him. Allowing that emotion would do him no good at all.

He certainly looked odd in the mask; it was much smaller than many of the masks he'd seen in China, but it covered most of his face. The long, bright brocade cloth that hung from the top and draped behind him held it in place. He knew it would attract much attention with its exotic design. He did not mind that at all, however, and he rather liked the idea that no one would know who he was underneath it until the unmasking.

Leonore was waiting for him when he arrived at the foyer. He would have laughed if he had not despair just under his surface calm. She, too, wore a golden mask, covering all but her lips and chin. But she was dressed as a medieval Italian princess, with a tall hennin for a hat, the tip of its cone draped with sheer silk. Her dress was as elaborately brocaded as his domino—gold on red velvet, and its long hanging sleeves were edged with ermine. The bodice of her high-waisted gown was low-cut, and her breasts looked white as cream in contrast to the deep red velvet. St. Vire sighed, wishing he did not have to go to the masquerade, but could stay home instead and explore the contours under her costume.

"My goodness," Leonore said when she turned to look at him. "A dragon?"

"Yes, oh Princess." He bowed, feeling at once relieved and frustrated. "It seems our costumes have dovetailed nicely." She had obviously not been so angry that she felt she must leave immediately. Something was keeping her here, despite her hatred of him. He did not want to hurt her more than he had already. What would make her leave? He did not want to kiss Mercia more than he had to, for she disgusted him.

"Yes," Leonore replied, then looked away from him. "Nicholas, I . . . I am sorry for my outburst this evening. It was wrong of me."

"Well, don't do it again," he made himself reply and detested the way he sounded—petulant and rude. He saw her flinch and hated himself even more.

"Of course," Leonore replied, her voice stiff—with anger, he supposed. He could not tell with the mask over her face. He offered his arm as they moved toward the door, but she did not touch him. He shrugged and opened the door.

When they arrived at Lady Comstock's house, Nicholas sensed Mercia's presence and searched the crowd. It was easy to find her; she wore a costume designed to reveal her charms rather than disguise them. She was dressed as Mozart's Queen of the Night—appropriately, he thought. He glanced at Leonore at his side. Lady Comstock, a respectable woman, would not invite people like those who had attended the Harlowe's masquerade; Leonore should be safe from any seducers. He left her to go to Mercia.

She knew who he was immediately—she was of his kind, after all. Her eyes measured him, and her lips widened in a smile.

"A dragon. Does it bite, I wonder?" Mercia murmured.

He bowed and kissed the cool flesh of her hand. "Yes, most definitely," he replied.

"All the time?"

"Surely, you know the fairy tales."

"No, tell me." She took a step closer and briefly touched his chest with her fingers.

"Dragons eat only princesses."

"Ah, I am safe, then, for I am a queen, as you see."

He made himself smile intimately at her. "But queens were often once princesses, so you are not safe at all." He noticed the young Sir Adrian Hambly was not at her side. "Especially when her young knight is not by to guard her."

Mercia shrugged slightly and let out a sad sigh. "Alas, my poor knight is . . . indisposed. He has not been well of late."

Nicholas clenched his teeth. No doubt she had drained the young man to the point of illness—or death. She had not changed at all; she was still the greedy, careless bitch she'd always been. She could use her body like a drug and cast a glamour so that her victims could not leave her. Utter hatred made him bare his teeth, but he turned it into a wide, avaricious grin.

"Then you are wholly unprotected. Beware, oh Queen! Dragons can carry off such ladies and devour them whole."

Mercia laughed. "But I have been known to ride dragons and so cannot be harmed." The musicians at the other end of the room started up their instruments. Nicholas put Mercia's hand on his arm and led her to the dance floor.

He smiled slightly and bent to her ear. "But you do not attend the opera often, yes? Perhaps you don't remember the end of *The Magic Flute*. Fire consumes the Queen and the earth swallows her up."

She cast him a sharp look through her mask. "Is that a warning, Nicholas?"

"For your own benefit, I assure you."

She frowned, but did not speak, for the figures of the dance separated them. Nicholas looked about him and saw that Leonore was dancing as well. She averted her face, and he was sure she had been looking at him. Now she smiled at the gentlemen who passed her in the dance, and a few of them gazed longer at her than necessary.

Angry heat flashed through Nicholas, and he suddenly realized he was jealous. He pulled his gaze away from Leonore. It was a useless emotion, and he should be glad she had some admirers, for then she would not be lonely once they parted. But the thought of Leonore in another man's arms, someone else kissing her and making love to her caused him to misstep. Clumsy fool! He would not think of what Leonore might do when she left him. It had not happened yet. Better he think of what he must do now rather than . . . he would not think of it.

The dance brought him back to Mercia, and she smiled sweetly at him as he took her hand.

"You are truly the gentleman, Nicholas. I appreciate your warning. But let me give you a warning as well: I grow impatient. It has been many months now, and your little pet wife has still not left you. Be warned that I can strike swiftly and close—as you well know."

Nicholas put on a bored expression. "So you've told me. If I dally with the woman, why should it matter to you? You have your little pets, also, and I know you won't give them up. Why should I?"

Mercia's smile grew hard. "Because they mean nothing to me, and I suspect your little wife means more to you than you say."

"Think what you want. As it is, she has informed me today she hates me, and no doubt she will leave soon."

"Will she?" Mercia gave him a shrewd look. "A jealous wife rarely leaves her husband, it seems to me."

"Oh, she will."

"I am not so sure, my dear Nicholas. But if you have any trouble, I can certainly rid you of her. Shall I demonstrate?"

He gave her an ironic look. "I thank you, no. I believe I can manage my affairs quite well." The dance ended, and an im-

probably mustachioed Turk eagerly asked Mercia for the next
one. She nodded her head at the gentleman, then left Nicholas
with a last, sly smile.

He stared after her. He was skirting close to the edge; he
could hear the angry impatience in Mercia's voice underneath
her slyness. Music began again, and he looked away to find
Leonore gazing at him. The next dance was a waltz, and he did
not want anyone but himself to dance it with Leonore. But
when he went to her side, she turned from him and accepted a
gaudily dressed cavalier's hand for the dance.

Nicholas's hands turned to fists at this cut direct from his
own wife, but he suppressed the urge to tear her away from her
partner. Instead, he turned and asked a lady standing next to
him for the waltz. She was a plump lady, disastrously cos-
tumed as a sylph, but he did not care. Any woman would have
done, only so that he could keep an eye on Leonore. But his
partner kept up a flow of chatter to which he must at least
reply from time to time. Between that and the whirling steps of
the dance, he was not able to keep his eye on Leonore at all.

What a fool he was! He made himself respond properly to
his dance partner until the dance ended. He looked for Mercia,
but she had disappeared. He breathed a sigh of relief. He felt
suddenly tired and wanted to go home. But he had not been
here very long, and with Mercia's barely veiled threats, it was
unsafe to leave Leonore alone at the ball, either. The ballroom,
stuffy and hot, seemed to close in on him. At the very least, he
wanted fresh air.

A windowed door, slightly ajar, led out onto a balcony.
Quickly, Nicholas slipped out and took off his mask and was
glad he did. The cold night air brushed his face; he breathed it
in and let it out again, and his breath hung in the air, a light
mist upon the darkness. No moon shone in the sky, for clouds
had gathered, and a faint humidity promised snow. A frozen
breeze wafted through his hair, cooling his disordered
thoughts, and he was able to think clearly for once.

He leaned against the low balcony wall, his hands rubbing
against the smooth stone. His senses had continued to become
more finely honed so that the wall's texture came through

clearly to his hand and to his mind. Sometimes a passage of music impressed itself upon his ears and surprised him with such emotion that his breath would catch in his throat.

But he'd thought he would become clearer in his mind as well, and he was not. The spell had not said that emotions would spring upon him like a trap so that he did not know how to escape to cool logic and intellect again. It was not the madness, which used to spin him around, taunting him with the merging of reality and illusion. Though he'd yearned for the ability to touch, hear, and see with a fine, sensitive appreciation again, he'd also been proud of his ability to be detached from the foolishness of emotions. He was a scholar and pursued knowledge and pure objectivity. It was not something he thought he'd be giving up when he regained his senses.

Now, however, he'd gone through the gamut of emotions: hatred, jealousy, and yes, love. He had always done what was expedient and logical. This return of his emotions gave him nothing but trouble, for now he needed to sort through them and had no time in which to do so.

And it was a dangerous thing, for it had caused him to become weak and indecisive, delaying his separation from Leonore. Not only did he have to think, but now his emotions demanded that he consider them as well. He was not, admittedly, good at dealing with them. He sighed. Perhaps that was one consequence of becoming human again. Acting from sheer expediency was a far simpler thing to do.

He would have to be vigilant. He could not let his emotions ruin his plans or endanger Leonore. His thoughts turned to Mercia, and he tamped down the anger he immediately felt. Staying a vampire was inevitable. He needed to think like one.

She had not bothered with Leonore so far, but Mercia was clever and impatient and might kill her soon. For all he knew, Sir Adrian was probably dead by now, or close to it, and everyone would assume the boy had died of some wasting disease. After that, who else would fall before Mercia's seduction? Perhaps she would even punish him, enticing his new friends, and he would see them die, one by one. And then, of course there was Leonore.

He would have to kill Mercia.

Relief washed over him. At last he could take some real action, and he could work toward it, however distasteful. There were many ways to kill a vampire—a long knife through the heart, fire, shutting one in a church, and of course, exposure to sunlight. He'd have to choose the most discreet and, if possible, the least dangerous. Mercia was strong, perhaps as strong as he, especially since he'd begun the spell for becoming human again. He would have to be very careful, but he was sure he could do it. Just a little more time, and Mercia would be dead.

Nicholas smiled grimly, put on his dragon mask, and entered the ballroom again.

Leonore refused to watch Nicholas cross the room. She was sure he had recognized Lady Lazlo somehow—perhaps they had arranged an assignation. Her face heated with anger, and she was glad the mask covered her face. If an amalgam of hatred and love could exist in her heart, surely it was a poisonous one, for it made her feel ill. She wished she hadn't apologized to him, wished she had not come to the masquerade at all. *Coward! Have you already forgotten your resolve to turn away your attention from him?* She took a deep breath and smiled at a passing pirate, who responded by asking her to dance.

She made sure to dance every dance that was asked of her, for it kept her occupied and did not allow Nicholas to approach her even if he wanted to. But she could not dance forever, and Leonore's legs finally trembled with fatigue. She sat on a nearby chair and politely refused one gentleman's offer of yet another dance. Unfurling her fan, she began to wave it, but it was taken from her hand and waved for her. She looked up. Nicholas.

He wore his mask still, and he did not smile. Yet, the tension she had sensed about him had lightened somehow. She wished she knew what had occurred to make him so, or even what had caused his strained manner of late. Leonore looked away from him. She should keep herself unconcerned with his affairs. The veil upon her hat stirred, and she felt Nicholas's breath close to her ear.

"Leonore," he said softly. "Let us go home. I do not wish to be here."

Relief washed over her. He had danced only once with Lady Mercia and had not disappeared with her tonight. Perhaps his affair with her was over. She bit her lip. How foolish she was! She should not hope so soon.

"Yes," she replied and rose from her chair.

Snow fell in thick, wet flakes as they stepped out of Lady Comstock's house into the carriage. Leonore was glad she had chosen the costume she wore, for it was heavy velvet and the ermine at her sleeves kept her arms and hands warm. Nicholas sat close to her, and she allowed it, even welcomed it. The barrier that had been between them seemed to have dropped for the moment, though she had all the reason in the world to want to keep it between them. She did not want to be hurt again, after all. Having Nicholas's leg pressed next to hers was comforting somehow, and the lack of tension in his body—tension that had seemed ever-present for the past four months—made her own body relax as well.

Neither of them spoke. Leonore did not know how long this comfort would last and was reluctant to disturb it. She gazed at Nicholas; he glanced at her, then sighed. But he put his arm around her shoulders and pulled her close to him, while his other hand took her hand and held it tightly.

By the time they arrived home, the snow had collected thickly upon the street. Nicholas put his hand under her elbow, steadying her as she stepped down. Carefully watching her feet so that she would not slip, she made her way to the door. But then Nicholas's sharp gasp made her look up and her hand flew to her mouth to suppress a scream.

The snow had covered most of the body that leaned against the door, but it did not cover the blood seeping from Edmonds's neck, or conceal the odd angle of his head and the open, sightless eyes.

Nicholas's arms came around her and pulled her close to him. Leonore burrowed her head into his chest, trying to block out the image still before her eyes. She heard odd, whimpering sounds and realized they were coming from herself. Her breath came fast, and she swallowed the rising nausea in her throat. Nicholas spoke, whispering something harsh, then his voice rose.

"Grimes, take her ladyship around to the back of the house and make sure she is safely inside."

"Y-yes, yer lordship." Leonore could hear the groom clear his throat. "Cor, is 'e dead, then, yer lordship?"

"Yes. Now snap to it, man! Take her ladyship inside." Nicholas pushed Leonore away from him slightly and stared at her. Dread showed clear in his eyes. "Get inside, Leonore. I will attend to this." She did not move. "Go, now." He gave her a push toward the carriage.

Leonore climbed shakily into it. She felt numb, not conscious of cold, and not remembering how she got to her sitting room once she entered the house. She felt a warm cup pressed into her hand and looked up into her maid's frightened eyes.

She took a sip of tea, then made herself sit up straight. Leonore dared not rise, for her shaking legs could not possibly hold her up. She put a firm, confident expression on her face, and pressed Betty's hand.

"You have heard. . . ."

"Yes, my lady. Mr. Edmonds, he . . . He . . ." The maid's voice shook. "Oh, Gawd, my lady, I'm that scared. Are we going to be killed in our beds?"

"No, of course not. I will not tell you to stop being frightened, Betty, for it is a dreadful thing." Leonore squeezed the maid's hand again reassuringly. "But I am certain it was some robber from whom . . . Edmonds . . . successfully defended us with his life. You may be sure his lordship will take care of it. Perhaps we will pay the watch to pass by our house more often, just in case." She had trouble saying the dead man's name, but she forced herself to say it.

Betty looked a little relieved. "Shall I tell the other servants, my lady?"

"Yes, do. I would not want them disturbed any more than they are already. You may tell them they can have every confidence that Lord St. Vire will make sure it does not happen again."

The maid let out a long sigh. "Yes, my lady." She curtsied and hurried out of the room.

Leonore put down her cup, her hand shaking so that the cup rattled on the saucer. She closed her eyes, leaning against the cushioned back of her chair. The heat from the fireplace seeped into her clothing, and her feet and hands ached with returning warmth. She wanted Nicholas here badly now, though she knew he was probably sending for the authorities. Part of her wanted the comfort of his arms around her so that she could press her face into his chest and block out the image of— No. She would scream if she thought of it.

But more than that, she wanted Nicholas to explain what she had heard whispered from his lips. She had thought he had called upon God for mercy upon Edmonds's soul, but he had repeated the word clearly, and she knew he had not spoken of God at all. It was a name, and one she hated.

"Mercia," he had said. "Mercia."

Chapter 16

God. Oh, God. St. Vire pushed open his chamber door and sank down upon the first chair he saw. He pushed his fingers through his hair, then drew his hands down again to press the palms against his eyes. *What have I done? What in God's name have I done?*

It was all his fault, he knew. Oh, he was certain Mercia had killed his valet. The body had her signature upon it—almost emptied of blood and a broken neck. She sometimes liked to do that last thing: It gave her a sense of power. It was her warning, her threat made real. He should have remembered it; he should have done something to have stopped her.

Too late. He'd set the events in motion with his desire to feel, see, and taste clearly again. He'd been arrogant, starting on the spell without thought of the possible consequences. His new friends were no doubt in danger, and his servants. If he hadn't started this course, Edmonds would not be dead now, and the threat of death would not hang over Leonore's head.

But how was he to know? He had little idea that emotions would rise in him to give birth to a damnably awkward conscience. It had confused him, and he had not been able to act in his customary logical, expedient way. Perhaps Mercia had been playing with him all along, slowly showing him her power and bending him to her will. She would kill Leonore. Not now; Mercia was impatient, but she savored the anticipation of the kill. It was her pattern, the way she always behaved. He'd forgotten it in the long space of time since he'd seen her in Paris. He had hesitated—now look at him! Nicholas pulled at his hair and groaned with self-disgust. He was wallowing in his newfound emotions, self-indulgent like a pig in swill.

Leonore. She was no doubt sitting by herself, frightened, and he had left her alone with her fear. At the very least he could go to her and give her what comfort he could. He'd already spoken with the local magistrate, Sir Justin Blake, with whom he had played many a friendly game of whist. Nicholas was certain the man would do everything possible to settle the matter of Edmonds's death. Then he and Leonore would leave this place, leave London for Avebury.

She was not in her bedroom, so he descended the stairs to her sitting room. At first he did not see her, for the chair in which she sat faced away from the door. A slight movement told him she was there, and he went to her. Her hat was on the floor, and her hair tumbled down around her shoulders. She stared blankly at him, her arms crossed across her chest. She breathed in small gasps, shaking as if with a fever, and her lips trembled.

"Nicholas . . ." she whispered. "Nicholas . . ."

He reached for her and she flinched. A sharp pain raked through his heart at her reaction, but he pulled her up out of the chair and into his arms. Her body was stiff and trembling against him.

"Hush, Leonore, sweet. Hush, my love." Nicholas stroked her hair and her back, and gradually she relaxed. Her breath slowed and became even. He led her to the sofa and cradled her in his lap. He kissed her on her forehead, her cheek, and gently on her mouth. "I've taken care of it. You need not worry; I have talked with Sir Justin—he believes it was some footpad who had overtaken Edmonds as he was coming back from his night out."

A large sigh caused Leonore's shoulders to lift and fall. For one moment she leaned into him.

Her body stiffened. She pushed against him and stumbled from his lap. She stared at him, and pain struck him anew, for her eyes were still frightened.

"Is it, Nicholas? Is it truly taken care of?"

He could not look at her. "Of course. Have I not said it?"

"Yes, but you said something else, earlier, when we found—You said her name."

"Her?"

"Mercia. Lady Lazlo. What does she have to do with this?"

"You must be mistaken." Perhaps he had said it—he did not remember. He remembered thinking Mercia's name when he first gazed at Edmonds's body. He made himself shrug.

"Don't lie to me, Nicholas. Don't lie!" Leonore's voice was low and shaking. He looked into her eyes, and they were filled with fear and anger. "I will not have it, not any longer. No facades, no lies. I cannot turn aside my face from what is happening in our marriage. I have tried, and I cannot."

She turned from him, staring into the fire, her hands clenched. "I do not understand you, Nicholas, though I thought I once did. You lavish gifts upon me and my family; you take me in your arms as if I . . . meant something to you. You kiss Lady Lazlo—I saw it!—and pay attention to her so that the gossip about you grows every day. Now Edmonds is dead, and you say her name when you saw his . . . his body. I don't think it was a footpad, Nicholas. What is the truth? What does Lady Lazlo have to do with your valet?" Leonore turned again, her eyes willing him to speak.

He leaned back upon the sofa, tipping his head and staring at the ceiling. What could he say? That he was a vampire? He loved her, but would she believe him? He wanted to tell her what he was; he had hinted and come close to telling her so many times, had almost blurted it out to her. He felt tired, tired to his very soul, and wished she would leave him alone.

"Go away, Leonore. Did I not tell you long ago that I was a bad man? So I am. This is all my damned fault. You would do better not to live with me. You deserve better."

"I cannot believe you killed your valet. That is nonsense. You were at Lady Comstock's ball tonight. I saw you and so did the other guests. Heaven only knows no one could have ignored that costume of yours." Her voice had calmed and grew steady.

He let out a short, angry laugh. "No, of course I did not murder my own valet. That would have been stupid, for I do not know how I will find another who polishes boots to perfection as he did." He lifted his head and gazed at her, watching her reaction to his sneering words. Her lips pressed together in a thin line before she spoke again.

"Stop it, Nicholas! You are not as vain as you make yourself out to be, either. That is yet another facade you wear, is it not? You act and pose, and none of it is really you."

"So you wish to know what the real Nicholas St. Vire is, eh, Leonore?" He sank back on the sofa and gazed at the ceiling again. God, he was tired of it all. A resentful anger burned in him. It did not matter if she knew what he was. Either way she would hate him, and if she made her repugnance clear to everyone, it might give her some safety. He shrugged and felt infinitely old, infinitely weary.

"I will tell you, my dear. I am a vampire. So is Mercia Lazlo. She killed my valet."

Silence, and then: "Nonsense!"

He raised his head and looked at her. "Really? And what do you know about such things?"

"I have read—"

"Nonsense!" Nicholas said, mimicking the same dismissing, angry voice she had used. He stood up and strode toward her.

Leonore took a step backward. He laughed nastily. "Frightened, are you? And so you should be. Do you think me mad? Perhaps I am. But I tell you, there are things you have not seen or experienced that exist in the world. Angels, demons, sprites, and, yes, vampires."

"No." Leonore stared at him, her breath coming short, and shook her head slowly. "No." Not mad, please not mad, she prayed.

"Oh, yes. Shall I show you?" He muttered some words, and a strange lizardlike creature blazed in the palm of his hand. "Can you—or anyone else—do this?" He threw the fiery creature into the fireplace, and the fire blazed high for a moment. "Or this?" He seized a poker and bent it in half, easily. He tossed it away from him, and it clanged upon the floor. She flinched at the sound and closed her eyes. A shudder went through her, and she stared wildly at him again.

"Not real," she whispered. "It is not real." It could not be—she was in a nightmare, she was sure. She swallowed. It was some kind of trick. Or perhaps she, herself, had gone mad. "If you are a vampire as you say, then your teeth—?" she said reasonably. A hysterical giggle almost bubbled from her lips. How ridiculous it sounded. But she looked at the fire and at the bent iron poker still before her, and dread seeped into her.

A frustrated expression crossed Nicholas's face. "So you cannot see them? But I can. Every time I look in the mirror, I can see what I am."

The mirror. Leonore remembered their wedding night when he had "accidentally" broken the mirror, the shards of glass—another mirror, she knew now—in his attic library. And the books in the library, the books of magic. She swallowed the fear that rose in her. No, no, he was teasing her, surely.

She looked into his eyes and saw no teasing there, only anger and despair. Her breath came out in a moan. All the things she had known since she had wed Nicholas—his condition, the way the sunlight hurt him, how he could not go out except at night. . . . And he was pale, more than was fashionable, though with his elegant appearance, all London assumed it was fashion. But surely, surely not . . .

Nicholas laughed again, a short and despairing noise. "Still you do not believe me!" He stepped closer to her, his eyes still angry and now abruptly intent. "You have read gothic novels, Leonore. Shall I show you how vampires use their teeth?"

Sharp fear and trembling shook her, but Leonore breathed deeply and stilled herself. "You will not, Nicholas. You will not, I know it." She did not know what made her say it, but her words were an acceptance of everything: the death of Edmonds, what Nicholas told her, here, now. Reality sank into her, sharp as a knife. She saw everything clearly, then tears obscured her vision. Grief pierced through her—she was dying, surely.

His fingers came up to caress her cheek and feathered down her neck. She shivered with both desire and fear and nearly wept with confusion and growing despair. His hand curved around her throat.

"But I have done it, my dear wife. Most certainly I have. Right here—" He tenderly stroked the hollow above her collarbone. "So soft . . . sweet."

"You will not," she repeated. "Not now." She spoke slowly, feeling her way through her emotions toward something deep within that she could not quite name. Her fear had somehow dissipated, leaving her numb, yet oddly clear-minded.

"How do you know that?" His voice turned sneering. "Did you not accuse me of betraying you?" His hand tightened.

She closed her eyes, then stared at him, at his angry eyes, full of self-loathing. "You care for me. You have said it, you have acted upon it, even when it was not necessary and even after your so-called betrayal." His hand fell from her throat.

"Oh, God. Oh, God, Leonore," he sighed, his breath ragged, and his mouth descended swiftly—to her lips. His lips moved across hers, and he kissed her deeply, sweetly. He parted from her, caressing her hip, bringing her close to him. "I am mad, I have lost all my reason, surely you know that."

She should run from him instead of standing here, letting him hold her. She closed her eyes. Surely she was mad, also. But madman or vampire, she did not care. She let him caress her, let him kiss her mouth, her cheek, her neck. He paused there, and she drew a deep, convulsive breath.

"Do it, Nicholas," she whispered. "If you are a vampire, do it."

A harsh sigh, almost a sob, broke from him, and he brought his lips down swiftly to her throat. She could feel his tongue touch her skin. She trembled, half in fear, half in desire, for the sensations were no different from when he had made love to her. His teeth slowly, sharply, scraped across the flesh of her neck.

A deep groan came from him, and he pushed her, hard, away from him. She stumbled and fell upon her knees.

"Go away. Go away, Leonore, before I hurt you." He raked his fingers through his hair, turning from her. Leonore pulled herself up and stood.

"You are not a vampire."

Nicholas gave a short, breathless laugh. "Oh, yes, I am. You don't know how close I came to drinking your blood this time. You truly don't. I can't wake before sunrise, for the sunlight will kill me, and if I enter a church I will experience an agony so intense that I will wish I were dead. Do you remember? I fainted like a vaporish bride at the wedding."

"Why did you marry me?"

"I did not want to be a vampire anymore."

There, he had said it. Relief flowed over Nicholas, making him feel dizzy. He had told her everything, what he was and why he had married her. She had not run from him, not yet. The leaden feeling that had lodged in his chest almost disappeared, and he felt light. He paced restlessly before the fireplace.

"Do you know what it is like, to have all your senses dulled? It is like seeing through a veil, touching through a glove. I hear, but melodies escape me; I taste, but no flavors stay on my tongue." He glanced at Leonore, who stood beside a chair, clutching it. "That is what it's like, being a vampire . . . except when the bloodthirst comes. Everything becomes sharp for the hunt, and only then. It is a madness. Soon the desire for sensation overcomes you, and you begin to live for the bloodlust, and slowly a vampire becomes mad."

"Of course, you would not want to become deranged," Leonore said, her voice a whisper.

"No, no, I did not," Nicholas said eagerly. Perhaps she understood; perhaps it would not matter to her. "I found a spell, one that would make me human again."

"And I was to be part of it, is that it?"

"Yes, it was necessary, necessary that you come to me willingly. . . ." He stopped, for Leonore was staring at him, her face still and white.

"How I hate you," she said.

Nicholas held out his hand to her, almost touching her, but she flinched from him. "Please, Leonore, I—"

"Don't touch me." She stepped back from him.

His breath left him. Of course. Of course, he could not expect it of her, that she would accept him, the monster that he was.

"I see," he said, swallowing the hope that had risen in him. "I see." The energy his confession had given him fell away, and he felt tired once again. He turned from her, not wanting to look at her. "I suppose it is best that you leave, or I."

He heard only a whisper of her yes before the door shut behind her.

Leonore did not know what she felt as she ran up the stairs to her room. Confusion, certainly; rage, repugnance, grief, horror, betrayal, and loss. And that persistent thing she should not feel: desire. She had told him she hated him, and indeed, she hated how she had been used and manipulated. But it was more a hatred and disgust for herself.

Her desire for him sickened her. She still wanted him even now—he, a creature that preyed upon others for their blood, a monster. When he had taken her in his arms, had kissed her and pressed his lips against her cheek and throat, she had kissed him in return and experienced the beginnings of the melting heat she always felt when he made love to her.

It was not just physical desire. She had looked into Nicholas's eyes, then offered her blood to him. She was a fool, and that sickened her, too. Still she had trusted him, believing he would not take what she offered.

And he had not. He had touched her neck with his tongue and his teeth, had kissed her gently, but that was all. Almost she could make herself believe that it was not true, that he was not a vampire and that magic did not exist. But there was that queer fiery creature he had held in his hand, and the poker he had bent in half. She also remembered the rosebud he had summoned from behind her ear and pinned to her gown. She had taken off the rosebud and put it in water . . . and it had bloomed and stayed fresh for three weeks. She had thought it was a special variety of rose, for no cut rose she had ever seen lasted that long.

Then there was Edmonds. She shuddered at the image that rose before her eyes and shook her head to dispel it. Nicholas blamed himself, but he could not have killed the servant, for Edmonds had been killed tonight—no, last night, for a glance at the clock in her room told her it was long past midnight. Nicholas had been at the ball the whole time; she had seen him except for a few short minutes. It took half an hour by carriage to reach their home. No one could have done the deed so swiftly whatever they might be.

Leonore pressed her hand to her head, wanting to press down her confusion. Nicholas had said Mercia had killed the servant. How could that be? It was true the woman had left before they had, for Leonore had seen Lord Eldon escort her out. But Lady Lazlo was a slight, petite woman, and she could not see how it was possible for her to kill a tall, strapping young man like Edmonds. Perhaps she had hired some ruffians to do the deed, but why she should want to kill a servant, Leonore could not tell. Perhaps the woman was mad. Or a vampire

She shuddered. It was late. Nothing made sense to her. Surely, she would understand better in the morning.

Leonore did not ring for her maid, for she did not want to disturb the servants more than they had been already. They would be near useless with fatigue tomorrow, for they would not be able to sleep well after Edmonds's death. She removed her costume herself, slowly, for it was heavy. But when she touched the white lawn nightgown that lay upon her bed, she dropped her hand from it.

She would not be able to sleep either, for she was sure the image of Edmonds's dead body would rise before her closed eyes and give her nightmares. She gazed at the connecting door to Nicholas's room and wished she did not know what he was so that she could feel comforted if he came to her bed. He would not come to her tonight, not after what she had told him, that she hated him. She shuddered. She did not know how she would react if he did and did not want to find out.

Indeed, she did not know what she would do. Nicholas had said she should leave. He would not want her, not now. A bursting grief rose in her, and Leonore let out a sobbing breath. It was grief for the illusions she had held of him, of course. She reached for her nightgown again. It caught on her elbow as she pulled the sleeve over her arm, for her hand still shook.

She had lost all control and could not stop herself from shaking. At last she had on her gown, and she climbed into her bed. The bedclothes had a slight, residual warmth from the warming pan that Betty had slid between the sheets, but still Leonore shivered. Her feet were freezing, and she shifted them to try and warm them.

She shuddered and shuddered again. Her eyes squeezed tight, and she put her arms around herself, pretending that Nicholas's arms were around her and that he was not a vampire. She craved him still, wanted the comfort of his body, the soothing way he stroked her hair and kissed her. She felt ill. She needed to leave this house, for she did not know what else to do.

Susan. . . . She would talk with Susan. She had grown into a sensible young lady. Of course, Leonore could not tell her that Nicholas was a vampire. But her sister loved her, and she could take comfort in that.

Tomorrow morning she would leave to stay in her parents' house. She didn't know how long . . . perhaps a week, or more. No doubt Nicholas would let it about that her nerves had suffered a severe shock from finding Edmonds murdered upon their doorstep, and that she felt too frightened to sleep at home. Nonsense, of course, and she despised such stratagems. But she supposed one must resort to them to keep up appearances.

Appearances. The curtain was rising once more, and now she must act yet another part. There was no escaping it, was there? She let out a breath and let her muscles ease into the soft mattress.

All the world's a stage, she remembered. But she wished the play would end so that she need not put on another mask.

Chapter 17

"I do not believe you."

"Why not?" Nicholas murmured against Mercia's ear. He trailed his finger along her jaw to her lips. She half closed her eyes and bit his finger, drawing blood. He felt a slight, sharp pain and almost frowned. His senses had not dulled, but stayed the same, though Leonore had been away a week. "My little pet Leonore has run from me and will not return. She told me she hates me and no doubt you, too. How could she not? She is jealous of you, for her own looks cannot compare to yours."

"Almost you convince me, Nicholas." Mercia said his name lingeringly, drawing out the last syllable in her lilting foreign voice. She pulled at the lapels of his coat so that he sat next to her on the chaise longue in her drawing room. "But how do I know you do not go to her when I am not watching?"

He took her hand and brought it to his lips. "You don't. You must trust me, of course." He gave her a wide smile.

Mercia pouted. "But I cannot trust you at all! You killed Louis, after all, and you took a wife not long ago."

"That again! But you must know it was because of sheer jealousy on my part that I disposed of Louis, for you would not leave him. Would you not have done the same?" He ran his hand along her neck, rubbing his thumb just at the base of her throat.

I could kill her now. But that would be a foolish, for her servants knew he was there. Mercia guarded herself well.

"Yes, of course." She nodded, then frowned. "But then there is your wife."

"Really, Mercia, I have told you she has left me," Nicholas

said, making his voice sound bored. "What would you have me do? I will not cause more scandal. Be content with what you have."

"And what do I have?" Lady Lazlo rose from the chaise longue and waved her hand at him in an impatient gesture. "You have not even come to my bed! What am I to think of that?"

St. Vire gave her an ironic smile. "You do not appreciate me, my dear, or my desires. You well know the deliciousness of anticipation. Isn't that how you use your . . . lovers? Slowly, you entice them until they are in your spell, and you draw out the killing to a fine edge until the end. Now why am I not allowed this in something less . . . final?"

"Is that what you are doing now, Nicholas? Drawing me out?"

"Why, yes." He pushed up her chin and kissed her, sliding his hand under her breasts. Her lips were cold as death. He wondered how Leonore could have borne his embrace if she felt the same repugnance for him that he now felt for Mercia.

"Mmm." Mercia gave him a sly smile. "Perhaps I will let you draw it out and let you seduce me. That might be amusing."

"Amusing . . . and tantalizing." He smiled at her and felt a rising nausea in the pit of his stomach. The devil only knew how long he would be able to stand pandering to Mercia's wishes. Long ago he could act out of expediency and occasional lust. But he had changed, and it took all his will to act as he had before.

"But I only said 'perhaps.' " Mercia twisted one curl of her black hair around her finger, her brow furrowed in apparent thought. "The thought of your wife is most distracting to me. The idea of trust—a difficult concept. I need a little security, you see. A show of loyalty. Perhaps if you shared your little pet, or eliminated her entirely, I would be content." She looked at him with cold eyes and smiled softly. "In three days. That would be a good amount of time, yes?"

Fear for Leonore almost choked him. Nicholas let out a long

breath and hoped the sigh sounded bored. That was it, then. Mercia would wait no longer.

"Oh, very well!" he said, making his voice petulant. "But I don't see your doing the same thing. In fact, I am sure you will find yourself another lover in time."

Mercia's smile widened in delight. "You are jealous!"

He took her hand and bit one fingertip. "Yes, of course."

"How wonderful! Will you do it straightaway?"

"Tomorrow," St. Vire replied and took his leave.

"I do not think I have heard you play that sonata before, Susan," said Jeremy Fordham to his betrothed.

"It is new," Susan said, smiling at him as she played. A maid lit a brace of candles against the coming dusk, and it shed a soft light upon Susan, making her hair a golden halo. Leonore could hear Mr. Fordham's sigh clearly from across the room.

Leonore glanced at the couple before her and set another stitch in her embroidery. Mr. Fordham—Jeremy—leaned upon the pianoforte, his eyes going from Susan's hair to her lips and eyes. He had followed her to the instrument, his hand reaching out, but stopping short before he touched her. He was clearly in love with her sister.

Leonore sighed and looked down at her hands in her lap. She missed Nicholas.

After a week had gone by, that was the only sure conclusion to which Leonore could come. She'd gained some objectivity away from him, and so was glad she had come to her father's house for a while. Besides, she needed to help with Susan's wedding arrangements since her mother seldom felt energetic enough to attend to them.

Then, too, she was able to stay away from most of the *ton*'s inquiring eyes. The report of Edmonds's death had spread, and the curious came to call. She played the part of the vaporish wife; Nicholas had let it out that his wife had suffered a tremendous shock from the discovery of the body. Of course she could not think of entering the St. Vire house for some time to come.

But Nicholas had not come once to her during the week she was gone. She was sure the gossips had noticed this, and she was glad for once that her situation gave her the excuse not to venture forth into society.

A week in her father's house reminded her why she had so eagerly left. Jeremy would take care of Susan now that they were betrothed, so she need not worry about her. But her mother still took to her bed with the megrims, and her father still came home intoxicated. She had felt her old stiff wariness return, and the wish that she were back with Nicholas cried clear in her heart.

How could she care for a creature like Nicholas? He was a vampire, impossible and horrifying. He had even taken her blood, though she didn't clearly remember it. Everything had fallen into place when he told her his true nature, and she understood the things she had glimpsed of him since the day she met him.

Laughter came from the couple at the pianoforte, and Leonore watched them, smiling slightly. Jeremy leaned forward and whispered in Susan's ear, and she giggled. He had a confident and elegant air—except when he was around Susan. Leonore almost laughed. He had a reputation as a ladies' man, but his usual grace of manner often fell from him and his speech stumbled a little when he spoke to Susan. It was as if he were so eager to please her that he couldn't decide quite what to do with himself.

It was a charming attribute, actually, Leonore thought. That and his obvious protectiveness over Susan made him an endearing young man. She had seen this protectiveness when her father had passed by them in the park the day after his rage. Jeremy had taken Susan's hand in a reassuring grip. Leonore knew she had little to fear for her sister once Susan was wed.

A familiar chord rang in her, one she had felt before when she had witnessed Jeremy propose to Susan. She thought of what it would mean for Susan to wed him, and how different it was from her own marriage.

But was it? Leonore gazed at her sister and Jeremy, thought of the young man's kindness, of how he had a protective air whenever he was near Susan. Her sister's words about Nicholas suddenly came to her. She had spoken of Nicholas's undeniable generosity and kindness. Leonore had thanked him once for a little toy sheep he had put upon her pillow for her to find. He had said it was a trifle, but he'd looked away from her briefly, as if embarrassed, and his hand's dismissing gesture had seemed awkward. Another laugh from the pianoforte made Leonore look up.

"Oh, Jeremy, how you tease! You know I cannot sing as well as I play. Even you sing better than I do."

"*Even* I? I thank you—I think." Mr. Fordham grinned.

A mischievous smile crossed Susan's lips. "You are welcome. It is the reason I consented to marry you, you see. We shall make a fine duet."

"And that is the only reason?" Jeremy reached over and ran his finger across Susan's cheek and over her lips. Susan blushed brightly, and he laughed.

Leonore bent her head over her needlework to hide her smile. Nicholas had teased her also and seemed to like to touch her face as Jeremy did to Susan. She glanced again at the couple at the pianoforte. She saw Susan's blush turn fiery and Jeremy's too innocent gaze at the ceiling. They must have exchanged a quick kiss when she was not looking. She bit her lip to keep from laughing and bent to her stitching with more diligence. The signs were obvious. He was deeply in love with Susan; Leonore was sure he would be a good, kind husband, like Nicholas.

A quick trembling shot through her, and her needle stabbed the ball of her thumb. She gasped. Susan and Jeremy looked up at the sound.

"It is nothing, really," Leonore said, smiling wryly, and took a handkerchief from her pocket. "I was clumsy and stuck my finger with my needle."

"Shall I get some sticking plaster, Leonore?" Susan asked.

"No, no, it has stopped bleeding already. Please, do play something on the pianoforte, Susan, and never mind me."

Susan raised her eyebrows, but Leonore smiled and shook

her head. Susan turned to the instrument again, drawing forth a light, tinkling melody.

Leonore wound her handkerchief around her thumb and closed her fingers over it tightly. Nicholas *had* been a kind husband. He had said he cared for her. She had not thought it, had not dared think that perhaps he loved her. Was it even possible that a creature like himself could do so? He had lavished gifts upon her, and she remembered seeing a disappointed look in his eyes whenever he thought one of his gifts had not pleased her. He had touched her the way Jeremy touched Susan, tenderly, as if she were precious to him, and more.

Nicholas comforted her a week ago, just after they had found Edmonds upon their doorstep. He had cradled her in his lap and stroked her hair, kissing her gently until her trembling had passed. He had done this before when she had been distressed.

A laugh came from Jeremy this time, making Leonore look up again. She watched Susan shake her head at his teasing. There was no reason why she could not have this with Nicholas, surely.

But he is a vampire, a monster, Leonore, have you forgotten that? said a small voice within her. No, she had not forgotten. But were his kindness and gentleness different because of it? Did she love him any differently now from before she knew what he was? She wet her lips, suddenly dry. No. No, she did not.

But Nicholas admitted that he had sought to marry her—to use her—because he no longer wished to be a vampire. If Lady Lazlo had not come to London, would Nicholas have told her what he was?

Ah, that was the crux of it, was it not? Lady Lazlo, whom Nicholas had said he disliked, but whom he had kissed and paid attention to as if she were his mistress—they had even talked of a liaison between them. What was she to Nicholas?

Somehow, Lady Lazlo had killed Edmonds. She was dangerous. Why did Nicholas pay such attention to her and neglect his own wife for all of London society to see? And yet, he still touched her, Leonore, as if he loved her when they were private at home.

Oh, dear heaven. Abruptly, Leonore rose from her chair, almost upsetting it.

"What is it, Leo?" Susan's voice sounded worried. Leonore focused on her sister's anxious face and Jeremy's concerned one.

"Oh . . . nothing, truly. I . . . I have been thinking it is time I returned to Nicholas . . . I have recovered from my nervousness about the . . . the incident at our house, and believe I should be with my husband now, instead of here. I . . . I should go back."

"If you wish it, Leo," Susan replied, looking at her curiously. "I know I can manage the wedding preparations myself now, for you have arranged it perfectly."

"Yes, yes, of course. If you will excuse me?" Leonore left the drawing room, hurriedly going up the stairs to gather her belongings for her return home—to Nicholas.

It was not quite dusk when she entered Nicholas's room, her lamp held high to guide her to his bed. She drew away the curtains, watching him sleep. She would tell him she understood, that she would not leave him again. Perhaps he would tell her he loved her, for she remembered how he called her his love. What else was he doing but protecting her from Lady Lazlo?

For that was surely what Nicholas had been doing. Leonore hadn't understood why he blew hot and cold upon her, pouring gifts into her hands and lavishing his caresses upon her body in private, and then abandoning her for Lady Lazlo's side in public. Lady Lazlo's languishing looks upon Nicholas clearly told her the woman's feelings. And if she were so dangerous that she killed Nicholas's valet, then it would be nothing to her to kill Nicholas's wife as well.

Nicholas knew Mercia and surely knew what she would do. Was it so improbable that he would send Leonore away from him so that Mercia would think him enamored of her, and leave Leonore alone? She gazed at her husband as he slept, waiting for the night to rouse him.

After what seemed an age, Nicholas stirred and turned toward her. He opened his eyes slowly, then he caught sight of her. Joy and consternation flashed across his face, then he frowned, pushing himself up from his pillows.

"Why have you returned?" he demanded.

His abruptness took her aback, for her mind had been filled with images of a joyous reunion. Foolishness, of course.

"I—I had to come back, Nicholas. I did not want to stay away from you. I don't hate you, truly I don't. I was angry and confused. . . ." Her voice faded away at his despairing look.

"You cannot stay here, Leonore. You must leave."

"Lady Lazlo—"

"Are you thinking she is my mistress? Then I wonder you are here."

"Is she, Nicholas?" Leonore took his face between her hands and gazed at him intently. Nicholas stared at her and said nothing. She drew close to him and pressed her lips to his. "Kiss me, then see if you can tell me. I know you will not lie."

A low groan blew against her lips, and Nicholas pulled her down upon the bed, kissing her deeply. He kissed her as if he could not have enough of her, held her close to him as if he wanted to take her into himself.

"I'm not good for you, Leonore; I have harmed you more than you know." he murmured against her neck.

"Tell me, Nicholas." She pushed back a lock of hair from his forehead. "Tell me."

"I should not have married you— Oh, God. She is mad. She will kill you if she finds you here." His eyes closed tightly as if in pain.

"Edmonds . . ."

His eyes opened wide with desperation. "Yes. Yes, like Edmonds." He moved away from her and sat up, running his fingers through his hair in a tired gesture. "But she wants *me* to kill you—tonight."

Leonore became still as cold ice clamped around her chest. "Does she?"

"Yes, the bit—Yes, she does." Nicholas rose from the bed and paced restlessly in front of the fireplace. "We must leave. She cannot find us together here. I have tried to find a way to get rid of her, but it's risky; she's too well guarded. Perhaps at home, at Avebury, you will be safe for a time, for I have set strong wards upon it." He groaned. "Though whether it will work against Mercia, I do not know."

He could kill me. Then: *No, no he would not. I must trust him.* But she was not used to trusting anyone, and the trust she had developed for Nicholas was too new and too recently shaken. *He could have killed me a long time ago if he were truly enamored of Lady Lazlo. He will not do it, he will not.*

"We must leave now, tonight." Nicholas turned to her and grasped her hands. "Pack quickly."

"But to Avebury! It will take two days! You cannot—"

He gave a short laugh. "Only in easy stages. But not if I drive! I always have horses stabled along the road. It will be uncomfortable for you and will take all night, but we'll arrive there before the dawn." He shoved her gently toward her room. "Go, now!"

Leonore ran to her wardrobe and pulled out dresses at random. She scarcely knew or cared what she put in her bandboxes.

By the time she was done and ready, the strings of her bandboxes held firmly in her hand, Nicholas was at the door. He wore a heavy greatcoat and boots and held a long riding whip. He gazed at her and let out a laugh. "Only two bandboxes?"

"I hurried, as you requested."

"Surely you cannot have many dresses in those. I will be surprised if you have any clothes to wear once we arrive."

"I did not think you would mind that," she snapped. She did not want to talk, for her nerves were on edge. She wanted to leave now.

He laughed again and grinned at her. "No, I suppose I would not mind at all."

They descended the steps of the house, and Leonore glanced at the carriage, then stared.

"A curricle! You must be mad!"

"Perhaps. But it is light and fast, and easier to get two horses changed instead of four. I think it will get us home in good time. You need not worry. I do know how to drive one, though I do not get much of an opportunity since it is a thing one tends to drive during the day."

"But how will you see? There is no lantern."

Nicholas gave her a crooked smile. "I am a vampire. I can see very well in the dark."

Leonore merely nodded and put her foot on the step of the carriage. He helped her into it and jumped up beside her.

"My only concern is that you will become frozen as we drive," he said, wrapping a fur rug around her.

"I shall be quite well, I assure you." She held up a large, heavy cloth bag. "Hot bricks. They heated in the fire while I packed."

Nicholas smiled and brought her gloved hand to his lips. "Admirable. Although I am afraid they won't last the whole journey."

"I will manage." Leonore waved toward the horses. "Let us go."

He gathered up the reins, and with a light flick of the whip the horses went forward.

All the snow of last week had disappeared, and an unseasonably warm sun had dried the streets yesterday. Leonore was thankful for that. Snow would have made their journey more hazardous. They wove their way through the streets and the traffic. The *ton* was out in force, seeking the night's entertainment. She could hear Nicholas muttering impatiently under his breath at the delays. His greatcoat's collar was up around his face, and his hat low upon his head. Only his eyes showed and flashed green when some errant light caught them.

Then they were through, and the road opened. Nicholas flicked his whip, and the horses picked up the pace. Leonore clutched the side of the carriage. She could hardly see in front of them, for though a gibbous moon shone in the sky, thin wisps of clouds obscured it from time to time and dimmed its light. But the whip flicked out again, and the horses began to gallop.

Nicholas let out a breathless, exhilarated laugh. "I have not done this in a long while," he said.

"That does not inspire me with confidence, I assure you,"

Leonore retorted. The wind whipped her hat, and she pushed it firmly upon her head. They were traveling, doing *something* to get away from Lady Lazlo's threats. At least they were taking action, and this lifted Leonore's spirits.

"Try to sleep. It will make the journey seem to go faster." She could hear the smile in Nicholas's voice.

"Sleep? I will be jolted to pieces by the time we arrive in Avebury."

But the curricle was well-sprung and bowled smoothly over the road. Leonore snuggled down into the furs. She did not sleep, but she did drowse, only to awake when they went over a rut in the road or when they stopped to change horses.

One last jolt brought her fully awake. The bricks had gone cold many stops ago as Nicholas had warned her, and her feet felt frozen in her boots. She looked at him, his face relentless in concentration. He stared into the night almost unblinkingly, his lips pressed together in a hard line.

There was no light on the horizon, but Leonore could hear early morning birds chirping above the sound of the carriage wheels. Fear rose in her. If they did not reach his house in time, Nicholas would surely die.

A large, dark shape loomed before them, and she heard him breathe a sigh of relief. "We are home," he said. He drove the carriage around to the back of the house to the stables, where a stable boy stumbled out and stared at them, wide-eyed.

"I am St. Vire. Take the horses and rub them down," Nicholas said to the boy.

"Y-yes, yes, yer lordship!" The boy scurried over to the horses' heads.

Nicholas leaped from the carriage and helped her down. Leonore was glad of his aid; she groaned when she stood up, for her back was sore sitting so long and her legs tingled with cold. She stumbled as she descended, but Nicholas caught her.

"Clumsy of me," she said. "I did not think I would be so tired. I am sorry."

He smiled. "I am sorry, too. Come, let us get some rest." He lifted her easily into his arms.

"Nicholas! Put me down!"

He laughed, and for the first time she thought she heard joy in it. "No. I wish to carry my bride over the threshold of my home. I wish it could be the front door, but I am afraid the door from the stables will have to do." Leonore could feel her face grow warm with blushes. She was glad it was too dark for him to see—and then she blushed even more, for she realized he *could* see in the dark.

"But you must be tired, too," she said.

"Only a little." He pushed open the door with his foot. "I am afraid there are few servants here, only for the stables and for maintaining the house. I don't even think I have a cook here." He set her down again on the other side of the threshold. "Welcome to Avebury." He kissed her.

She smiled at him. "Thank you. Shall you want some tea?"

Nicholas laughed. "Ever practical. No, though if you wish some, feel free to have some yourself. The kitchen is to the right; if you are lucky, you might find a scullery maid to brew you a cup. Please excuse me, however. I need to see to the horses; I hope the hard driving has not harmed them."

"I can manage, I am sure," replied Leonore.

"Of course." He moved toward the stables, then turned. "And ask to have the blue room prepared for you. It's next to mine in the west wing. You'll have to walk a bit; it's on the other side of the house. The servants stay on this side."

The stable boy was rubbing down one of the horses when Nicholas entered the stable. He nodded at the boy and checked the horses. Both were breathing easily now, and both were munching their feed contentedly. He patted one on the back, and the horse flinched and moved away. Nicholas sighed. He liked horses, but they did not like him, for he was sure they sensed his predatory nature.

But St. Vire's heart was light. Leonore had come back to him, and she did not hate him—or so she said. That was something good, even though it was a complication—Mercia would follow them once she understood he had not killed Leonore. There was hope, too. He had returned home, his birthplace, his own territory. Here his strength was greater, his magic more potent. The environs of Avebury was a place of much power, more ancient than his own vampiric nature—older than Mercia, who had lived for more than a hundred years. The closer he was to his home, the stronger he felt, though a fast, hard journey would have tired him greatly, and would have exhausted a human. If it came to a contest of strength, surely he could kill Mercia as easily as she could kill a human. She would be foolish to come here, for she must know he would be the stronger if they fought.

He smiled, his heart lightening even more. He would not mind staying in Avebury with Leonore. He could pursue his studies in magic and have his books brought here from town. The evenings he could spend with Leonore would be comfortable, with no pretence between them. She knew what he was and had come back to him. Perhaps, despite her week's absence, the spell could continue and he could become human once again.

If, of course, Mercia did not come. He would have to study the ways to keep vampires away from his lands, so that if he became human again, she would not come back to overpower him and hurt Leonore. St. Vire sighed. Or kill Mercia.

He gave the stable boy one last approving nod and left the stables. He took the stairs two at a time, eager to see Leonore again. Perhaps she would be in bed already, but he wanted to be sure she was comfortable. Then he would begin his studies.

A brace of candles lit her room, and though a fire flickered in the hearth, he shivered when he strode into the room toward the curtained bed. It was almost as if a cold draft had blown through it, for the back of his neck prickled. . . .

"Nichola-as . . ."

His breath left him, and he froze as fear caught his throat, almost choking him. The voice—low, lilting, and foreign—

"Mercia." Her name came from him in a low, feral hiss. He turned and heard her soft laughter.

"I thought I might come to welcome you . . . and your little *pet* . . . to this most gracious home."

Oh, God, no.

Mercia had one slim hand around Leonore's neck so that her head arched back. Her thumb moved back and forth above the quick pulse at his wife's throat. It would be so easy for Mercia to kill Leonore—one quick movement. . . .

Nicholas made himself smile slightly. "A trifle . . . vulgar . . . don't you think, Mercia—inviting yourself to my little party like this?" He glanced at Leonore. Her arm was twisted behind her, and she was on her knees before Mercia. Leonore's eyes were wide, but she breathed evenly and did not struggle. *Brava, my love. Don't show your fear. Mercia delights in it.*

Mercia looked thoughtfully at him. "But how ungenerous of you to keep me from my entertainment. I thought I would at least come to see how you eliminated your little pet wife."

"You sadden me, my dear. I see you do not trust me at all."

"Of course not," Mercia said conversationally. "I have seen how you fawn upon her. Now you bring her to your ancestral home. Can I truly be sure you haven't more than some fondness for her?"

Nicholas sighed. "Haven't I told you I despise indiscretion? Of course I brought her here! If I killed her in London, do you not think there would be speculation and gossip? Here, there would be fewer eyes and fewer questions."

Despair made Leonore close her eyes, and hope slowly seeped from her. *Please, he does not mean it. He cannot mean it.* She felt Mercia's hand close a little tighter on her throat. Leonore's neck ached with the way it was bent, and her back ached with fatigue. She wanted to cry out, but did not. A wave of defiance, the defenses she had built all of her life against her father's drunken rages, rose up in her, and she angrily decided she would not give Lady Lazlo the satisfaction of a response—even it it meant her death.

And yet: *I am going to die.* Lady Lazlo had come upon her in her chamber, quietly, swiftly, with the strength of a she-wolf. The tea cup in Leonore's hand had fallen and shattered on the floor, and hot tea had scalded her hand. Even now the broken shards of porcelain jabbed her knees through her carriage dress, and the tea, now cold, soaked through the cloth.

"Indiscretion! Always you speak of indiscretion! I am not indiscreet!" said Lady Lazlo sharply.

Leonore opened her eyes again. Her sight seemed sharpened, and everything stood out in clear relief: the bed, the fire, the table with the candles on it. She watched Nicholas, his still, pale, beautiful face, his expression cold as ice. He glanced at her. It was a quick, hooded flicker. She almost thought she saw fear there. Almost. Hope flared again, and she quickly tamped it down. She must wait and watch. Patience, patience.

"If you say so, Mercia." Nicholas shrugged. "I wonder what happened to Sir Adrian? He seemed such a promising young man."

Lady Lazlo made a sound of distaste. "He bored me. I am afraid he did not last long. Some wasting disease, the doctor said." Leonore swallowed and felt the woman's fingers tight against her throat. "Were you jealous?" Lady Lazlo said brightly. "Oh, I hope you were jealous!"

"Of course I was, my dear." Nicholas gave her a slow, seductive smile.

"How marvelous! Perhaps I will release your little pet wife, and we can have a bit of fun with her before you kill her. I would like to see that, you know, see you kill her."

Nicholas kept the smile on his face and shrugged. "If that is what you wish," he said carelessly. He could not let down his guard one moment. How quickly could he move and keep Mercia from killing Leonore? He shifted his feet and saw Mercia's hand tighten on Leonore's neck. Not quickly enough for him to run to her and snatch his wife away. Hope sank in him.

He gazed at Leonore for a moment. She was still, staring at him. It was as if she was trying to tell him something without words. She smiled at him slightly, and he understood clearly, suddenly, that she loved him. Why else had she acted as she had when she knew he had kissed Mercia? Why else had she returned to him? He felt dizzy, and he took a step back, putting his hand upon the mantelpiece to steady himself. Hope, foolish hope, warmed him just as the heat from the fireplace warmed his back.

Hope. Fire. He remembered the old Taoist priest and his gift. He had forgotten the thing that made him different from other vampires. He clasped his hands behind him and breathed a few words within a deep sigh. Heat flared in the palm of his hand. Nicholas gazed at Mercia and smiled sweetly at her.

"You gave me such joy when I saw that the stupid boy was no longer at your side at the masquerade," he said and let his eyes linger upon Mercia's face and breasts. He saw her hand loosen from Leonore's neck, and Mercia's smile turned seductive.

"Did I?" she murmured.

"Oh, yes. You were sublimely beautiful, regal, the Queen of the Night. Remember how I teased you? I admit my words sounded spiteful when I spoke of how the Queen had expired in flames, but the fires of jealousy had consumed my heart."

Mercia's face softened. "Oh, Nicholas! I had not thought . . . your wife . . ."

He took a step closer to her; her hand was lax upon Leonore's neck. "I wanted to make you jealous. Tell me I succeeded, lovely, sweet Mercia."

"Oh, let us kill her now, Nicholas. We do not need her at all." Mercia's eyes glowed with incipient bloodlust, and Nicholas's hatred for her flared high.

He grinned fiercely and laughed. "Too late, Mercia." His hand swept from behind him and flung the fire-salamander at her.

Mercia shrieked thin and high, and her hands flew to her hair. Leonore fell to the floor. Nicholas seized her, shoving her away from Mercia.

The little dragon curled around Mercia's hair, dancing down her shoulder to play amongst the folds of her gown. It burned and an acrid stench filled the air. She shrieked again. Leonore pressed her face into Nicholas's chest and shook with horror. He held her tightly, then pulled her farther away.

"We must get out of here, Leonore."

She gazed at him, but he was not looking at her. She followed his stare; the fire had caught onto the rug by the door and climbed quickly up the doorjamb. Lady Lazlo was gone. Burning cloth the color of her gown twisted and fluttered in the air. The fire roared, and the heat nearly scorched Leonore's skin. They would be burned alive if they stayed here.

"Move, Leonore, now!" Nicholas pushed her away from the fire. He went to the bed and stripped off the sheets.

"Where?"

"The window!" He tied the sheets together and secured one end to a bedpost.

Leonore ran and fumbled with the window catch. It opened wide, and she heard a roaring behind her.

"Nicholas!" she screamed. He was standing, looking at the fire. He turned to her. "If you do not come, you will die!"

"If I come, I will die." He nodded toward the window and smiled wryly. "It is nearly dawn."

"Stupid man!" she shouted. "If you do not go with me, I swear I will stay here."

"Damn you, Leonore, go!"

"No! I am afraid of heights."

"*Now* you tell me!" He ran to her and took her hand, almost dragging her to the balcony.

"You go first," she said. "In case I should be frightened and fall." He gave her a penetrating stare, then glanced at the fire in the room. She heard the roar of the fire, closer now.

"Very well," he said and climbed over the balcony wall.

Leonore cast a glance at the room behind her and shivered, despite the heat that poured out the windows.

"Leonore, give me your hand!"

Nicholas stretched his hand out to her, apparently holding onto something underneath the balcony. She grasped his hand, swung her legs over the low wall, and slid down into his arms. Quickly she twined her legs around the bedsheet rope and held tight to it with her hands.

"I have it!" she said. "Go now, Nicholas!"

She heard a thump and looked down. He was on his feet, looking up at her. It was dizzyingly far down, but she closed her eyes and concentrated on descending. Finally, she felt his hands around her waist, and her feet touched the ground. He turned her around, kissed her hard upon the mouth, then cradled her in his arms.

"You little liar," he said into her ear. "You are not at all frightened of heights."

"True," she said. "But you would not have come down with me if I had not said it."

"True." He sighed. He took her hand and led her away from the house.

Leonore gazed back at the mansion. The fire had spread quickly, and she could see flickers of flame curling around the edges of the windows. Nicholas gave another sigh, deeper this time. Leonore turned to him. He had closed his eyes and suddenly swayed on his feet.

"Nicholas!" She put her arms around him, and he leaned against her.

"I am tired, Leonore."

The chirping of birds came to her, and she looked toward the horizon. The sky to the east had lightened. Fear seized Leonore's heart, harder than the fear she felt when Mercia had squeezed her throat and twisted her arm.

"No. No, Nicholas, we will find some shelter." She looked frantically around her, but no place could hide them from the coming dawn. And the house . . . The fire blazed high now; it had spread through more of the west wing. Perhaps if they went to the east—

Nicholas slumped heavily upon her; she stumbled, and he fell to his knees on the grass. She hugged him to her.

"No, please, Nicholas, stand up! We'll go back, the east wing—"

He opened his eyes and gazed at her. "Too tired." His eyes widened. "The dawn. Is that the dawn?"

"Yes, yes it is. Oh, please, Nicholas, don't, don't—"

A small laugh rushed from him. "I have seen the dawn at last," he said. He swayed again and gasped. "It hurts."

She clutched at him, but he was too heavy. He slid to the ground.

"No, oh, dear God, no! Please, Nicholas, don't, don't—" Leonore pulled at the lapels of his coat, but she could not lift him. "No! What have I done? I—I didn't want you to die in the fire—Please, Nicholas, wake up!"

He opened his eyes slowly, focusing upon her. "Never mind, Leonore," he whispered. "It is better. . . . And I have seen the dawn again."

"Stupid man! How can you say it is better?" She leaned over him, trying to shade him. It was useless. She looked over her shoulder at the thin sliver of sun barely painting the clouds above a faint orange. A touch drifted over her cheek.

"I love you, Leonore," Nicholas whispered. He closed his eyes. "I am sorry."

Grief, hard and hot, seized her throat. "No. No. Please, Nicholas. Don't, please don't die." She took his face in her hands and kissed him frantically. No breath came from his lips. "Don't! Don't leave me!" She put her hand upon his chest. Only a faint pulse, and it grew more faint as she tried to feel it.

Leonore stared at him, at the sunlight drifting slowly over his pale, beautiful face, burnishing his hair. "Oh, dear God," she whispered. She hadn't even told Nicholas she loved him. She had meant to, but she hadn't been able to, or found the right time. Now he was dying.

"Please, Nicholas, listen to me. I don't want you to die." Her voice was hoarse, plaintive and pleading all at once. "See, you must not die. Not now. I love you, don't you see? You can't. Please don't—please don't." She lay next to him, her head upon his chest. She closed her eyes. "I love you."

A fire burst in her chest, sending scalding tears coursing over her cheeks. Leonore clutched Nicholas's coat, weeping into the front of it with hard, wracking sobs. She wept all her loneliness, all her love and grief into him, all the terror and agony of fear she had just experienced. But no arms came up around her, and no kisses comforted her.

She did not know now long she lay there, weeping—minutes, hours. The colors of the dawn had disappeared; the morning sky showed gray. It was raining, but she did not know when it began. It soaked her dress, and she shivered with cold—or grief—she knew not which. The rain gradually slackened and ceased, and she could feel the sun's warmth upon her back. She cursed the sun for what it had done to Nicholas and wept again.

"You are ruining my neckcloth."

Leonore jerked up her head. It was barely a whisper. His chest moved beneath her hand.

"Nicholas . . ." She let out a breathless laugh.

"I think you have wept all over my shirt, too."

"You *beast*!" she cried angrily and thumped his chest with her fist. "How can you speak of shirts and neckcloths when I thought you were—when I have been—you stupid, vain, impossible man!" She hit his chest again.

His hand grasped her wrist in a weak grip, then tightened. "Ah, ah! None of that, my love." Leonore stared into Nicholas's green, smiling eyes, then gazed at Nicholas's smiling mouth. "How beautiful you are! Perhaps it is the sun—that is the sun, is it not?—upon your hair. I think you should kiss me, sweet one, and stop staring at me like an idiot."

"No!"

"Yes!" Nicholas rolled over and pinned her to the ground. He gazed at her avidly, as if drinking in the sight of her eyes and lips and hair. "Ah, how beautiful! I never knew, never saw—ahh, Leonore. . . ." He bent his head and kissed her gently, then with more heat. "Your lips, I can feel them . . . soft, sweet, warm," he said against her mouth. "Beautiful, so beautiful . . . I love you, Leonore. God, how I love you."

Leonore breathed a long, sobbing sigh and put her hands behind his head, pulling him down into a fierce kiss. His lips moved upon hers sensuously. A cold drop of water splashed upon her cheek. She pushed him away.

"You are wet," she said, breathing hard. He sat up, gazing at her, an odd, wondering look in his eyes, as if he had just discovered something miraculous and new.

She closed her eyes briefly. "Thank you, thank you," she whispered, the words a prayer. Nicholas was alive—he was alive! A hard trembling shook her, and she felt tears roll down her cheeks. His arms came around her, warm and comforting, despite the dampness of his coat.

"It is no wonder I am wet, with all the weeping you have done over me," Nicholas said, kissing the tears from her cheeks.

"It was the rain."

"Of course it was," he murmured. "Hush, now, my love. You need not cry any longer."

She rested her forehead on his shoulder. "I thought you had died." She raised her head again and looked at him. His eyes became distant, and a frown creased his brow.

"I . . . I think I almost did. I thought I saw . . . heard . . ." He shook his head and returned his gaze to her. "It does not matter now." He looked around him and squinted at the sun that peeked from behind the clouds. "This shouldn't have happened. It has not yet been a year since we married." He shook his head again. "I do not understand it."

"Does it matter?" Leonore said and smiled tremulously at him. "You are alive . . . and I love you."

He gazed at her, his eyes bright. "Do you, Leonore? I had hoped—I was not sure—"

"Yes, and yes, and yes!" Leonore kissed him, fully and deeply. "I have loved you for so long, but I was afraid to say it," she said when they parted. "Will you forgive me for being so foolish?"

"No," Nicholas said, grinning. "You must make it up to me first by telling me you love me—every day will do, I think. And giving me perhaps not less than, oh, five kisses per day. No, six is better, I think. Then I will consider forgiving you."

"It will only puff up your vanity if I do!" Leonore stood up, shaking out her dress. It was damp and clung to her legs. She saw Nicholas staring at her, a seductive smile upon his lips. She blushed. "I suppose I can allow it . . . from time to time."

"Starting today," Nicholas said, then sighed and looked toward the house. No fire burned the west wing now, for it seemed the rain had doused it. A few trails of smoke rose from the broken roof. "But not in the west wing. Our rooms are ruined, and I shall be very lucky if I can retrieve a few books from the library above them. We'll have to stay in the east wing and perhaps share a room."

"I will not mind," said Leonore. "If you do not."

Nicholas smiled at her and kissed her once more. "No. I shall share my life with you. What is one little room added to that, after all?"

Epilogue

The early autumn sun streamed into Nicholas's study. He shook his head, sighed, and shut the ancient *grimoire* he had brought from London. Shoving the notes he had been writing into a drawer of the escritoire, he stood up. He looked out the window at Leonore walking out toward a copse of trees, carrying a bundle under her arm and lazily swinging her hat to and fro in her hand. He really did not want to be indoors any longer today.

He caught up with her in good time, for he ran all the way, enjoying the breeze that sifted through his hair. He marveled again at the blue of the sky, so bright that it hurt his eyes to look at it. Leonore turned to look at him when he touched her shoulder and smiled before she kissed him fully on the mouth. He took her hand when they parted and walked with her to the trees ahead of them.

"I have been foolish, Leonore," he said. "Perhaps even stupid."

"Yes, my love," she replied dutifully.

"*What* an obedient wife!"

"I do try," she said and grinned at him.

He sighed. "I've been impatient and arrogant, also. I discovered it was never necessary to wait a year to regain my humanity."

"Oh?" They came to the trees, which shaded them from the hot sun. Leonore unrolled her bundle—a large blanket—sat down upon it, and took out a book from inside her hat. Nicholas sat beside her.

"The solstices and equinoxes were the important times. It was not just that I had to wed a willing virgin . . . but she had to love me, knowing what I was." He shuddered and closed his eyes. "I almost destroyed you—destroyed both of us. I shouldn't have been so sure of my knowledge; it was wrong— prideful and arrogant. If you hadn't come back to me at the right time—if you had not forced me to climb down from the balcony. . . ." He opened his eyes and saw her watching him. "Can you forgive me?"

"No," she said. "You must make it up to me first by telling me you love me—every day will do, I think. And giving me not less than, oh, six kisses per day. Then I will consider forgiving you."

He laughed huskily. "Is that all?"

"No." Leonore took his hand and placed it on her slightly swelling belly and put aside her book. "I want you to make love to me whenever I ask it."

"Now?"

"Yes," she said and kissed him. Nicholas moved his hands to her breasts, more full than they had been five months ago, pushing away her bodice. She sighed and ran her hands down his thighs.

He loved her then, gently, careful of the new life he had begun in her. He almost forgot himself at the end, gasping and pressing himself deeply into her as Leonore gave a last moan of pleasure.

"I think I will begin forgiving you," she said breathlessly.

"Thank you," Nicholas replied. "Very, very, very much." He felt a slight fluttering pressure where his belly met hers, and he moved reluctantly away. "He—or she—is probably not thanking us at all."

Leonore laughed, then grew silent. "Nicholas . . . do you mind not having your vampire powers?"

"No," he said, smiling at her. He reached over and caressed her cheek. "Some magic is learned, after all." A puff of air burst beside Leonore's cheek, and she started. He opened his hand and a white rosebud lay in his palm. She stared at him, wide-eyed, while he tucked it into her hair.

"Besides, loving you is magic enough," Nicholas said and kissed her once again.